W0038297

By JACOB Z. FLORES

NOVELS
3
The Gifted One

PROVINCETOWN STORIES
When Love Takes Over
Chasing the Sun
When Love Gets Hairy

Published by DREAMSPINNER PRESS
http://www.dreamspinnerpress.com

When Love Gets Hairy

JACOB Z. FLORES

Dreamspinner Press

Published by
Dreamspinner Press
5032 Capital Circle SW
Suite 2, PMB# 279
Tallahassee, FL 32305-7886
USA
http://www.dreamspinnerpress.com/

When Love Gets Hairy
© 2014 Jacob Z. Flores.

Cover Art
© 2014 Michael Breyette.
www.breyette.com
Cover Design
© 2014 Paul Richmond.
http://paulrichmondstudio.com
Cover content is for illustrative purposes only and any person depicted on the cover is a model.

ISBN: 978-1-62798-364-8
Digital ISBN: 978-1-62798-363-1

Printed in the United States of America
First Edition
January 2014

To Provincetown and to all the wonderful people I've met on the tip of the Cape.

A part of you lives within me and on the pages of this book.

Chapter One

WHEN NINO Santos woke up, he expected to hop out of bed, as he normally did, and spring to the floor to complete his customary one hundred push-ups. Afterward, he'd venture out of his room to start his day by peeing, making a protein shake, and then heading for the gym.

That was how the day *should* have started.

Instead, Nino had to figure out just why there was a small, furry man asleep in bed next to him. And snoring like a motherfucking freight train.

What the hell?

When he first awoke, he'd thought the ball of fur was a dream, so he shut his eyes and slapped his face really hard, twice. When he opened them again, the short, hairy, out-of-shape man remained, except he'd now flopped over onto his back and begun scratching his balls underneath the sheet that partially covered his nakedness. The smile that stretched across the man's stubbly face told Nino the gesture obviously felt damn good.

When did he meet this guy? And did they fuck? He couldn't remember. Sure, he'd often tricked with guys whose names he couldn't recall. That happened *all* the time. He had no interest in who his hookups were or where they lived, even if every single homo who came to Provincetown seemed to want to share that information. Nino didn't care, but he at least faked it really well.

Conversation after his initial come-on was idle chitchat. He never really listened to what most guys said. It was all just filler until the moment his tricks stopped talking and started sucking his cock.

But to not remember the fuck itself, especially when it involved a type of man he'd never once been interested in before, made his head spin.

Nino slid out of bed and crept over to where his clothes lay in a heap. As he quietly pulled his jeans up to his waist, the bear in his bed grumbled to himself and rolled over onto his right side, exposing his hairy belly and what looked like a nice piece of meat. The guy's cock looked impressive, but the fur-covered stomach, not so much.

His type had always been the smooth, young, tall jock. Guys who took care of their bodies and were more like Nino, whose job as a model required he look good 24-7. Since he kept his body in peak perfection, he expected the same from the guys who he allowed the pleasure of his company.

He just didn't sleep with guys who were short, hairy, or obviously older. Like the sleeping little beast sprawled underneath his expensive sheets.

At least he never had before last night.

Just how the hell did that happen?

Last night he had gone to the beach for the bonfire party Quinn and Gary threw to celebrate the beginning of Bear Week in Provincetown. The couple loved the bears, and they got the most play when the bearded balls of fur came to town. And, like every year since Nino first moved to the Cape, Quinn and Gary threw a big party to rejoice in the bounty of hairy sex they would have for the week.

Although he supported his friends' right to poke the bears, he hadn't wanted to go. He hated Bear Week and loudly complained about it every year. He didn't enjoy the plus-sized men who sashayed around town shirtless and in sarongs. Their presence destroyed the idyllic beauty he typically enjoyed—half-naked, hot men just waiting to service him.

When Bear Week arrived, that perfection was shattered and replaced with hairy rolls of fat, so he usually holed up in his apartment. The only action he got for seven days came from his hand and the porn he hoarded on his computer. He'd anxiously count down the days until the furry fellows departed. Once the last ferry sounded its horn at the end of Bear Week, Nino would reemerge onto Commercial Street and resume his quest for man flesh after his weeklong hiatus.

That was what he had planned on doing again this year, but Quinn had insisted Nino attend the party.

Out of all his friends, including Van, only Quinn knew about Nino's recent troubles. Keeping secrets from Van wasn't something Nino normally did, but Van was too busy being in love. He hadn't wanted to bother his best friend with his issues when Van was acting like a disgusting teenager with Zach.

His friend deserved the happiness he'd found, even if it made Nino want to vomit.

Quinn knew this, and he didn't want Nino to be alone. Out of respect for Quinn's concern, Nino had gone to the party.

Why hadn't he stuck to his guns and stayed home? Especially now that he spied the empty condom wrapper lying beside the bed, where the little bear sawed more wood than a paper mill. Being alone last night would have been better than waking up to this disaster.

He'd not only fucked a bear, but he'd let the guy stay the night. He had always brought tricks back to his place, fucked the shit out of them, and then sent them on their merry way. He'd never *ever* allowed some random guy to sleep over. Doing so broke rule number three of the Rules of Nino's Life, a six-rule system he'd followed for years.

What had happened last night that made him break his rules?

He broke other people's rules quite frequently, but he'd made it a point to never breach one of his own.

But now he had, and he'd done it with a bear.

How fucked up was that?

He wanted this bear out of his bed, out of his apartment, and out of his life.

Right the fuck now.

TEDDY MILLER ignored the annoying voice that kept demanding he wake up. He had no intention of complying. Artillery shells from some unseen enemy fired inside his brain, and his tongue was rawer than if he'd been licking the hairy ass of a grizzly muscle bear all night.

While he'd normally find that idea really hot, the hangover that slowly churned the contents of his stomach quickly snuffed out the fires of his usual passion. Why did he have to drink all that trash-can punch at the party? He hadn't guzzled down alcohol like that since college. He definitely wasn't getting out of bed any time soon.

He craved sleep, and sleep was what he planned on getting.

"Get up!" the voice repeated more forcefully. "Now."

Teddy turned over and burrowed underneath the covers.

Bringing Irene with him to P-town had been a mistake. She had promised him she'd let him do his thing if he'd let her tag along, and though Teddy loved Irene, she tended to be a royal pain in his hairy ass.

He just couldn't tell her no whenever she looked at him with her baby blues and pouted.

She'd been there for Teddy since college, when his heart was broken for the first and last time. She had brought him back from despair, like any good hag. Having Irene had been a lifesaver. Since then, she'd been his constant companion.

Because of that, he'd relented and let her come. But now that she insisted he get up by rudely shaking him awake, he had half a mind to tell her to get the fuck out of the condo.

"Goddammit, Irene," he mumbled. His throat burned as if he'd had a cock lodged down his gullet all night. He only remembered hard alcohol crossing his lips instead of a nice, hard dick. "Leave me be, will you?"

"No, I will not," Irene's strangely masculine voice told him. "And I'm *not* Irene."

Teddy's eyes fluttered open. Instead of the beige Ikea bed stand that passed for furniture in his rental, a solid oak nightstand with brass drawer pulls sat beside the bed. The closet that stood open just beyond held more clothes than he'd brought with him from Boston, and as his gaze continued to sweep the bedroom's interior, the olive walls with the white trim and wainscoting revealed to Teddy that he definitely was not in his condo.

When he finally noticed the half-dressed man who stood next to the bed staring down at him, Teddy immediately sat up. His already aching head thudded in response. "Who the fuck are you?" he asked the shirtless man with zero percent body fat and rippling washboard abs. His perfect body made Teddy even more ill. "And where the hell am I?"

"I'm Nino," the man answered as he looked away. "If you want anything else from me, you'll have to cover up first."

"What the hell are you talking about?" Teddy asked before he realized he was buck-ass naked. Immediately, he grabbed the white satin bedsheets and wrapped them around his body. Nino's wrinkled upper lip told him Nino apparently didn't appreciate gazing upon a more lived-in body.

From Nino's chiseled perfection, he guessed the man hadn't eaten a hamburger in five years, which probably explained why he was being such a dick. Hunger could do that to a person.

"Better?" Teddy asked as Nino slowly turned back to him.

Nino answered with only a nod.

"Now, would you mind telling me where I am?"

"Where do you think you are, Sherlock? At home in your bed?"

Teddy was really starting to hate this guy for more than just his perfect body.

"I assume this is your place, then?" he asked.

Nino clapped. "You must be smarter than the average bear. It didn't take you too long to figure that one out."

Teddy officially hated him now. "You're being a real douche. You know that, right?"

Nino looked off into space for a moment and then nodded in agreement. "That I am," he answered. A grin spread across his lips that seemed to make him even more perfect. There was a mischievous yet innocent quality to the smile that caught Teddy off guard. It made his cock stiffen.

What the fuck was *that* about? He hadn't been attracted to Nino's type since college.

The all-American guys with smooth, flawless skin were like pictures in a magazine. Pretty to look at but two-dimensional and flat. That was why Teddy preferred men with more meat on their bones and fur that covered their chests and arms. The extra padding seemed to be an outward sign of truly grounded people who knew who they were and what they had to offer.

Perfect people with no body hair were often fakes. The lack of fat and fur somehow had a direct correlation to their personalities. As if by shaving off the unwanted hair and pounds they somehow cut themselves off from what it meant to be a normal person with flaws.

While he'd once chased hairless pups in college, he'd long since abandoned that pursuit.

Or at least he thought he had.

His hard cock apparently had other ideas. It liked what it saw in Nino and wanted an up close and personal meeting. That unnerved Teddy. He rarely strayed from the norm because routine gave him security. Deviations bothered him.

Change and Teddy Miller were not exactly the best of friends.

"SO THE two of us hooked up last night?" the naked ball of fur asked from Nino's bed.

The question threw Nino even more than waking up next to this guy. How could he *not* know he'd had sex with Nino? Nino completely understood why *he* would block such an event from his mind. After all, he'd grown accustomed to bedding guys with six-packs, not ones who carted around a pony keg.

For this unfit fucker, sleeping with Nino was one for the record books.

He had half a mind to strip and give the little guy a good gander at what he'd had the pleasure of touching last night. But there was something about the way he looked up at Nino with such wide eyes that triggered a childhood memory he'd long since forgotten.

This dude reminded him of Teo, his teddy bear.

As a child, Nino didn't have very many friends, but Teo was always there for him. When Nino got home after another harsh day of being pushed around by the popular kids, Teo always sat on his bed with open arms, waiting to give Nino his hug. He'd spent many afternoons telling Teo his problems, and Teo had always listened. They were best friends, at least until Nino outgrew his awkward caterpillar stage and became the butterfly he now was. When that happened, he had moved Teo from his bed to his closet and ultimately to the church donation box. When his parents took Teo away, he'd never given him another thought.

At least until this very moment.

The way this guy sat there, staring at him, reminded Nino of his teddy bear. He fought the urge to crawl into bed and snuggle inside the furry arms that used to make him feel safe as a child.

After what he'd been through the past few weeks, Nino could use a hug from his childhood pal right now.

"Um, are you okay?"

The voice jarred Nino out of his memory. He scanned the room, double-checking that he was still in his apartment in Provincetown and not back in the shack he once called home in Sao Paulo. When he was convinced his world was as it should be, Nino finally replied, "I'm fine."

"Well, you don't look it. You went white there for a minute. Like you saw a ghost."

Nino didn't like that he had momentarily let his guard down in front of someone he didn't even know. He rarely did that even for Van. It was past time for this guy to leave. "Yes, well, I was just deciding whether I should try to wash all your hair out of my sheets or just throw them out and start anew."

"I see you're back to being a douche," the guy retorted. "Your last name must be Massengill."

Nino liked the comeback. He rarely found someone who could verbally spar with him. Van tried, but he usually failed miserably. Even though Nino appreciated wit, he valued his private space and the six rules of his life more. This guy had to go. "My last name won't matter. We won't see each other ever again."

"Fine by me," the guy replied. "I don't usually find myself in this situation."

His comment piqued Nino's curiosity. Was this guy even more of a loser than Nino thought? Did he not even hook up with guys more in his league? "And what situation is that?"

"Waking up in a bed with a plastic."

"A what?" Nino asked as the guy got up from Nino's bed and walked over to his crumpled clothes. His body wasn't all bad. Despite the fur and the gut, this man obviously spent *some* time at the gym. Just not as much as Nino did, or the guys Nino usually fucked stupid.

"You know," he finally responded. "Guys like you. Perfect bodies. Flawless hair. Zero imperfections." He shoved his legs through his underwear and shorts at the same time before pulling his shirt over his head. "I've never been into guys like you. Far too superficial for me. I like substance, and plastic doesn't really have much of that."

What the fuck was going on here? Did he wake up in some parallel universe where the fatties somehow took over the world? Where people with flab turned up their noses at those who took care of themselves?

"Are you shitting me right now?" Nino asked. If he had a rope, this guy would be hanging from the ceiling fan. "Who the fuck are you to judge me by how I look?"

The furry son of a bitch snorted. "Are *you* serious? You've been judging me since you woke me up, based on how *I* look. Are you telling me that you can judge me but I can't judge you?"

That was exactly what Nino was saying. Now that the hairy fuck knew the score, he could take his fur-covered ass out of his apartment.

"Well, it goes both ways, sweetheart," he said to Nino. "You see me as a fat slob not worthy of you, and I see you as a vacuous prick not worth the words I'm speaking." As he slipped his hairy hobbit feet into his sandals, he glanced over at Nino. "Do you even know what vacuous means?"

Nino fought the urge to punch him in the throat. "I do," Nino said. "It means you're the little piece of shit this douche is flushing out of his apartment."

"Good one," the guy said with a chuckle before he exited the room. "For a plastic."

After Nino slammed the door to his bedroom shut, he headed for his bed and yanked the sheets free. There was no way he would ever touch anything that had come into contact with that fucking little cunt.

Nino *was* judging him. That was what he did. He just was no longer used to being judged, especially by someone who could benefit from a diet and a good trainer. He'd spent too many years improving himself, making himself better than what he once was, to be belittled ever again.

To cross paths with a man immune to Nino's looks and who apparently didn't give one fuck about his hard-earned hardbody intrigued him. But it also had another rather unpleasant effect. Deep within him churned turbulent emotions Nino had long since suppressed.

He had almost forgotten what it felt like to be rejected, and he didn't like the reminder one bit.

Chapter Two

IN THE shower, Nino scrubbed himself with his block of pumice. He normally used it to slough off the dead skin and keep his flesh smooth and blemish free. Today, he vigorously scrubbed his chest and arms, legs and thighs, and even his cock and balls in order to remove all traces of his furry little one-night stand. And it hurt like a motherfucking bitch.

As he scoured the arms that had most likely held that hairy bastard to his body, Nino couldn't believe he'd allowed him to get under his skin.

When was the last time that happened?

He prided himself on being the rubber to other people's glue. He'd long since learned how to ignore what people thought and focus only on his concerns and his needs. It had been a vital self-defense mechanism in Nino's youth.

When the kids at school teased him for being poor and made fun of the rags he called clothes, he'd learned to tune it out. Their comments became background noise on the playground. When they called him *gordo* and asked him how he could be so fat if he was so poor, their words turned into music on the radio that he silently sang to himself. When his older sisters told him he was *feio* and useless and that he would never find someone to love him because he was so ugly, their taunts took flight on the wind. He couldn't hear their insults if they floated in the sky with the clouds.

Just why did the words of some guy he didn't even know bother him so much? Schoolmates and siblings had tormented him for most of his life. He could handle himself.

What was it, then? Nino shut off the water and exited the shower. Was it the fact that someone thought he was an empty-headed himbo? Was it that Nino was seen as superficial and shallow? Was his pride simply wounded? And why the fuck did he even care?

Nino considered the answers to his questions as he studied himself in the mirror.

He puffed out his chest, noting the added definition to his pecs from his new chest exercises. He flexed his biceps, pleased with the lean curvature of the muscle. As a model, it was important to look good but not too massive. He'd managed to strike a good balance. He ran his fingers down the ridges of his abdominals and pinched the skin at his obliques. He couldn't pinch an inch, which was important, and when he turned around to look at his back and his ass, he was pleased to find his back nicely defined and his butt perky and toned.

But when he zoomed out, when he didn't focus on each part of his perfectly maintained body and instead took the whole person into account, Nino couldn't help but wonder if the little guy had been right.

Had he become plastic?

He'd managed to transform the chubby, ugly, poor kid into a model. His appearance, the very aspect people once ridiculed him for, became his bread and butter. Not only did he wear expensive clothes, but very important fashion designers paid him handsomely to walk down the runway or pose for photographs wearing the clothes they had designed. Nino's fat body had become a temple of Adonis that many men worshipped, and even though he didn't believe in relationships, Nino had men lining up for a chance to be his man.

All they got, though, was a one-time fuck and an express ticket out of his bed after he shot his load across their asses.

He embodied the very characteristics he was once teased for not possessing, and he'd achieved what many thought impossible. So why did his trick's words haunt him?

As he continued to stare at himself, Nino couldn't find the answer. He hated that little bastard for causing such turmoil, but for some reason, Nino hated himself even more.

Now *that* he just didn't understand at all.

AFTER NINO finished getting dressed, his foul mood seemed to be coming to an end. He might not have the answers to the questions that had plagued him in the shower, but he found he didn't really give a damn about them anymore.

They mattered as much to him as the corpulent cow he'd kicked out of his apartment.

Well, he wasn't really a cow, but so what? He hated him, so he *was* a cow as far as Nino was concerned.

That nameless little fuck was condemned to a life of mediocrity, while Nino was destined for far greater things. He was fabulous, and not only did Nino know it but so did his portfolio, chock full of photos that charted his rise from his humble beginnings in underwear to a male fashion model.

He might be experiencing some technical difficulties in his career at the moment, but his agent assured him all would be well. The modeling jobs would come rolling back in once all this shit with Ford Michaels blew over. That was why he wasn't going to let anything get him down anymore.

That just wasn't who Nino Santos was.

He was a force to be reckoned with. He had the ability to rise above the concerns that might bring a lesser man to his knees. He'd come so far that there was only one direction Nino ever felt comfortable traveling, and that was up.

The doldrums that had gripped him for the past few weeks had to be cast aside. Embracing life and having fun were the only ways to combat what the mad gods above threw down at him. If he didn't make a big deal about it, then his problems were no big deal. He'd come through on the other side of the shit tunnel of life, smelling like roses and with a big fucking smile plastered on his face for the cameras to capture for posterity.

Nino snatched his white Oakley sunglasses—which were his favorite pair because they made him look so damn fine—from his chest of drawers. He ran his fingers through his curly locks, sending them sprawling about his head, and exited his bedroom, ready to meet the day head-on.

Although he hated Bear Week, he wasn't going to allow any more of those furry fat asses to stand between him and his need to get his fuck on. Somewhere out in P-town a hot, hairless jock just waited for Nino to defile him, and Nino intended on finding him, even if it took him all day to hunt his prey down.

But as Nino walked down the hallway in his apartment, a rustle from the kitchen caught his ear. Nino bristled. The guy was still here, no doubt eating him out of house and home. If he had to, he'd grab the guy by his short hairs and toss him over the porch railing to the alley below.

"What the fuck are you doing here?" Nino asked as he turned the corner of the kitchen. But it wasn't the hairy little guy from this morning foraging through his cabinets. It was his best friend and former roommate, Van, who stared back at him with arched eyebrows and a puzzled expression.

"Well, I see someone woke up on the wrong side of the bed this morning," Van commented with a snicker.

Why was there a shit-eating grin on Van's face? Nino didn't like it, but he didn't dare ask. Van only looked this pleased with himself when he was about to make Nino's life miserable. Right now, he needed that about as much as he needed to find another bearish guy in his bed. "What are you doing here?" Nino asked as he sidestepped the meaning behind Van's silly expression. "I thought you were too busy getting nailed by Zach to venture out of the new apartment."

"Zach's spending the morning writing his latest novel," Van answered as he continued going through the kitchen cabinets. "Besides, he's already fucked me twice this morning, so I'm good to go till lunch." Van stopped and thought about his answer. "Well, till I get home at least."

Nino rolled his eyes, to which Van replied with his typical raspberry. "You still haven't answered my question. What are you doing in my apartment, besides raiding my kitchen? You don't live here anymore, in case you've forgotten."

"How could I forget that I no longer live with such a surly sourpuss?" Van asked with a cheesy grin.

Nino ignored Van's dig. Van obviously wanted to get into one of their fake arguments, where they teased each other mercilessly, but Nino wasn't in the mood. He feared further taunts this morning might make him snap. Instead, he gestured for Van to answer his question.

"Fine," Van complained. "I'm just grabbing the last of the dishes I left behind. Don't worry. I'm not taking everything. Although with how little you eat, I could take the whole kitchen and you'd probably never notice."

"I would if you took the blender," Nino told him. "Gotta have my protein shakes."

"I thought that's what your tricks were for," Van said with another big smile.

He shook his head. "I provide my tricks the protein. There's no reciprocation on my part."

"I almost forgot," Van replied. "It's always about you."

The words smarted, even though their intent had been one of playful ribbing. Did Van think Nino was a plastic too? He contemplated asking if that were true. Should he also tell Van what had happened?

He couldn't. That would make him too vulnerable, and Nino didn't do vulnerability. Not even with Van. Instead, he changed the course of their dialogue. "Not working at the Carpe Diem today?"

Van shook his head in response as he resumed taking plates out of the cabinet and depositing them in the box that rested on the counter. "Jonas gave me the day off. He and Sebastian have plans this weekend, so I'll be in charge of the guesthouse while they're gone."

"I'm glad to see your career change is going well," Nino commented. Although he supported Van's decision to abandon his porn job for love, he couldn't fathom changing anything about his life for someone else. Most people were fickle and came in and out of one's life on a whim. Gay men were even worse. They had the attention span of a puppy suffering from ADD.

"Thanks," Van finally answered as he closed one cabinet and moved on to the next. "I was a little scared when I gave it up last year, but I've never been happier."

Nino was loath to admit it, but Van's words were true. He'd been there when Van had his heart broken and saw how it changed his best friend. These days, though, Van walked around as if his shoes were made of clouds and went about his day with an idiotic grin plastered on his face. The sappy spectacle was nauseating, but he didn't begrudge Van his happiness. His friend had earned it.

"So, what's new with you?" Van asked as he took some cups out of the cabinet. A twinkle reflected in Van's eyes, the same one Nino had first noticed when he entered the kitchen. He wasn't in the mood. Why couldn't Van realize that?

"I haven't seen you out and about for a while."

"It's Bear Week," Nino responded and saw no reason to clarify further. More than anyone else, his best friend knew how much Nino despised a week devoted to the heavy and the hirsute. The occasion was nothing to celebrate.

"Yes." Van nodded. "It is."

After his reply, Van just stood there, staring at him. He evidently expected some grand reveal, but Nino had no idea what Van wanted him to come clean about. If he would just speak his mind, they could save themselves a lot of time. But the more he thought about it, the less he wanted to get into it with Van. His eye twitch, the one that only acted up when he was severely stressed, wouldn't let up. If confronted with something unpleasant right now, he was liable to start a fight. The last thing he needed was to get into an argument with Van.

"Well, lock up when you're done," he announced as he headed for the front door. "I've got guys to do."

"So, you're into bears now?"

Van's question stopped Nino in his tracks. "What are you talking about?" he asked as he turned around. Van's smug expression gazed back at him. "You know I'm not."

"Uh-huh," Van replied. He rounded the kitchen counter to stand in front of Nino. "Now, tell me another lie."

"You're hot, and I want to fuck you," Nino deadpanned.

"A different lie." Van crossed his arms and stared at Nino.

"I could tell you a whole butt full of lies, but you seem to have something pretty specific you want me to say." Although Nino didn't want to have this conversation, Van wasn't going to let the matter drop. "What is it?"

"I'd like you to tell me about the pocket bear that marched out of here as I came in."

Nino's shoulders slumped. He'd hoped the little bastard had left before Van got there. He didn't want to have to tell *anyone* about what he did last night, much less admit what happened this morning.

"It's nothing," Nino fibbed as he turned to leave.

"Now, *that's* the first new lie you've told me in years."

Instead of responding, he left. That was the best course of action, considering his mood. Besides, he had more important things to do, like finding a brand new hole to pummel. That might be the only way out of his current funk.

Chapter Three

TEDDY DREADED going back to the condo. Once he did, he'd be hit with the bitch storm that was Irene upon arrival. She'd be pissed that he had left her at the beach last night, even though he didn't remember leaving, and then lambaste him for not calling when she'd left three voice mails and about fifteen texts. At least that was the count when he last checked his phone.

But he didn't want to think about Irene or the storm that brewed back at the rental. For now, it could wait. Instead, he wanted to enjoy his stroll down Commercial Street and take in a sight he hadn't allowed himself to experience for a couple of years.

Bear Week in Provincetown.

Hairy hunks of men of all varieties trudged up and down the street.

Over by the Purple Feather, a group of muscle bears suggestively licked the snaking drips of ice cream from the cones they had just purchased. They laughed and groped each other in front of the store before walking away, arm in arm, down the street. Why couldn't everyone be like these guys and not be so damn body conscious? They loved and lusted after each other with hearts as big as their barrel chests.

"Honey, that shirt will be perfect for tea," said a bear exiting a shop to Teddy's left. He and his friend walked just in front of Teddy. They had more than a few bags wrapped around their wrists as if they were purses. "I wish I'd found one there I liked."

"You did. They just didn't have your size," replied his friend, who was perhaps one extra-large size smaller than the other.

"Oh, bitch! I know you just didn't say I was fat!"

He chuckled at the exchange as the larger bear playfully pawed his apologetic friend. Few events made him laugh more than two burly bears acting like Goldilocks.

"Ooh, let's get new leather harnesses for the Vault at Large," the larger bear said. The Vault at Large was a popular bear-themed leather party over at the Crown & Anchor.

"Bitch, you don't want a new harness, you just want that hot tattooed sales boy to fit you for a cock ring again. I mean, really? How many times are you going to make him touch your junk this week?"

"As many times as it takes," his friend replied before they disappeared into FK Leather.

Teddy was sad to lose the pair. He briefly entertained the idea of following them into the store, but he didn't want to appear like some bear stalker. Besides, leather just wasn't his thing. It wasn't that he found hairy daddies with cute, cuddly bellies unattractive in leather; it was preparing for such an event that he didn't care for. Getting into gear seemed quite the feat for Teddy. He never attached his harness right, and the cock strap always hurt and pinched the base of his dick.

If his cock was going to be hurting, he'd rather it be from some hairy loving.

Now *that* was a party he'd gladly attend.

Unlike the one he couldn't remember from last night, where he ended up in bed with one of the biggest and most attractive douche bags he'd ever encountered in his life.

How the fuck had that happened?

Even though he hated the smug bastard, he had to admit the boy was smoking hot. For a plastic, arrogant dickwad.

Perhaps Irene knew the details of how he ended up with Nino. Unfortunately, in order to get them, he'd have to call her or head back to the condo. He had yet to gird his loins for such an encounter. Dealing with Irene required football padding and a cup. All he had was a queasy stomach and a killer headache, which meant he didn't have the required defenses.

What he needed was sustenance, so he stopped by one of the local shops to buy an ice cream cone. He hoped the dark-chocolate scoop of delight might replenish his strength and clear his hazy memory of the night before. Food always seemed to help him when he needed to work through a problem. He'd been that way since he was a kid, when his bitch of a mother made his life a living hell.

Whenever she invited her stripper friends over to their apartment after a night of flashing her titties to the world, he'd consume a bag of chips or candy while she and her friends got high in the living room. The simple act of eating allowed him to escape the fact that his mother was either doing drugs or some random guy she brought home. Who knew if the late-night guest was someone his mother was interested in or someone who had paid for her services?

The food gave him the will he needed to get past the horror.

That was what he needed now. He required the focus food gave him so he could figure out how he had ended up in bed with such a strikingly attractive asshole of a human being. Waking up with someone he didn't even remember wasn't like him. At all. In the past, he'd always been careful whom he tricked with.

He preferred getting to know the guy first before they dove into each other's bodies. He understood that was probably a byproduct of being raised by Amanda Miller, but he was fine with it.

He had no desire to turn into the strung-out slut his mother had been so hell-bent on becoming.

That was why waking up at Nino's bothered him. It also explained why he'd been such a dick to the man, even if he deserved it. Teddy's actions deviated too much from his usual routine, something he prided himself on following. His customary behavior not only gave him direction, but it was one of the qualities that made him the polar opposite of his mother.

She was loose; he had more restraint. She was hung up on body image, so he didn't give two cents about the way he looked. She sold her body for a living, and he earned a living with his mind, as a lawyer. She was chaos. He was order.

To find himself in bed with someone he didn't know and who was obviously just as body conscious as his mother churned the ice cream in his stomach. Instead of the treat giving him focus, it gave him indigestion instead.

Teddy sighed.

The ice cream wasn't going to help him remember. He recalled everything else from yesterday quite clearly—Gary's invitation to the party, getting wasted at the Tea Dance, grabbing some pizza at Spiritus, and then heading home to get ready for the party.

After that, there was nothing but a gaping hole in his memory.

Teddy had no choice. If he wanted answers, he had to head back to the condo. And to Irene. There he might find what eluded him, if he survived whatever Irene had in store for him when he got back.

TEDDY HAD prepared himself for a lot of things when he got back to the condo. He anticipated Irene launching into a verbal assault as soon as she saw the whites of his eyes. He expected gnashing of teeth and maybe even some spittle flying from her angry snarl. He even guessed she might be sitting on the patio, smoking a cigarette and flinging the still-lit butt at him. She had done that once after he abandoned her at a gay club in Boston. He had left with a guy he'd been talking to on the gay dating app called Cyber, and she had been furious. He pictured her leaning out from the second floor as she'd done then, tossing objects at him from above like in some idiotic sitcom.

He definitely never imagined this.

When he slid open the patio door, instead of a banshee screaming obscenities, Irene stood in the kitchen, making breakfast. She dished up scrambled eggs onto two plates and placed them on the kitchen table. She didn't scream or shout; she simply smiled and told him good morning. Her blonde hair didn't lie in a tangled rat's nest that communicated she'd been waiting up all night. It was pulled back in a 1980s-inspired side ponytail. She dressed in constant homage to the decade of her birth and dedicated her fashion sense to the decade's hair bands, New Wave music, and hideous clothing. Right now, she wore her "I Love the 80s" T-shirt. As if the way she looked didn't communicate that enough.

Still, she looked at peace. What the fuck was up with that?

"Good morning," he told her as he walked into the kitchen, where she poured him some orange juice. He looked around for Louie, his French bulldog, but his handsome boy was nowhere to be found. "Where's Louie?"

"Gary took him to the dog park," Irene told him after she handed him the glass of juice. Her face was gentle and free of the usually caked-on makeup popular during the eighties. Today, she looked more like a woman of the twenty-first century. Well, minus the hairdo. "He thought Louie might want to socialize with other mutts." Irene hated Louie, and the feeling was mutual. Most Frenchies were gregarious and friendly. Louie was reticent and antisocial. The only person Louie cared for was Teddy. Everyone else, Louie treated with disdain.

Preferring not to talk about the dog that always peed on her shoes, Irene set her attention to her task, buttering the toast that had just popped out of the toaster.

"You cooked?" he asked. Why did that have to come out so incredulously? She was trying to be nice, and he had just poked the bear. That wasn't very smart. Still, Irene had never been one of those hags who catered to her gay. She'd always been the other kind, the one who made it her life's mission to get her boy to behave himself and punished him like a child when he didn't act according to her standards. Even so, Irene loved him. She just had trouble expressing her feelings in a productive manner. It was who she was, and he had accepted that a long time ago.

"I did," she said triumphantly as she finished applying the butter. She motioned for him to sit at the table, and he did as instructed. Teddy had no intention of unleashing the beast by continuing to be combative.

"Thanks, Reenie," he said as she placed the plate in front of him. She then took the seat to his left. Unsure of what else to do or say, he started to eat. As he ate his eggs and then his toast, he kept stealing glances out of the corners of his eyes. When was the other shoe going to drop?

Irene just sat there, eating. She wasn't being difficult or launching into a never-ending series of questions. He had no previous training with this Irene. She had caught him completely off guard.

"Did you have a good time last night?" she finally asked after she finished off her eggs. She tore the crust from her toast as she awaited his answer.

"I'm not sure," he admitted with a shrug. "Don't remember much."

She nodded as if she expected that to be his answer.

"How about you?" he asked, terrified his question might wake the sleeping beast.

"It was okay," she said. "There were lots of hot guys there."

She ended her last statement with a sigh of exasperation. Teddy understood the meaning. Not only was Irene a hag nag, she also found herself almost exclusively attracted to gay men. She was a beautiful woman, once someone got past her ridiculous style, and could land *any* straight man she wanted, if she were at all interested in them.

Instead of setting her sights on a more attainable goal, she had spent most of her adult life trying to find a gold-star gay, otherwise known as a gay man who'd never been with a woman. She dreamed of converting him. Whenever she prowled the clubs for a homo to call her own, he referred to her as Goldie, after her search for that perfect gold star. Naturally, she hated the nickname, but the comment usually calmed her down and made her rethink her choices.

At least for a week or two. She'd been that way ever since college.

"You didn't think so?"

Irene's question startled him. Teddy pulled himself out of his thoughts and stared into her inquiring blue eyes. "I'm sorry. What, now?"

"You didn't think there were a lot of hot guys there?"

Teddy shrugged. "I really don't remember."

She looked at him crossways. It was how she looked at him when she was trying to determine if he was pulling her leg or not.

"I'm serious." He placed her empty plate on top of his and then walked over to the kitchen sink. "I have zero memory of last night."

"Why do you think that is?"

He turned on the water and washed their breakfast dishes. "I was kinda hoping you'd be able to tell me."

"Did you take any drugs last night?"

If the sink had a nozzle, he'd have drenched her head to toe for that comment. She knew his stance on drugs. After all, he'd seen what they had done to his mother. He'd never done *any* drugs in his life. It was stupid to ask him such a question.

"I'm sorry," she apologized rather quickly. "I was just asking. You're usually so in control. I've never seen you act like you acted last night. I didn't know if P-town brought that out in you or not."

"What do you mean?" he asked. Irene's statement concerned him. Just what had he done last night? Obviously, Irene had seen something. If he found that out, then maybe he could understand how he woke up next to the heir to the Massengill fortune.

"We were only together for the first thirty minutes or so," she revealed. "So I didn't see everything. But you got shitfaced pretty quickly. The last time I saw you, you were running around naked and humping random guys' legs."

"Are you shitting me?"

Irene shook her head. "If you don't believe me, ask some of the guys we met at tea yesterday. They were there and snapped pictures of you. I tried to stop them, but you were acting too much like a fool. I finally gave up and let you be. Next thing I knew you were gone. Without a word." Her eyes turned hard, as if she were trying her best to keep her usual anger contained. "I called several times and even texted you, but you never even replied."

Her hard gaze softened, and her lips made a slight pout. It was not only pitiful but also extremely genuine. He'd been a jerk to Irene and quite possibly the worst person alive.

Maybe even worse than Nino.

"I'm sorry, Reenie," he said as he drew her into a hug. "I promise I didn't see any of your texts till I woke up. Otherwise, I would have told you I was okay."

She nodded. She obviously didn't believe him one hundred percent. Her half-closed eyes told him that much, but instead of whining about it, she let the matter drop. He liked this Irene. Where the hell had this woman been all these years?

"Was he at least cute?" she asked as she pulled away from the embrace.

"I guess," Teddy replied with a shrug. "If you like physical perfection combined with a personality no deeper than a puddle."

"I do," Irene said with a nod. "And just how hot are we talking about?"

Teddy swatted her on the behind and immediately regretted doing so. Most physical contact from a gay man, including him, revved up her sexual engine to warp drive. She bit her lip seductively at the gesture and moaned. He needed to shift her loins back to neutral. Fast.

"Rein it in, Goldie." He wagged his index finger at her. "I like cock as much as you do. Remember?"

Irene took a deep breath, and when she exhaled, the flames of her passion reduced from a raging fire to a slow burn. It always took Irene a few minutes to get her insane hormones under control. Why did he sometimes think she was only acting this way, though? As if there was some secret she was hiding? They weren't supposed to keep things from each other.

"So, you were saying," Irene at last said. "How hot was he?"

Continuing down this conversational path wouldn't be good. It would only add fuel to her fire to discuss Nino's perfect body with strong, lean muscles and his flat, muscular stomach.

Hearing about his full head of curly hair or his piercing brown eyes set under dark, bushy eyebrows could potentially get her motor going again. If he described Nino's perfect smile, the one that made him look like both a choirboy *and* a bad boy, well, it would all be over. She'd be rocketing through space from the fire he'd ignited in her lady parts. Because whether she faked it or not, she did love a hot man.

Also, the good-boy bad-boy combo rolled into one guy got her hotter than anything else. Teddy had to admit, he liked those qualities as well. A little too much.

That must be why Teddy couldn't stop thinking about him. Nino might have been a prick, but he was probably one of the most gorgeous pricks he'd seen in a long time.

"He was okay," he said, finally answering Irene's question. But Nino wasn't a subject he wanted to discuss anymore. It was time for a newer and better topic. "What are we going to do today?" he asked, and while Irene went through her laundry list of ideas, Teddy's thoughts immediately traveled back to Nino.

How was he going to get that to stop?

Chapter Four

WHILE IRENE was upstairs changing for their excursion into town, Teddy sat on the patio, waiting for Gary to return with Louie. He hadn't seen his pooch since before he had left for the beach party last night, and as far as Teddy was concerned, that had been too long. He needed a serious dose of some Louie loving, which his pooch always had in plentiful supply.

For him at least.

Just how did Gary get Louie to go with him in the first place? Louie rarely did as anyone else instructed. Whenever someone tried to get him to move or to come, he rested on his back legs and stared at them as if they were idiots.

Louie had most likely been crossbred with a cat. That was how ornery he sometimes was. He didn't care if Louie was half feline. He loved his handsome boy, and he couldn't imagine his life without the smushed-up face and bat ears.

Just then a car turned down the gravel driveway, and Gary's green Honda Civic crunched its way down the path. He immediately jumped to his feet and was halfway down the walkway when Gary opened the car door to let his little rascal out.

Louie leaped out of the passenger seat, his tongue lolling to the left and his ears pulled back flat against his head. He bounded on furry white paws up the three steps until he met Teddy halfway. Teddy knelt down, and Louie hopped into his open arms, where he proceeded to lick Teddy's face before sniffing intently at his clothes.

"What do you smell there, my handsome boy?" he asked Louie.

"I'm guessing your trick from last night," Gary offered.

Teddy stuck out his tongue at Gary in response.

"Normally, I'd say I've got just the place for your tongue," Gary said as he motioned for Teddy to put his tongue back in his mouth. "But since we're old friends and all, I'll spare you the pain of knowing you can never taste my sweet white ass."

"Thank heavens for that," Teddy replied with a wink. He and Gary had known each other since Gary and Quinn's days in Boston. They used to live in the same apartment complex until Gary and Quinn inherited the row of condominiums, where they resided and also managed. Teddy owed the sweet deal he got on this condo every time he came to P-town to that friendship.

"Is this the thanks I get, Theodore Miller?"

As always, Gary addressed him by his full name. It was a personality quirk he'd initially found very strange. Now, it was just a part of who Gary was. He couldn't imagine his friend any other way, even if Gary's face had now grown dark with mock irritation. He strolled down the wooden walkway toward Teddy and Louie, sashaying more like his drag alter ego, Penny Poison, than his friend. When Gary was feeling this feisty, it was difficult for Teddy to know where Gary stopped and Penny started.

"I not only give you a considerable discount on our five-star accommodations, but I take your ungrateful little bully to the dog park. And you don't even have the common courtesy to at least *pretend* to pine for my ass."

Before Teddy could respond, Louie answered with an "Arf!" He evidently didn't like being called ungrateful, even though that was what he was. After making his comment, Louie continued his persistent snuffing around Teddy's legs. He apparently caught a whiff of something on Teddy he liked.

"First of all," he told Gary as he pushed Louie away from trying to smell his crotch, "as much as I do appreciate you and Quinn letting me stay here at a discounted rate, I'd hardly call the place five-star. I'd give it three and a half at best."

Gary gasped in pretend incredulity.

"Secondly, I doubt your ass is as sweet as you are constantly advertising. It's not exactly a bowl of Skittles."

Louie stopped trying to sniff him long enough to punctuate that comment with a hearty snuff. While Teddy laughed at Louie's appraisal of Gary's smelly ass, Gary glared down at his dog with playful derision.

"And lastly, my Louie is an angel," Teddy stated as he forced Louie to stop sniffing him as if he were hiding doggie treats in his underwear. When Louie finally obeyed, he rewarded his little friend with a scratch to the sweet spot on his backside. In response, Louie gazed up at him as if Teddy hung the stars and the moon.

"When did you turn into such a foul being, Theodore? The man I once knew worshipped the very ground I walked upon."

"True. But that only lasted for five minutes," he added with a wink. "Now I greet you with the contempt only a good friend can muster."

Gary sighed in defeat. Although he had a wicked tongue, Gary could rarely keep up with Teddy. Few people could. "Fine, I give up," Gary said before kissing Teddy on the cheek. "With how vigorously you wag your tongue, your blowjobs must be incredible."

Teddy laughed as he led Gary to the patio in front of his condo. "I haven't had a complaint yet."

"I'd imagine not," his friend said as he sat down. Gary then peered through the patio door, squinting his eyes to see past the sun's reflection on this amazingly hot day. "Where's Miss Frost?" Gary finally asked before sitting down. Teddy took the seat next to Gary. As usual, Louie jumped up into Teddy's lap, sniffed intently at his clothes, and then proceeded to fall asleep.

"You don't like her," he said. It was a statement rather than a question. If Gary liked someone, then he addressed them by their full name. Gary didn't use nicknames. That was why he was always Theodore instead of Teddy. If Gary didn't like a person, he referred to them by their last name only, which explained his referencing of Irene as Miss Frost.

"I think she's a beautiful woman," Gary replied.

"That's not what I said. And you know it."

Gary looked down his nose at Teddy. "You think you know me so well, don't you?"

"Only because I do," he admitted. "Now spill. Why don't you like Irene?"

"You know I don't speak ill of people," Gary began. That was a big fat lie. He loved Gary, but Gary's love of gossip was legendary, especially about people he didn't care for. "But that woman gets on my last nerve."

"Why?"

"Do I have enough time to list all the reasons before she descends from on high?" Gary asked, nodding to the upstairs bedroom where Irene slept.

He smacked Gary's leg. "Be nice."

"I am nice," Gary replied. His lips pulled back into a mischievous grin. "To those who deserve such treatment. I'm still debating if you're worthy. I know Miss Frost is not."

"What did she do to you?"

"You mean besides act like Debbie Downer at the party? All she could talk about to anyone who got within earshot was how insane you were acting. How she couldn't believe that you were behaving like some college frat boy on spring break. How disappointed she was in you. Then she proceeded to hit on and completely alienate most of my guests. None of them wanted her big old breasticles smashed against them. Did she care? Not at all." Gary stopped and locked eyes with Teddy. "Then she had the audacity to tell me that green was *not* my color."

And there it was. The true reason behind Gary's dislike of Irene wasn't her mostly irritating behavior. It was the fact that she unintentionally put down Penny Poison, whose signature color was green. The last person who dogged Gary about Penny was Gary's one-time drag partner, Suzy Wroughtinkrotch.

That had ended in complete and utter disaster. The two could barely coexist in Provincetown. Whenever they crossed paths on Commercial, people scattered to avoid being collateral damage.

"She doesn't know about Penny," he said. "She didn't mean to offend you."

Gary snuffed, and it reminded him of Louie. There was no way he was going to tell Gary that. His friend's feathers had been ruffled enough.

"I can guarantee you that if she knew, she wouldn't have said a thing."

"Regardless," Gary said. "Common decorum dictates that you don't comment on what people you don't know look good in. Hold your tongue. Save your ass. That's what my momma always told me."

"Irene's never been one to hold her tongue. Please don't hold Irene being Irene against her. She's really a very wonderful woman. Once you get to know her. She just has…." Teddy stopped. He didn't quite know how to communicate her sexual craving for gay boys or her mother hen qualities. "Issues."

"That's a bit of an understatement," Gary added with a huff. "But for you, Theodore, I promise to be as polite as humanly possible."

Teddy groaned.

"What's that for?" Gary asked.

"You're only polite to people you don't like," Teddy said. "To everyone else, you're a bit of a bitch."

Gary smiled, quite pleased with Teddy's appraisal of his character. "I am," he finally said with a glint to his eyes. "And I love it!"

While Gary continued to bask in the glory of his bitchiness, Teddy leaned forward in his chair and peered through the patio door into the condo beyond.

"What are you doing?" Gary asked.

"Checking to see if Irene was downstairs yet or not."

Gary stared at him. The right side of his mouth hooked upward. His friend had obviously caught a whiff of secrecy and scandal, and the glint in Gary's eyes communicated that he just had to know the juicy details. "Well, out with it, then," Gary said as he waved his hands at Teddy to get his attention. "If you don't want your hag to hear this, it's got to be good."

"Tell me about the party last night," Teddy said when he turned back to face Gary.

Gary looked confused. "You don't remember?"

Teddy shook his head, and Gary chuckled. "Theodore, I *so* love being in sole possession of knowledge someone seeks. It grants me power that I intend to use." Gary scooted himself closer to Teddy, kicked off his flip-flops, and perched his feet up on the table. He then wiggled his toes in Teddy's face. "Rub my feet and maybe I'll remember."

"Gary," Teddy warned. He hated massaging other people, especially their feet. His mother used to make him rub her feet or shoulders after her late nights at the strip club. "You know I don't do massages."

Gary grinned. "I know. But if you want me to answer your questions, you must appease me. It's tit for tat."

"I don't want your tits," Teddy told him. "Or your nasty feet."

Gary moved his feet off the table and sighed. "I guess you don't want to know what you did at the party, then."

"Come on, Gary," Teddy complained. "Just tell me."

Obviously done being difficult, Gary said, "Fine, I'll tell you, but I expect some sort of recompense."

"As long as it's not a foot massage, you got it."

Gary nodded his acceptance of the conditions and said, "You were very drunk."

"I know," Teddy interrupted. "And dry humping guys on the beach. That much Irene told me, but I don't remember how I...." Why didn't he want to tell Gary about waking up in Nino's bed? It wasn't exactly unusual. Most gay men had been there and done that. Gary included.

"How you what?"

Teddy shook his head. "You go. Then me."

"Okay, then," Gary continued. "Do you remember making out with that guy?" When Teddy shook his head no, Gary went on. "I don't know his name, to be honest. We invited a lot of bears to that party, but you two were about to break several indecency laws the last time I saw you."

"And then?"

"And then what?" Gary asked. "You were gone. I assume you went back to his place for a rousing game of hide the pickle."

He made out with a bear? And went home with him? That couldn't have happened. He had woken up at Nino's, who was most definitely *not* a bear. There was just no way he would've had two anonymous hookups in one night. He wasn't that much of a slut.

How did he go from making out with a bear to going back to Nino's place? It just didn't make any sense.

"What's the matter?" Gary asked. The playful teasing they'd previously enjoyed disappeared. His friend's eyes reflected only concern.

"Nothing, really," he finally admitted. "But I didn't go home with that bear."

"You didn't?" Gary asked. "Then where were you?"

"I went home with someone else."

The twinkle in Gary's eyes revealed his delight in the unexpected turn of events. "Who?"

Should he tell Gary about waking up in bed with Nino? He'd made it quite apparent over the years that he'd never be attracted to someone like that douche bag. Guys with perfect bodies were dicks. Personal experience taught him that, and he had no intention of ever going back there.

"No one important," he finally told Gary. He needed to forget Nino. Not keep talking about him. "The guy was just a jerk, and I wanted to figure out how I ended up with him."

"It's impossible for you to have ended up with someone like that," Gary revealed. "I didn't invite any jerks to the beach party."

"Well, one slipped by you," he announced. "But that's beside the point. There won't be a repeat performance."

Gary nodded. He obviously read Teddy's body language enough to know he would reveal no more. "Well, Theodore. If he really was that much of an ass, then you're better off."

"I know," Teddy agreed. "I just don't like having a gap in my memory. You know how I am. It makes me feel—"

"Like your mother," Gary said, finishing his thought.

He nodded.

"Well, you're not your mother. You and Ms. Miller couldn't be more different from each other."

Teddy lifted Louie from his lap and placed him on the deck. Louie expressed his dissatisfaction with being disturbed by snuffing twice at him. "Oh hush," he told Louie as he rose from where he sat and kissed Gary on the forehead. "Thanks, sweetie."

"Anytime."

"What's going on out here?" Irene asked as she emerged from the condo. She eyed Teddy and Gary suspiciously.

"Nothing, Miss Frost," Gary said coolly as he rose from the chair. "Just an exchange between friends."

Irene didn't respond. She only glared at Gary. Evidently, she liked him as much as Gary liked her. If he didn't interrupt this fast, Gary and Irene were likely to start bitch slapping each other. A part of him wanted to see who would win if they did.

"You ready?" Teddy asked her as he walked to her side.

"You bet," she replied, not taking her eyes off Gary.

Gary got up and started walking back to his place. "You two have fun. I hope to see you at tea later."

"We will be there," Teddy called out to Gary as his friend walked away.

"Let's go, then," Irene said as she handed him Louie's leash. "I've been cooped up in the condo enough today. I'm ready to have some fun."

Teddy attached Louie's red leash to his collar, which Louie greeted with much excitement. He wagged his butt and moved forward. He enjoyed exploring unknown territory as much as he loved to nap. He looked up at Teddy and then placed his nose to the ground, signaling to his owner that he was ready to go.

As Louie led him and Irene down the steps and across the pebbled driveway, Irene chattered on about wanting to go sit by the ocean. After a few steps, her words were lost in the breeze and drowned out by his thoughts.

He desperately wanted to learn the events of the night that had brought him to Nino's. He had to find out *why*, after all these years, he had allowed himself back into the orbit of a man who was no good for him. The last time he ventured beyond the bears, his heart and his spirit had been broken.

Teddy couldn't do that again.

Chapter Five

ON HIS stroll down Commercial Street, Nino immediately regretted his decision. He'd rather be back in his apartment having the conversation he'd avoided with Van than be where he was at this moment—stuck in a river of sweaty, hairy men.

Shouldn't most of these big guys be out of the heat? It was in the upper nineties, which wasn't exactly ideal bear climate. But instead of escaping the scorching sun, they'd come out of their caves in droves. They ambled about in the street, giddily snapping pictures of each other and squeaking like little girls whenever they ran into a friend or fuck buddy from last year. What the fuck was that about? It didn't make sense for such big guys to turn into such big girls. He'd never understand their hairy ways.

He got that they enjoyed food. That much was obvious from more than just their sizes. They consumed everything set before them with wild abandon. Like that couple coming down the street toward him. Both guys were working on ice cream *and* saltwater taffy. Was it any wonder most bears exited clothing stores with bags filled with supersized clothes?

Also, why did they have to parade about shirtless with sweat running down their shaggy, swollen bodies? The dark patches of moisture around their ass cracks were not appealing. At least not to him. Apparently, the bear sticking his hand down the shorts of his portly partner disagreed. He seemed to enjoy the feel of sweaty ass crack, but did he really have to sniff his fingers in front of everyone? If Nino had eaten breakfast, it would be all over the sidewalk right now.

Why did bears love sweaty ass and armpits so much? Nino enjoyed working up a sweat in bed. That was a blast. But to not wear deodorant and reek of onions? No, thank you. Like everything else about one's body, smell was something that had to be masked by careful application of manufactured scents.

Anything less was a huge turnoff for him.

"Well, there's my cute little thing," growled a shirtless bear standing outside of Shop Therapy, a local store that primarily sold tie-dye apparel. Although Nino stood about an inch taller than the man who leered at him, the man had at least a hundred and fifty pounds on him. Comparatively speaking, Nino guessed the man was right. He was "little," but he most certainly *wasn't* his.

"Thanks," Nino said, trying to continue down the street. The big fellow had other plans. He pushed off from the wall of the store and got in Nino's path.

"How are you today, sweetness and light?" the guy asked as he extended his paw for Nino to shake.

He eyed the hand and the man attached to it. He had zero hair on his head, but his chest and arms were fully covered in a rich, dark pelt. He even had those dreaded wings of hair stretching out from his underarms and swooping back to join the thick brush that coated the man's back. And did that twinkle in his eyes mean he was hitting on Nino? This guy apparently didn't realize he was barking up the wrong tree.

"I'm good but in a hurry," Nino replied, trying to be polite but also not wanting to take the man's sweaty palm in his. "Now, if you'll excuse me?" he asked as he nodded for the man to move aside.

"You don't remember me, do you?" His meaty smile turned into a frown. "It's Jay."

He didn't know Jay, and he was certain the expression on his face communicated that. If he'd met someone this large in person, he'd remember such an encounter. This man was obviously mistaking him for somebody else.

"Sorry," Nino replied as he tried to get around Jay. "I think you're mistaken."

"Only if you've got an identical twin," Jay called to him as he walked away. "We met last night on the beach. At Gary and Quinn's party."

Nino stopped. Just what he needed, another bear he didn't remember. Could this day get any worse? What the fuck else happened last night that he wasn't recalling? He needed to call Quinn for the details. After which, he planned on squeezing the life out of Quinn for making him go to that damn party.

"Do you remember me now?" Jay asked from behind him.

Nino turned around to find that Jay had strolled down the sidewalk toward him. The man's face beamed with the possibility that Nino might remember who he was. It made him look like a goofy, dimwitted giant from a children's fairy tale. "No," he told Jay, whose smile became a pout. "I had a lot to drink last night."

Jay let out a big, hearty laugh. "That you did," he nodded. "But it's Bear Week in P-town. It's all about letting your hair down and having fun."

What hair? The man was bald. He had no hair to let down. Well, at least none on his head. He had hair to spare everywhere else.

"So, what you up to?" Jay asked, since Nino hadn't picked up the conversation.

Looking for a guy to fuck was what Nino planned on saying. He didn't want Jay to take it as an invitation, though. Then he'd have to break the big lug's heart by admitting he couldn't be any less interested in sleeping with him if he tried. "Just out and about," Nino finally replied.

Why was he being so nice to Jay and putting up with the interruption? He'd never let anyone delay his pursuit of ass before. Earlier, he'd been downright surly with Van, his best friend. Why did being around this big guy make him act nice? Was it the kindness Nino saw in his eyes? Or was it the fact that he looked miserable when Nino admitted to not remembering him?

First he'd slept with a bear, and now he was being pleasant to them. What the hell was going on with him?

"Well, I was supposed to meet a friend for lunch," Jay said, answering a question Nino hadn't asked. "But he bailed on me. He apparently got lucky last night and needs to get home to shower."

"Good for him," Nino replied, even though he had no real interest in this conversation. What he really needed was to fuck some hot stud who wanted to be drilled long and hard. The parade of bears going up and down Commercial Street made him doubt he'd ever find what he'd come looking for.

"My roommate got lucky last night too. As if he'd ever have a problem scoring!"

"And what about you?" Nino asked before he could stop himself. He almost punched himself in the face. He wanted to end this conversation, not drag it out by asking stupid questions he didn't really care to hear the answers to.

Jay laughed. "Nah, I'm an acquired taste."

"What does that mean?" There he went again. Asking dumbass questions.

"Look at me," Jay said as he stood there with his arms wide. His pregnant stomach hung over his shorts and drooped at least two inches lower than his waistband. The wings of fat on his plump arms dangled southward, and instead of taut pectorals, Jay had a pair of man boobs that were at least a B cup. "I'm a pretty big guy."

No shit. Where was Jay going with this? This place was crawling with plenty of other guys who looked like Jay. "And? That's what Bear Week's about. To celebrate you in all your hairy, big-ass glory."

Jay chuckled as he slapped his hand on Nino's shoulder. The guy hit so hard Nino stumbled to the side a few steps.

"Sorry," Jay said as he helped set Nino back on steady feet. "I forget my own strength sometimes."

"Don't worry about it." Nino straightened out his Dolce and Gabbana T-shirt that Jay had unintentionally knocked out of perfect alignment. "Now, you were saying?"

"About what?" Jay asked. He looked extremely confused.

"About you being an acquired taste."

"Oh, that. Well, I know Bear Week is about us big girls, but I'm not really into other bears. I like my guys with less meat on their bones and to not be so—" He paused, looked around, and then whispered, "hairy." Jay shuddered at the mention of the word hair. Evidently, he found it as disgusting as Nino did.

"Are you serious?" he asked Jay, unable to hide the surprise in his question. He then eyed Jay's fur-covered body and arched his eyebrow at the man.

"I know," Jay giggled. "I'm hairy too, but it grows back too fast. If I shave or wax it, I get stubble in about a day. I'd rather be hairy than all prickly. I wish I could be smooth like you," he added wistfully. "I don't know what it is about smooth bodies, but they really turn me on."

They turned him on too. "I know what you mean," Nino admitted with a smile. "I like for my hands to run down soft skin, not be scraped to shreds by sandpaper."

"Amen, sister!" Jay yelled as he held up his hand for a high five.

Nino chuckled to himself as he delivered the five Jay anxiously waited to receive.

"You know, you'd be my type if you weren't so damn pretty," Jay said with a wink.

"What?" Nino asked. "You prefer the uglies?"

Jay smiled broadly as he shook his head. "You're a silly pup, you know that?"

"Then explain."

"There's just no way I have the self-esteem to be with someone like you. You're just too perfect-looking, and next to you, I'd look like leftover Spam that's been sitting in the sun for a week. I'd feel too imperfect and most likely get too jealous. I'm not saying I date ugly guys or that I think I'm ugly. I'm a pretty attractive guy in my completely humble and unbiased opinion. I'm just more interested in guys who have more visible imperfections. Makes me feel better about myself, I guess. To be with someone like you," he said as he gave Nino the once-over. "Well, no matter how fun the ride might be, I'd probably eat myself into a diabetic coma afterward."

He'd never met someone as self-aware as Jay. To find this combination in such an unexpected package caught him off guard.

Weren't the guys with the perfect bodies supposed to be the most secure people in existence? Their looks made them accepted by society as a whole, so they usually had less to worry about with trying to fit in.

Jay, who was at least a hundred pounds overweight, let it all hang out. He didn't feel compelled to hide who he was or what he liked from anyone.

Nino envied that quality. He hadn't been himself for so long that he doubted he could even remember who he had been to begin with.

"I like you, Jay," Nino said. He was as surprised by his words as Jay was to hear them.

"Aw, well, thank you, sugar," Jay said. "But I already told you that I'm not interested."

Nino laughed. "Good. Because I'm not interested in you either."

"Great!" Jay said with another heavy whack to Nino's shoulder. "How about we just be friends, then?"

He already had a ton of friends in town, including Van, who he cherished above all else. He really wasn't looking for another pal, especially in a tourist. He'd never hung out with them before. He only used the men who came here to relieve his sexual tension. That was about all they were good for. By definition, their presence in the town and in his life was temporary. They could never be permanent fixtures because they'd be gone by the end of the week.

This was Provincetown, though, and people always raved about how they made friends in unexpected places here, and nothing would be more unforeseen than for him to become friends with a bear.

"Sure," he finally answered. "Why not?"

"Great!" Jay said and punctuated the statement with another vigorous smack. "Just promise you won't fall in love with me, and we'll be fine."

A smile involuntarily stretched across his face. "I promise."

Evidently satisfied with the response, Jay nodded. "Now, how about we grab some lunch? You look like you could use a good meal."

Why did people always tell him that? He took good care of himself and wasn't waifish or thin. He just ate well and exercised.

Since he could tell from the wide grin that Jay was only teasing, he let the matter drop. "Sure," he finally replied. "As long as you're paying."

"Typical queen," Jay said with an exaggerated eye roll. "Always looking for a free meal."

He laughed. He liked Jay, which surprised the hell out of him. He typically didn't take to other people this fast. He preferred to hold back and reserve judgment before he decided if someone was worthy of being his friend.

The only person he'd ever liked this quickly was Van.

BY THE time Nino and Jay had walked all the way down Commercial to Bubala's, Jay had turned into a puddle of sweat. He'd wanted Nino to take him to where the best burgers in town were served, which made Bubala's the obvious choice. Their burgers were not only tasty but were big enough to satisfy even someone with Jay's appetite.

The problem? It was located on the west end, and he and Jay had met on the east end. That made for a rather long stroll, and the journey hadn't pleased Jay one bit.

"These fucking burgers better be the best I've ever eaten," Jay complained as he now hobbled instead of walked to the patio in front of the restaurant. He also took his shirt out from where he'd tucked it at the waistband of his shorts and, after a few failed attempts, finally managed to pull it over his damp skin. Sweat stains immediately bloomed across the fabric. "If they're not, I'm gonna sit on you."

"Don't worry," he reassured as he waited for Jay to catch up to where he stood. "They're the best in town. I promise."

"They better be," Jay warned. "For your sake."

Nino shook his head in pretend exasperation. "Stop whining, ya big baby. And get your ass over here."

"I'm coming, bitch," Jay announced rather loudly as he slowly inched his way forward. "In case you haven't noticed, it's like a zillion degrees out here, and you've dragged my fat ass all the way out to butt-fucking Egypt."

"I've never been to Egypt, but if it's full of butt fucking, I'm there."

Jay flipped off Nino as he finally arrived at the patio entrance. "Well, what are you waiting for?" he asked. "An engraved invitation? Let's go eat."

Nino gestured for Jay to look around at the crowded patio. Bears were everywhere, taking up all the tables the restaurant had set up outside. "The place is packed," Nino pointed out. "You boys eat up a lot of square footage when you come to town. Wait times for prime seating are always doubled."

"Oh, hell no!" Jay exclaimed as he motioned one of the servers over.

The young blonde girl, who was likely no more than eighteen, immediately sprinted over to them. "What can I do for you, sir?"

"We'd like a table," he told her. "Now."

"There are tables available inside," she announced. "But none on the patio."

"We'll wait," Nino chimed in. The girl nodded and started to walk away.

"We'll what?" Jay asked as he called the young girl back. "What's so special about these patio tables?"

"Are you kidding me?" he asked Jay, who stared at him with deadly serious eyes. He apparently wanted a good explanation as to why they had to wait. "When you're on the patio, not only are you seen by all the hot guys parading by, but you get to see them too. If one's hot enough, an afternoon delight can usually be arranged."

"Is that the only reason, you horny bastard?" Jay asked, apparently unconvinced by his rationale.

"*Only* reason? That's the *best* reason there is. If we sit outside, you might just find the hairless pup you've been looking for."

That point caused Jay to reconsider. He surveyed the restaurant, as well as up and down the street, to see what eye candy he might miss if he went inside.

"The inside is air-conditioned," the young girl said. "If that matters."

"Hell, yes, that matters," Jay told the girl as he motioned her to show them to their inside table. "This big bitch is about to melt."

"Jay," Nino complained, but Jay held up his hand for Nino to be silent.

"I'm not going to die of heatstroke on the off chance that one of us will get some play. If I get that hard up, I can always head down to the dick dock later tonight. Now shut up and march!"

Jay then pointed for Nino to follow the waitress. Nino surprised himself by dutifully complying. Not even Van managed that.

Once inside, they passed by tables filled with plus-sized patrons. Their plates were piled high with more food than Nino could eat in a day. His stomach turned to see gluttony met with such relish. When they sat down and were handed their menus, he regretted those thoughts when he peered over his menu at Jay.

He seemed to be a genuinely good guy, and Nino had said he'd be his friend. He wouldn't be such a good friend if he let such thoughts continue to run rampant. He'd been made fun of for being overweight. He needed to be less shallow and do what he'd so often wished the kids who bullied him in school could do: see what lay on the inside.

That would certainly make him less of a plastic.

His bad mood from earlier this morning returned. Thinking about what happened and the furry little shit who said he was superficial made him want to find the little guy and tear his head from his shoulders.

"What's got your panties in a bunch?" Jay asked from across the table. "You're not pissed that I made us sit in here, are you?"

Jay actually looked worried that he was the cause of Nino's distress. "No, not at all," he replied. "Just remembering something that happened this morning."

"Well, what happened?" Jay asked as he set his menu down.

"Nothing important."

"I call bullshit on that," Jay said. "Look, I know we just met and all and that you don't know me from Adam. If you don't want to tell me, that's fine. Just don't lie to me."

If anyone else, besides Van, would have called bullshit on him, he'd have gotten up and walked away. People just didn't get away with talking to him so candidly. So why did Jay's comment make him like the big guy even more?

"Okay, fine. It wasn't nothing," Nino admitted.

"Thank you," Jay said with a triumphant grin. "Now, do you want to talk about it?"

He wanted to discuss this with somebody, but he couldn't even bring himself to do so with Van. He didn't have it in him to spill his guts to a complete stranger. Not even to Jay. "No," he finally answered. "I don't. I hope you're not offended."

"Not at all," Jay replied with a shake of his head. "We all have our shit to deal with. If the time's not right to share it, then it's just not right. When you're ready, you will. With me or one of your other friends. That's what friends are for. To listen when you need to talk or to give you the space you need to get there."

Once again, Nino smiled at Jay before he could help himself. How did Jay get that kind of power over him? Maybe it was the sincerity in his words or just the fact that Jay was a decent human being, but Nino enjoyed Jay and his company immensely.

There weren't very many people Nino could say that about.

"I'M FULL," Nino told Jay as he set down his fork.

Jay eyeballed him suspiciously as he continued to munch on his burger and fries. "You've got to be fucking kidding me. You had a side salad and only ate half of it."

"What can I say? I don't require much food."

"You're not a plant, you know," Jay said while pointing a french fry at him. "You can't survive on water and sunlight. You have to actually consume food to stay alive."

"I think I've done quite well for myself, momma bear, so don't you worry."

Jay glared at him for his comment. He reached underneath the table, and even though Nino couldn't see the gesture, he understood what Jay was doing. He was grabbing his crotch. "I've got your momma bear right here."

"That's not very good table manners," Nino chided.

In response, Jay opened his mouth to reveal the food he was still chewing.

"Now, that's just gross," he groaned as he turned away from the offensive display.

That was when he noticed the young guy two tables over. He was smoking hot and thankfully not a bear. His nose might have been a bit too big for Nino's liking, but the sculpted arms that emerged from his tight muscle shirt allowed Nino to look past that flaw. He also had a full head of thick black hair that begged to be pulled while he was being nailed, and his lips were luscious and soft. The guy could probably suck a penny through a straw.

Nino's cock turned rock hard when he imagined those sweet lips gliding over his dick. When his thoughts shifted to bending the guy over the table and fucking him right in the middle of Bubala's, his boner almost ripped a hole in his shorts. He definitely needed a quick come and go.

"Who's snagged your attention?" Jay asked as he turned in his seat. When he spotted the guy, he nodded. "Very nice." He turned back to face Nino. "Definitely a guy I'd fuck."

"Who wouldn't?"

Jay chuckled. "Good point." He picked up his heavily sweetened tea and took a big sip. "You gonna go for it?"

Nino smiled at the guy, who continued to stare in his direction. "Most definitely."

"That's a good boy," Jay said with a grin. "But before you abandon me, you must hand over your phone."

Nino switched his attention from the guy he was going to be fucking in a few minutes to Jay. "You want me to do what, now?"

Jay didn't repeat his request. He simply presented his hand palm up, waiting for him to do as instructed.

"Fine," he said as he dug his phone out of his pocket and handed it over to Jay. When the phone was turned over, he glanced back at the guy. He was now chatting with his chubby friend and nodding toward their table.

"I can't get into your phone," Jay complained. "It's pass code protected."

"Tell me something I don't know," he said without looking at Jay. His new trick needed to think he was all that existed in Nino's world. Well, at least until Nino blew his wad up his butt or down his throat.

"And your pass code would be?"

"I'm not giving that to you. That's why there's a pass code."

"Oh, stop being a little bitch," Jay said as he tried to regain Nino's attention by snapping his fingers in front of Nino's face.

"What?" Nino asked. He was getting a little irritated. He was on the hunt, and one thing Jay needed to learn was not to come between him and his prey. Friendship only went so far.

"What. Is. Your. Pass code?"

"Go. To. Hell," he retorted. "I'm not giving that to you. It completely invalidates having one."

"Oh, for Christ's sake," Jay said, completely exasperated. "Do you want to fuck that nice tight ass over there or what?"

"Damn straight I do."

"Well, then give me your pass code, because you're not getting your phone back until you do."

"I could just take it from you."

"You could," Jay commented as he opened the waistband of his shorts and dangled Nino's phone over his crotch. "But will you still want it after it's been nestled next to my sweaty, stinky junk?"

There was no use continuing the debate. Jay won hands down. "One zero eight four," he announced.

"Good boy," Jay said as he entered the code and unlocked Nino's phone.

"Now would you mind telling me what the hell you're doing?"

"I'm entering my phone number in your contact list," Jay replied, as if it were obvious. "And I'm sending myself a text so I have yours.

Now, we'll be able to meet up again when you're not busy fucking the snot out of that one all week."

"I'll only fuck him once," he told Jay. "I don't do repeat fucks. That would break rule number five."

Jay handed Nino back his phone. "What the hell are you talking about?"

"I live by six simple rules, designed to make my life happy and drama free."

"Sounds too complicated," Jay said with a wrinkled nose. "You should just go with the flow instead of forcing rules on yourself. Seems silly to do that, if you ask me."

Nino locked eyes with Jay. "I didn't."

"All right, cool it with the psycho eyes," Jay said as he waved Nino away. "Go get him, tiger. We'll talk later."

Nino nodded as he stood up and strolled over to the table, where the hot jock and his bigger friend watched him approach. Could they look any more like schoolgirls? Well, the hot jock would in a few minutes, when Nino was balls deep up his ass and the guy was moaning like the bitch he was.

"Hey," he said as he slid into the booth next to the attractive guy. "I'm Nino."

Why did this guy suddenly look confused? He glanced over at his friend with an open mouth. Nino didn't really understand the expression, but he was pleased to see that the guy had nice teeth. He hated getting sucked off by a snagglepuss. They typically scraped the shaft while they gave head.

"What's your name?" Nino asked.

"Um, I'm Terry," the guy mumbled. "But this is my friend John."

Nino glanced over at John, whose face lit up like a seventy-five watt lightbulb. "How are you doing, John?"

John answered with a sigh, "I'm doing great. Now."

"What's your friend's name?" Terry asked.

"Who?" Nino asked.

"The guy you were eating lunch with," Terry replied with a nod to Jay, who was paying the bill. "I think he's superhot. Would you introduce me?"

If Nino had been standing, he would have fallen over right there in Bubala's.

This guy with the hot, tight body was a chubby chaser? He belonged with someone like Nino, who wouldn't squash him when he topped his ass. This guy didn't seem to think so, though. The faraway look in Terry's eyes as he ogled Jay's butt told him Nino stood a better chance of nailing Ellen DeGeneres.

He had nothing this guy wanted. Was he really being snubbed for the second time today?

This morning he'd been rejected for his lack of substance. That was difficult enough to deal with. Terry was rejecting him entirely on his appearance. That had never happened to him before. He always got whomever he wanted, but apparently during Bear Week, an alternate universe took over the town, and the world Nino had always known no longer existed.

"Will you do it?" the guy named Terry practically begged.

Nino didn't play wingman for anyone, even Van, but he just couldn't deny Jay a shot at this sweet, young thing.

"Come on," he told Terry as he rose out of the booth. "I'll go introduce you."

"Thanks!" Terry said as he followed Nino across the restaurant. "And when you're done, you can go back and talk to my friend. He's really into you."

"Great," Nino replied. He doubted he carried off the comment with any sincerity, but Terry was too gaga over Jay to notice. When Nino glanced over his shoulder at John, who waved at him from the booth, Nino exhaled.

How was he going to get himself out of this one?

Chapter
Six

NINO THANKFULLY escaped Bubala's without incident after introducing Terry to Jay. The newly paired duo walked hand in hand down the street, and though he had no interest in Terry's chubby friend, John, he couldn't bring himself to hurt the guy by telling him the truth. So he spared John's feelings by lying. Which wasn't like him at all. He usually told it like it was. If he wasn't interested, he didn't sugarcoat it. Most guys got the "fuck off" look and went on their merry way. But did he do that to John? No. Like a dumbass, he pretended to have some place to be, and instead of leaving it at that, he gave John his number.

The guy's eyes had shone brighter than floodlights. And if that wasn't enough, he actually liked sparing John's feelings. What kind of crazy train had he boarded? Whatever it was, he needed to hop the fuck off. Sure, what he'd done proved his trick from this morning wrong. He wasn't some unfeeling plastic. He was, in fact, the better man. Score one for Nino. That gave him some satisfaction, but at the same time, he had just seriously screwed up.

By giving the guy his number, he broke another of his six rules.

Exchanging numbers complicated things, and he never gave it out to guys he fucked, much less men he didn't even know. His dalliances were one-time events, and for someone to have his number meant they could hound him forever in hopes of obtaining a repeat performance.

John wouldn't be getting one sweaty roll in the hay, much less two, but now that John had a means to contact him, he'd have to come up with multiple lies to get out of seeing him whenever John called.

He'd only have to keep that up until the guy went back to wherever the hell he was from, but it didn't make it any less of a hassle.

If he'd simply followed his own rules, he wouldn't be in this mess.

And the fact that this was the second rule of his he'd broken in twenty-four hours seriously pissed the shit out of him.

When had he suddenly developed a conscience? He didn't give one shit about other people's feelings. Now, all of a sudden, he was doing things he'd *never* have done last week, much less yesterday. His life needed to get back under control, the way he liked it.

This new man he'd suddenly become needed to die a quick death, and the only way he could figure to return to the man he used to be was by refocusing his efforts on the hunt. If he found some willing, greedy bottom to take what he planned on unleashing, he'd feel more like himself again. More centered.

A good come always cured what ailed him.

But he wouldn't find his usual prey out here on the street, among the heavyset hairy man parade, and he didn't have time to scour Provincetown for a fuck. He needed it now.

Desperate times called for desperate measures, so he turned on his phone and eyed the Cyber icon. He hadn't used the dating app in a few months. The last time was this past winter, when a blizzard made venturing out into town impossible. The app had given him what he needed, access to horny guys holed up in their rentals who wanted to hook up.

After perusing some of the profiles, he'd found a hot, young stud visiting from Boston. He was renting down the street from where Nino lived, so he had invited the guy over for a quick pump and dump. The trick hadn't been one of the best, but it cleared his pipes and his troubles, which was what he'd needed at the time.

His problems with his job had started around the holidays, shortly after his last shoot with Ford Michaels. And he'd used the trick to help him move past his terrible mood. It had worked then. He hoped it did so today too. His modeling career still lingered in limbo, and his sudden personality shift made him wonder if some alien invader hadn't taken control of his body. Just like this past winter, he needed something to remind him who he truly was.

Within minutes of touching the icon, Cyber loaded and downloaded all the profiles of guys currently online and looking to screw. Just like the men scuffling about him on Commercial, most of the profiles featured an abundance of beards and body hair. He could look past the whiskers if he had to, but the excessive fur coats made him wince.

After scrolling through four pages of profiles, he found one for a guy named Brody who looked like a winner, and Brody was only about four hundred feet away. Brody's photo showed three or four days' worth of facial hair. On Brody, though, the dark-blond scruff made him even more attractive, which he found odd. Still, the guy's blond hair, light-green eyes, and boy-next-door good looks made his cock harden. At almost thirty, he was older than Nino was typically attracted to, but the smooth body featured in the profile picture sealed the deal.

He wanted this guy. Badly.

So he sent him a message.

NINO: Hey, man. What's up?

As he waited for a reply, Nino moved off the street and away from the hairy bustle choking the street around him. He stood on a small path off Commercial that led to the public beach area a few steps away. Laughter emanated from the beach just down the walk, as well as the barking of a small dog. Well, it wasn't a bark in the truest sense. It was more of an arf.

BRODY: Just looking around. U?

Nino grinned at the screen. Brody's response meant the guy was interested and wasn't strictly a fan of the chubby and the furry. If he hadn't been interested in Nino's stunningly hairless good looks, Brody either never would have replied or just responded with a curt hello.

NINO: Same here. But I think I've found what I'm looking for.

BRODY: Nice. U wanna host or u wanna come here?

The cum in Nino's balls churned. His tension had reached epic proportions, and this guy was his solution.

NINO: I'll come to you.

Brody sent his information. He was staying in one of the rooms at the Boatslip.

NINO: Be right there.

After receiving Brody's okay, he turned back onto Commercial Street and made his way as quickly as he could through the crowd of sweaty, hairy flesh that continued to clog the street.

"WHY WOULDN'T you take me to the Boatslip?" Irene complained as she spread out on the beach blanket. "This beach blows. And not in a good way."

Teddy didn't want to admit to Irene that he was keeping her away from the half-naked men lounging around on the deck at the Boatslip for their own safety. Being surrounded by so many hairy gay men would not only make Irene cream her panties, but turn her into a sex-crazed succubus.

She'd be impossible to be around, and Teddy didn't want to have to deal with that right now.

"I just thought some quiet time would be nice," he lied as he unclasped the leash from Louie's collar and let the dog run toward the ocean and chase the waves.

Irene surveyed the empty beach, which was littered with more rocks than people, and then returned her gaze to him. She peered over her sunglasses. Her eyes narrowed into slits of displeasure. "Quiet's one thing. Being the only losers on this stretch of sand is another."

"I think it's peaceful." He swept his gaze out to the bay just as a cool breeze blew across the water. It wrapped around Teddy like the soft hands of a lover, delivering gentle kisses across his bare chest, and as he typically did when held within the arms of another, Teddy inhaled deeply.

During sex, he did that to capture as much of the scent as possible. In this instance, though, his lungs didn't fill with the heady odor of musk and sex. On the air that traveled off the ocean and into the town behind him, Teddy caught a whiff of more than just salt and sea air. He detected a soothing sweetness, as if somewhere out in the water floated a garden that honeyed the wind with its nectar.

The scent reminded him of someone. Who was it, though? Teddy closed his eyes, focusing on the intoxicating salty sweet mixture. Trying to force the buried information to the surface, he used the smell that so enthralled him to recall the event from which this emotion sprung.

An image floated up from the darkness. A lean, muscled neck. Smooth, exceptionally soft skin. Strong hands that surfed down his back and cupped his ass. Teddy distinctly recalled breathing in deeply at the crook of the man's neck.

When the image pulled back, curly locks and gorgeous chocolate-brown eyes filled his vision. It was Nino, looking down at him with a smile that melted him as if he were butter.

Teddy's eyes fluttered open.

The image and the emotions tied to it startled him. Looking up into Nino's face made him feel special, reminding him of his first boyfriend in college. It had taken him a few years to get over that particularly painful time in his past, and he didn't appreciate the fact that Nino had somehow brought those emotions to the surface.

The connection, though, could be explained. Nino and He-Who-Must-Not-Be-Named shared a lot of similar physical qualities. That *had* to be the reason why.

There simply was no other explanation.

"What's gotten into you?" Irene asked from the blanket next to him.

"What do you mean?"

"You look like someone just slapped you in the face."

"That sounds about right."

Irene turned over on her side, resting her full head of blonde hair on her upturned left palm. The side ponytail from this morning had been crimped. Did they even sell hair crimpers anymore? "Care to share?" she asked.

Teddy exhaled. "I was just thinking about…." He paused. He didn't know how Irene would take the revelation. She'd helped him pick up the pieces after the breakup, so she knew firsthand how devastated Teddy had once been. "Him."

Irene's eyes widened in surprise. Even after all these years, she obviously didn't need Teddy to clarify who he was referring to. "What brought that unfortunate blast from the past to the present?"

Teddy was about to answer when Louie emerged from the ocean, sopping wet. He bounded toward them, collecting clumps of sand across his paws and underbelly as he ran. When Teddy realized whom Louie was gunning for, he told him to stop. Louie had no interest in obeying. Instead, he gleefully jumped on Irene, who cussed at the sandy, wet bomb that landed on top of her. After bounding off Irene, Louie made a beeline for Teddy, where he hopped into his owner's loving lap.

"Louie!" he complained as he tried to dust the sand from his blue swimsuit and from the beach blanket that had previously been spotless. Louie simply snuffed and licked Teddy's face as if he'd done nothing wrong.

Irene responded with her usual grace. She catapulted off her blanket and glared at them. "Damn it, Louie," she screeched. "Now I smell like wet dog!"

Louie turned up his nose and faced the other way.

"Look at me when I'm screaming at you," she seethed. Louie did not comply. Instead, he lay down in Teddy's lap and closed his eyes. "I hate him." She glared at Teddy as she shook the sand from her body.

"He's just being friendly."

"Friendly, my ass!" Irene railed. "He did that on purpose."

"No, he didn't," Teddy replied, even though he knew better. Louie took great pleasure in tormenting Irene, and as Louie looked up at him with one eye open, what looked like a huge grin spread across his muzzle.

"Bad dog," he whispered to Louie, who closed his open eye in response. "Now I'm gonna have to clean you off."

"Toss him in the ocean," Irene commented. "That'll teach him."

"Irene!" he scolded as he removed Louie's collar. He needed to shake the sand off the once-pristine red material. "He's a Frenchie. He'd drown."

"I know," she replied with an evil grin.

Teddy didn't bother to argue. It wasn't worth the aggravation. Instead, he took the extra blanket out of his backpack and set to work on drying Louie's coat. As he dried Louie, his dog's eyes suddenly opened and his ears perked up. He sniffed the air intently and rose on all fours.

"What do you smell, my handsome boy?" Teddy asked. "You catch a whiff of some butch Rottweiler or German Shepherd? I know you've got a thing for the bad boys."

"He's not the only one," Irene said after she had once again settled on her blanket.

"What does that mean?" he asked as he tried to corral Louie, who seemed intent on following the scent he had picked up.

"You've only been in love one time in your life, and that was with He-Who-Must-Not-Be-Named. They don't come badder than that."

"Louie, stop!" Teddy commanded. Louie immediately sat down but continued to sniff the air like he smelled a grilled pork chop. Or a cat. To Irene, he said, "And it won't happen again."

"What? Falling in love or falling for a bad boy?"

"Both," he replied. Irene's knitted eyebrows told him she didn't believe a word he said.

"Look, Teddy, I love you. You know that. But the only person you're fooling is yourself."

"And how am I doing that?"

"Whenever you feel even the tiniest hint of something beyond attraction, you run in the other direction. Why else do you think you bed so many bears?"

"Besides the fact that they're hot and think that I am too?" Teddy asked in reply.

"I won't deny any of that," she said with a nod. "But Br—" She stopped herself, remembering the one rule they had whenever discussing Teddy's failed relationship. "But He-Who-Must-Not-Be-Named wasn't a bear, was he?"

Not even close. His body had been smooth as silk, and his blond hair and green eyes used to drive Teddy into a sexual frenzy he'd never experienced since. "No, he wasn't," he finally replied.

"That's why I think you gravitate to the bears. They're so friendly and fluffy and so very different from *him* that you aren't in danger of falling like you did the last time."

Irene might just be on to something for once. Since He-Who-Must-Not-Be-Named, he didn't dare hook up with another man with a perfect body. Being in love with someone like that, when he looked the way he did, had proven too difficult. He'd done his best to feel good about himself after years of being torn apart by his mother.

But when he fell in love all those years ago, he opened himself back up to his inherent insecurity in his appearance, and when his heart had been broken, it took him too long to find himself again.

"Where's Louie?"

Irene's question immediately caught his attention. "What do you mean?" he asked as he searched the beach. He didn't see his dog anywhere. "Where the *fuck* is he?" he asked as he jumped to his feet.

"That's what I asked you," Irene replied as she joined him in his search.

"He was right beside me," Teddy said. "You don't think he went—" He couldn't even finish the thought. There was no way Louie had run into the ocean without him seeing. Although Louie loved the water, he never ventured into it too far.

"No," Irene reassured him. "He's a dumbass, but not that much of a dumbass."

"Then where?" A thousand cold needles pricked his skin. Louie was like his child, and he couldn't bear to be apart from him.

"You know him," Irene said as she gathered up her stuff. "He's just sniffing around."

Teddy appreciated Irene's reassuring tone, but he also heard the fear in her voice. She might hate Louie, but she loved Teddy. She would search heaven and earth to find his precious boy. "We've got to find him."

"We will," she said as she stuffed her belongings into her backpack. "We'll search all day if we have to, and if that doesn't work, someone will find him and call the number on his tag. You'll be notified in a few hours."

Irene was right. Provincetown was filled with animal lovers. Someone would call, and he would be reunited with Louie. As he bent down to pack up his belongings, his heart caught in his throat.

Louie's collar rested on the blanket. He'd taken it off to clean it, and on the collar was the dog tag.

When Irene saw it, she gasped too.

If they didn't find Louie themselves, they might never see him again.

NINO DIDN'T have time for this. He had a trick to get to and pound the shit out of, but this damned French bulldog wouldn't leave him alone. No matter how many times he told it to shoo, it arfed at him and continued to follow him down Commercial Street.

He had to admit the little guy was cute. He'd owned a dog once. A mutt named Ginger. She had followed him around the streets of Sao Paolo while he whistled songs he'd heard on the radio. They had been best friends, and being together made them happy. He'd never been so loved in his life. Not even by his family. Their love had always been conditional. Based on what Nino could do for them. Not Ginger. She always gazed up at him as if he were the most important person in the world. Kind of like the way this pooch was staring up at him now.

Why was this dog looking at him that way? He'd never met this guy in his life, and he'd have remembered this little stinker. Even though lots of people in town owned Frenchies, a breed that seemed preferred by most homos everywhere, this little guy at his feet looked to be one of a kind. But it didn't matter how cute or unforgettable this pooch was. Nino preferred bigger dogs with long snouts. Like his Ginger.

There was something about the lean and strong frame that appealed to him. He'd entertained the idea of getting a dog, especially since Van moved out, but ever since Ginger died, he'd been unable to love another four-legged fur ball. Losing her had torn his heart from his chest, so he always did his best not to get attached to another sweet doggie face.

But for some reason this guy's squashed nose and huge-ass ears made him giggle, even though he was also making Nino late for his fuck.

"All right, boy," Nino said as he turned to face the dog. "You need to go back to your owner. Now."

The dog sat down in front of him. He was apparently going nowhere. Typical bulldog. Stubborn to the core.

"You're not a very good dog, are you?"

His new furry friend arfed in response. When had he suddenly become irresistible to the short and the hairy?

Nino walked a couple of steps backward, testing to see if he could move without being followed, but the persistent pup matched his steps. When he stopped, the dog stopped. Evidently, he wasn't going anywhere without a shadow.

He surveyed the crowd of bears who streamed around him in hairy packs. He scanned the crowd, looking for a frantic owner searching the street for his lost baby. He could find no panicked, wide eyes anywhere.

"Apparently no one's missing you," Nino announced to the dog that looked up at him and snuffed. "Did your owner abandon you because you're a pain in the ass?"

At this, the dog arfed again and then proceeded to sniff his leg. He inhaled at his flesh so roughly that he sprayed Nino's leg with dog snot.

"That's gross," Nino said as he wiped his leg. "I'm used to sharing a drink with a new boy before he splooges all over me. And you, my friend, are definitely *not* my type."

Undeterred, the dog continued his sniffing quest. Apparently, Nino had picked up some scent his new pal liked.

"Cute dog," some random bear commented.

"He's not mine," Nino responded. "You want him?"

The man didn't reply. He simply smiled and waved good-bye to him and his furry little stalker.

"Not even strangers want you," Nino said as he looked downward. The dog's brown eyes stared up at him with complete and utter devotion. "Why are you looking at me like that, you crazy dog? You don't even know me."

His friend sniffed the air around Nino and chuffed. If Nino didn't know any better, he'd have said that the dog was arguing with him. As if he knew Nino by smell alone, which was entirely impossible.

"All right. You win." Nino sat down on the curb, and the pooch immediately crawled onto his lap, making himself at home. "Jeez, you're worse than most of the guys I meet. Crawling on my junk the first chance you get."

He stroked the pooch's back and then scratched at his backside, which elicited a dreamy stare from the Frenchie. He apparently enjoyed butt play. A dog after his own heart. "I guess you're not too bad."

As he continued to dole out the loving the dog craved, Nino searched the dog for identification. "You don't have a tag. That means you've got a dumbass for an owner."

His friend snorted.

"You don't like when I talk about your master, huh?"

His reply was a snuff.

"Okay, fine. I won't call your owner names. Even though he is a dumbass."

The dog once again snorted a mist of dog boogers. This time in Nino's face.

"You did that on purpose. Didn't you, you little fucker?"

Suddenly, the dog's ears perked up, and he looked back down Commercial. "What do you hear, boy? Is that your owner?"

"Louie!" A voice called out. The panic was unmistakable.

"Here, Louie, Louie," someone else said. The voice belonged to a woman. Probably some straight couple who came to P-town to gawk at the gays.

The dog, who he suspected was called Louie, continued to stare through the crowd of bears, sniffing the air. He was apparently waiting for his owner to appear, so Nino joined him. Who was the idiot who had taken his dog out without a leash or a dog tag?

Whoever they were, he planned to give them hell for making him late for the hookup he desperately needed.

"I DON'T see him anywhere." Teddy almost collapsed in the middle of Commercial Street. What would he do if he never saw Louie again?

"We'll find him," Irene said from his right. She marched down the street with him, searching the shadowed alcoves of the stores where Louie might be quietly resting, away from the oppressive heat and sun. Since they had arrived in Provincetown a couple of days ago, they had passed many pets and their owners sitting under the trees or on the stoops of the various restaurants and stores that lined both sides of the street.

With any luck, Louie might be curled up in a corner. Or intently sniffing the butt of some new friend. Louie loved ass almost as much as Teddy did.

"Louie!" He called out, stopping to listen for the arf that would allow his heart to resume beating. When he got no response, he shouted out Louie's name again.

"Here, Louie, Louie," Irene said before she made whistling noises.

Irene needed to stop whistling. She couldn't carry a tune in a bucket, and Louie hated it when she whistled. His little man always pinned back his ears and took off in the other direction. Along with everything else, Louie was apparently a music critic too. That furry little stinker butt. If he ever saw him again, he was going to smack his little white heinie for taking off on him. After he loved on him a whole bunch first. And maybe even after a treat. But he'd definitely be disciplined somehow.

Who was he kidding? Teddy wasn't going to do any of that. He could never get mad at that handsome little face.

"You lose a dog?"

Teddy's head snapped in the direction of the person speaking to him. The man had a cute, chubby face and a big, friendly smile. "Yes," he answered quickly.

"I spotted a dog. A honey-pied Frenchie?"

Teddy's heart caught in his throat. That was his Louie. He opened his mouth to tell the man just that, but his constricted throat made words impossible. He nodded instead.

"He was with some guy who claimed the dog wasn't his. In fact, he was trying to give the cute little guy away."

Give away Louie? If he found the man, he was going to pound him bloodier than a raw steak.

"They're back that way." The man then pointed toward the blue-and-white sign that hung over The Pied, a popular bar for after the tea dance.

"Thanks," Teddy muttered before sprinting through the crowd. His heart beat in his ears as his feet pounded the street. He had to get to Louie before that dumbfuck who'd found him sold his boy to the highest bidder. Frenchies could net someone big bucks, since the breed wasn't exactly cheap.

If he didn't make it in time and his Louie was gone because of his rookie mistake on the beach, he'd *never* forgive himself. But he couldn't think that way. He'd find Louie. He had to. He lived and died by his cranky pooch. He wouldn't trade Louie for anyone or anything. No matter how badly Louie's farts stung his eyes in the middle of the night.

Louie was his boy. His family.

The crowd ahead of him parted slightly, and a white pelt blinked into view before the passing squadron of bears once again blocked him from sight. Why wouldn't all these fuckers get the hell out of the way? "Louie!" he cried as he darted around an advancing wall of hairy men. He then had to sidestep a couple of extra-sized boys, who glared at him. What did he care if he almost knocked one of them down? They were in his way, keeping him from his Louie.

At last, the crowd before him parted. Not just a little crack like before, where he only glimpsed a flash of Louie's butt. But a wide corridor formed ahead of him as the crowd stepped out of his way. No doubt because of the furious pace at which he ran. And the insane and determined scowl that probably twisted his face. He must have looked like a thief trying to escape a mall cop by the way people were quickly getting out of his way.

When he spotted his cute little bugger sitting in some man's lap, Teddy almost broke down. Then he noticed whose lap Louie was sitting in.

It was Nino's.

IF NINO had a gun, he would have shot himself. Point blank in the head. Of course, the furry little fucker's owner would be the furry little fucker from this morning. That was just his goddamn luck these days. Wasn't it?

Louie wagged his butt vigorously. He obviously recognized his owner, but he refused to get off Nino's lap. He did manage to arf at his approaching master. He then turned his squashed face up to Nino and snuffed. Why did this dog look so damned pleased with himself?

"There you are," Louie's dad panted.

"Here I am," Nino replied.

"I'm not talking to you, fuck face. I'm talking to my dog."

Nice comeback. No matter how much the hairy little piece of shit pissed him off, the guy's attitude served him well. Also, he looked different from this morning. Was he holding in his stomach or something? He definitely still had a belly, but it didn't jut out as far as he recalled. The man was still hairy. Excessively so. The stubble on his face appeared darker and thicker in just the few short hours since Nino had seen him last. The man's father must have been a Sasquatch.

"What are you doing with my dog?"

"With your dog?" Nino asked. "The one you seem incapable of taking care of?"

"I can take care of Louie just fine." The man's eyes shot through him. Apparently if he had a gun he would have fired it at Nino too. Nino liked getting that kind of reaction out of this jerk. And why wouldn't he? He now had this man's precious little pooch in his lap, and little Louie seemed quite content where he was sitting.

Another point for Nino.

Maybe the dog wanted to upgrade to a better and leaner master. Louie could certainly do better. That would definitely put him ahead by at least another two points.

"I don't think you can take care of him," Nino said at last. "Dogs without a leash are a no-no in P-town."

"And so is trying to sell stolen dogs for profit."

What the fuck was this guy talking about? "I didn't steal your damn dog. I was minding my own business. On the way to a pretty hot fuck, if you'd like to know, when your little Louie comes trotting after me."

"Yeah, right," he said. "You expect me to believe that my dog just happened to chase after you? The *one* guy in this town who I can't stand? That's what you want me to believe?"

"You can believe in the tooth fairy for all I care. The truth is the truth. I didn't steal your dog."

Little Louie snuffed in support from Nino's lap.

"Don't you come to his defense," the guy said to his dog. They apparently had one-way conversations. Like the way he used to talk to Ginger. How did he know that, though? How was he able to read both the dog and the man so well?

He typically couldn't read an open book. Mostly because he didn't care. And he didn't care right now either. Not about this guy or his dog. But when he gazed down at the funny-looking pooch, Nino had to admit he cared about Louie a little bit.

When the hell did that happen?

"You know, the man attached to the lap you're in is a dick."

Louie yawned at his owner's comment and made himself even more comfortable in Nino's lap by falling asleep.

"Your dog's as bored by your tirade as I am," Nino announced. His eyebrows arched, as they typically did when smug superiority descended. He usually reserved such gestures for Van, the one person who he enjoyed verbally sparring with. It was part of the relationship he had cultivated with his best friend.

Then why was he continuing to banter with this guy? This guy wasn't Van, and he didn't waste time idly chitchatting with most people. Not even the guys he actually planned to fuck. He and this hairy mess might have already hooked up, but there wasn't exactly going to be a repeat. Something both of them could agree on.

It was probably the *only* thing they'd agree on.

"How about you just take your dog from my lap and be on your merry little way?" Nino asked. He wanted to get the hell out of here and back to his trick. If he missed the opportunity to fuck Brody in his tight butt, there'd be hell to pay. "I'm sure there's a meal you're no doubt dying to get back to."

A cool mist settled over the man's eyes. He'd apparently hit a nerve with his comment. Good! His work here was officially done, then. The guy opened his mouth to respond, but before he could utter a word, a blonde-haired woman emerged from the crowd. What the fuck was up with her 1980s hairstyle? She looked like a combination of Debbie Gibson and Tiffani. Where the fuck did that mess come from?

"Teddy!" she exclaimed. "There you are."

This guy's name was Teddy? Really? Teddy the bear? God, he'd never wanted to vomit more in his life.

"I was wondering where you ran off to," she said as her eyes swept over Louie in his lap. She rested one hand on her hip and sneered. "And I see you've found the little bastard."

"Yes, I found him," Teddy replied without looking at his friend. The coolness of the man's stare thawed, and the sly grin that pulled at his lips betrayed his true emotion. Teddy was preparing to hurl an insult. "Louie's apparently been slumming."

Nino suppressed a laugh. Not because of the comment. It was tired and lame. But he found it amusing that Teddy the bear seemed to enjoy their war of words too. How fucked up was that shit?

The blonde's face changed as she studied Nino. A coquettish smile danced across her lips as her ravenous eyes set upon him. "Hi," she said. Her dreamy-eyed stare revealed her attraction, and if Nino wasn't careful, she'd devour him whole. "I'm Irene."

What the fuck was he doing being all social and shit?

He didn't have time for this. He had other more important places to be. Like buried pubes deep up a nice tight hole. "Nice to meet you," he said as he took Louie in his arms and stood. "But I need to get going."

"Aw," Irene complained. "We were just about to get better acquainted, and you were about to tell me your name."

"My name's Nino," he said. She held out her hand, loose at the wrist. She evidently wanted Nino to shake it or kiss it. He had no intention of doing either. "Sorry," he told her. "I've got a date."

"With syphilis, no doubt," Teddy retorted.

Nino laughed despite himself. This guy was good. If he didn't hate him so much, they might actually be good friends. But he did hate him. Rabidly. Besides, he could never get past Teddy calling him a plastic. That was unforgiveable in Nino's book. And once he set himself against someone, there was no coming back from that.

"No STDs for me, thanks," he said while handing Louie over to Teddy. The groggy pup snuffed about being disturbed, but in his daddy's arms, he promptly fell back to sleep. "I'll let you pick those up for yourself. If there's someone willing to sleep with you, that is."

"I have no trouble getting guys," Teddy announced. "You know that better than anyone."

Irene's mouth fell open. "The two of you—" She stopped. Surprise apparently stole her breath. After swallowing down her shock, she continued. "Hooked up?"

"I like to think of it as date rape," Nino told Irene. Her eyes grew even wider at his remark.

Teddy nodded. "I agree. I don't remember any of it. Which means that your new buddy Nino here took advantage of me."

The tone of Teddy's voice changed. It no longer bit. Or even stung. It turned light and playful. Like when he and Van joked around. The only way this day could get any weirder would be if Louie woke up and started speaking in a bad French accent.

"This is the guy you were with last night?" Irene asked. She seemed completely incapable of understanding this turn of events. As if Teddy and Nino together sounded like the most absurd plot twist she'd ever heard. Should he be offended or agree with the sentiment?

He and Teddy were definitely *not* made for each other. That was for damn sure. Besides, Nino didn't do relationships. Never would. Especially *not* with a bear.

"All right, I'm out of here," he finally said after a few moments. "Places to go. People to do."

"Don't be a stranger," Irene said.

A stranger? Nino planned on running in the other direction if he ever saw either of them again. Instead of admitting that, he replied, "See you when I see you."

"Which means never," Teddy clarified.

Nino smiled. This guy knew him too well already. "Like I said. When I see you."

"Thanks for finding Louie," Teddy said as he gazed down lovingly at the snoring dog. "And for not selling him."

"You're welcome," Nino replied before he could stop the polite words from exiting his mouth. What he needed was a stapler to fasten his lips shut. "I wouldn't have gotten very much for him anyway."

Teddy nodded and laughed before turning around and departing with Irene. They strolled together back up Commercial Street. When Nino started walking in the other direction, he began to whistle. He hadn't done that in years. Not since Ginger.

Chapter Seven

BY THE time Nino knocked on Brody's door at the Boatslip, he was already thirty minutes late. Standard tricking protocol dictated that he'd check Cyber again and send him another message before coming over. Just in case Brody had already found another dick to play with. But Nino wasn't in the mood to follow the rules. He'd always been far more comfortable breaking them, and since he'd broken far too many of his own rules today, it was more than time to return to the heartless prick he pretended to be.

Life had always been better for him when he did that.

So what if Brody was in his room riding some random cock? He could wait his turn. Hell, he could even slide his dick in there alongside the other guy. He'd double fucked a slutty bottom before, and he'd do it again. Anytime.

"Just a minute," someone announced from inside the room beyond the pale-blue door. The voice had a masculine quality to it. Nino liked that. There were few things that turned him off more than a high-pitched girly voice attached to a hot body. The two just didn't mix well. His voice had once been several octaves too high, one of the many things he had been teased for. If he could learn to sound more like a man, then so could anyone else.

When the door finally swung open, Nino couldn't stop the advancing smile that marched across his face. Could he look any more like a grinning idiot? He probably could, but damn, Brody was even hotter than his Cyber pic.

He stood almost eye level to Nino, which put him at just over six feet. That meant he'd be able to bend Brody into a lot of positions and still keep his cock firmly up his butt. That was always nice. Golden flecks of pigment made his light-green eyes mirror the golden hue of his hair, which had been perfectly styled and slicked back. But the most amazing part of Brody was his crooked smile. It hinted that there was a devil inside such a heavenly looking man.

What more could Nino ask for?

"You must be Nino," Brody said as he leaned against the doorjamb. His slight beard accentuated the rough cut of his jaw, and his impish smile still hung on his parted lips. Nino wanted to claim that mouth by planting his cock down his throat.

"That I am," he responded. He mimicked Brody's stance, propping himself up on the opposite side of the door.

"You're late."

Nino nodded. He didn't give excuses, and he wasn't going to start today. "We still doing this or what?"

Brody chuckled, the devil inside him spirited away as he continued to laugh. In fact, the flirty charm disappeared almost entirely. Why was Brody so amused with himself?

"Sorry, Charlie," Brody said. "But you missed your window of opportunity."

"What do you mean? You're here. I'm here. Let's get naked and do what comes naturally to two hot guys like us."

"Are you serious right now?"

Nino arched his left eyebrow, which was his trademark flirt. He then grabbed his crotch to display the hard-on he'd sported since Brody opened the door. "What do you think?" he asked as he gave his cock a nice, firm tug.

"Nice," Brody responded as he smiled at the outline of Nino's cock. Nino made sure to accentuate the length and thickness by pulling the fabric of his shorts taut. When Brody's gaze once again returned to Nino's, Brody's plush brows knitted and his eyes became slits. Even after his impressive display of his equipment, which most guys immediately fell on their knees to sample, Brody was apparently still trying to determine whether he was going to let Nino in or shut the door in his face. If Nino was rejected for the third time today, he'd likely jump off the back balcony and dive headfirst onto the deck below.

After a long sigh, Brody stepped back and waved Nino inside.

Nino strolled into Brody's room, thankful he didn't have to take a flying leap off the balcony. Not that he really would have. But still. His ego didn't need any more potshots today. As he surveyed the room, he was surprised to discover that rubber play sheets adorned one of the beds. Apparently, Brody liked sliding around on the slick material when he was getting plowed. He could *definitely* work with that.

As he pulled the shirt from his body, Brody's voice interrupted him. "Hold your horses, cowboy."

Nino stopped, his shirt halfway over his head. "What do you mean?" he asked, his voice muffled by the fabric.

"I mean don't get ahead of yourself."

What the fuck was going on now? "I'm not following you," he said as he lowered his shirt. "I thought we were doing this."

"We would've been," Brody told him. "If you'd gotten here on time. But you didn't. So we're not."

Nino eyed the sliding door that led out to the balcony beyond. It looked like he might be headed over it after all. "Then why did you ask me in?"

"Because you looked so desperate. And I really didn't want to send you off with your tail between your legs. I'm not that kind of guy."

What the fuck was going on? He'd never been rejected this much in his life. Had his luck bottomed out? Was he now also a pathetic loser in the game of life *and* career?

"Look," Brody said as he walked over to grab his wallet from the dresser. "I think you're a hot guy. And the two of us could definitely have some fun making this room reek of sex."

"Then what's the problem?"

"The problem is I'm late to meet friends at tea," Brody said with a nod to the balcony. Surprisingly, Nino hadn't noticed the music downstairs, but now the deep bass beat from the speakers rattled his bones. "How about you come with me? We can socialize, have some drinks, and then if the mood is still with you," he added with a nod to Nino's crotch, "we can come back upstairs and enjoy some naked time."

"Or we could just ditch your friends and tea and start naked time early."

Brody shook his head. "Not gonna happen. Unlike you, I don't keep people waiting."

Nino sighed. "I didn't do that on purpose. There was this lost dog—"

Brody grabbed Nino by the hand and led him toward the door. "You can tell me your excuse as we head to tea. I don't like being late."

He followed Brody out the door and down the stairs to tea. What was he doing? He didn't give excuses, but that was just what he had been about to do. He thought he'd been losing it before, but this took the cake. What happened to his attitude? Where did the old Nino Santos go?

He'd once been a hot commodity. Guys either took what he had to offer or they didn't. Now he'd fallen even further than he had all day. Giving excuses and escorting some random guy to tea.

When would his downward spiral stop?

NINO HATED tea during Bear Week. It wasn't the crowds; he could deal with that. Guys were usually packed shoulder to shoulder during Twink Week, which was the week he cherished above all, but during Bear Week, space was at even more of a premium.

Every square inch of the outside deck of the Boatslip was packed with large, hairy men with perspiration dripping from their bodies. It made passage through the crowd difficult. And messy. He hated getting bear sweat on clothes he treated with care. Fashion was his livelihood, after all, or at least had been until the modeling gigs had dried up. That was why he treated his clothes as if they were special, because wearing them and being photographed in designer clothes made him special.

Especially in a crowd of button-down flannel shirts, camouflage shorts, and baseball caps. Who the fuck but bears and bull-dyke lesbians wore that shit anymore?

These silly bears avoided fashion as adamantly as Nino steered clear of carbohydrates. He embraced good clothes as gleefully as the bears welcomed an all-you-can-eat buffet.

But being here wasn't about these damn bears. It was about Brody. Sure, he'd allowed himself to be dragged here pretty much against his will, but it didn't change his plans. He intended to get Brody back upstairs so he could lose himself in the fuck. Brody was likely the only man in Provincetown this week who was the kind of guy he'd usually be interested in. He wasn't about to let that opportunity slip by him.

He needed to focus. Get through tea with all these bears and keep the finish line in sight. That finish line being Brody's nice, tight ass, which wiggled in front of him as Brody led him through the crowd.

As they approached a particularly dense patch of bears, Nino grimaced. Experience told him this wasn't going to be pretty.

Whenever he'd come to a bear tea in the past, he'd had to throw away some pretty decent clothes. Bear sweat had an unusual knack for not only leaving stains but also a stink that could never be washed out. No matter how many times the clothes were run through the washer.

He was going to smell like sweaty bear ass for days if he wasn't careful.

Brody, however, didn't seem to mind as they penetrated the forest of fur. He slid by the growling bears with relish. They patted his bottom or stopped him for a grab and a smooch, and instead of trying to extricate himself from their greedy paws, he languished in their embraces by wrapping his smooth, tanned flesh around their much larger frames.

"How are you doing, you sexy fuck?" one of the especially amorous bears asked Brody. He cradled Brody's ass in the palm of his left hand.

"It's Bear Week in P-town, Hal. How do you think I'm doing?"

"Normally, I'd say great," Hal replied as he eyed Nino. Why did he look like a disapproving daddy bear? "Tired of us bears already?" he asked as he turned back to Brody.

If Nino'd had a razor handy, he would have shaved Hal bald right there in the middle of tea. Who was Hal to be judging him? He wasn't the one who had body hair trailing up his neck fat or shooting out his ears. He also didn't have a round belly like Hal. Thank God.

Brody was more like Nino than Hal ever would be.

"Never," Brody replied. "I'm taking this one out for a spin around the block."

When did people start talking about him as if he wasn't present? He'd always been the one to start and end the conversation. He needed to put a stop to this. And fast.

"Except I'm the one who does the driving," Nino chimed in.

Hal chuckled, as did his group of friends. What was that about?

"We'll see about that," Hal said with a wink at Brody.

Brody acknowledged the gesture with his crooked grin and then tugged on Nino's hand, which Nino had surprisingly allowed him to continue to hold.

"Let's go find my friends," Brody said as he pulled Nino away from Hal and his group.

"See ya around," Nino said over his shoulder. He made sure he grinned extra wide to let the hairy daddies know Brody was with him. For now at least. Once Nino had what he needed from Brody, well, he'd never see Brody again. That was how he rolled.

But the knowing wink Hal offered up to Nino as he walked away troubled him. It was like Hal knew something Nino didn't.

WHEN BRODY finally found his friends, Nino's jaw dropped. Among the smiling group of guys was Jay. And Jay's new boy toy, Terry, from Bubala's.

"Nino!" Jay screeched as he descended upon him. He scooped Nino up in his arms and delivered the strongest bear hug Nino had ever experienced in his life. The force of the impact dislodged Nino's white Oakleys from his face. By the time Jay set him back on the deck, Terry had picked up the glasses and handed them to Nino.

"Thanks," Nino told Terry as he straightened out his shirt. Before the day was through he was going to need an iron to flatten out all the creases from Jay's rough handling. If Jay didn't crush him first.

"Long time no see," Jay said with a hearty pat to Nino's back.

"It's just been a few hours," Nino replied. He glanced over at Terry, who was currently mooning all over Jay. "I see you two have hit it off."

Jay chuckled as he wrapped his big arm around the smaller Terry's waist. "What can I say? Terry here is so delicious I've been gobbling him up all day."

"I bet," Nino replied as his stomach turned. He didn't want to think about Jay's naked body flattening out Terry. He was happy his new friend had been pounding some ass, but he really didn't need the visual.

"Let me introduce you to everyone." Jay pointed to two pale bears almost as big and hairy as himself. "This is Carl and his husbear, Rick. They're from Toronto. Which you could no doubt tell from their pasty asses."

"Fuck you too," Carl growled playfully.

"Nice to meet you," Rick said. Nino returned the greeting as he shook both men's hands. God, he needed to stop with the Social Suzy routine. But if this was what it took to get inside Brody's ass, he'd endure it. For now.

"And over here, we've got Dave, Brad, and Steve, who drove down from Vermont. They own a B and B and have been together for—" Jay stopped and looked at them. "How long's it been now, guys?"

"Ten years with me," Steve said.

Dave wrapped his arms around both men. "Brad and I were together five years before Steve came into our lives."

"Came being the operative word," Brad giggled.

A trio of bears? Was there a bed big enough for all three? "Pleased to meet you."

As the words came out of Nino's mouth, he inwardly shuddered. He'd never been this social in all the years he'd lived in P-town. Tea wasn't for meeting new friends. It was for finding the next trick. Was Brody worth all this trouble?

"How do you two know each other?" Brody's question distracted Nino from his internal monologue.

"We met last night at the beach party I was telling you about," Jay announced to the group, to which they all ahhed in unison. "Nino doesn't remember that. He was too shitfaced to remember me when I ran into him on Commercial today."

"If only we were all so lucky," Carl teased.

"I'd call you a bitch, but that would be an insult to bitches everywhere," Jay joked. Carl retorted by flipping Jay off. "But as I was saying, even though Nino didn't remember me, we did have some brunch together today."

Brody nodded, apparently pleased for some reason. "That's great. Jay's a nice guy."

"Yes, he is," Nino agreed. He surprised himself by the genuineness of his comment. He apparently really did like Jay.

"Aw," Jay said. "Before you go and make me blush, I wanna know how you two know each other."

"Cyber," Brody said.

"Ah, the app that brings more homos together than a glory hole." Jay turned to Nino and winked. "Feeling better now that you've busted your nut? You were sort of a moody cunt this morning."

Nino grimaced. He disliked having his business shared in front of people he didn't know. Then again, he hated making friends with people in general. All in all, this day had been unique and crappy at the same time. "I'll let you know when I do," he finally said.

Jay gasped in overexaggerated astonishment. "What do you mean? The two of you haven't done the gay handshake yet?"

"We would have," Brody cut in. "But someone here was late."

Jay nodded as if that made complete sense. Nino still didn't understand why punctuality had been such a big deal. Since when did friends trump a good fuck? That would be a never in his book.

"Brody hates being late," Jay admitted, as he rubbed Nino's shoulder. Jay apparently sensed his confusion. "Especially when it involves his friends."

"I just don't get that," Nino admitted. "Friends and fucking are two separate things. Why does one affect the other?"

Jay gazed at Nino as if he were a silly child. Brody and all the other guys in the group shook their heads. He'd apparently said something they didn't agree with.

"Friends should come first," Brody said. "Fucks come and go. Friends don't."

"Maybe in your world," he told the group. "In mine, people come and go as often as tricks do."

The guys in the group frowned. Not at his words but at what he'd admitted. Their blank stares reminded Nino of pity, and he didn't do pity. "What?" he finally asked. A fire raged in his belly.

"That just means you haven't found the right friends."

"Bullshit!" he exclaimed. The raging fire surged upward from his stomach. It now scorched his throat. "I've got good friends here. I just don't see the need to collect friends as if they're baseball cards. And I don't live my life by what my friends do or think. It's my life. I do what I want."

"Where's that gotten you?" Brody asked.

"Where I am today," Nino announced proudly, but the guys around him looked unconvinced.

"You're alone," Brody pointed out. "You claim to not want friends, yet here you are with a group of guys you've never met before. That doesn't sound like someone who doesn't want friends. It actually sounds like someone who *wants* friends but doesn't know how to be one."

"Brody, that's enough," Jay warned. He tried to offer Nino a comforting pat, but he shrugged off the contact. The fire Brody's words had started within him blazed out of control. This was why Nino didn't meet new people. They somehow thought it was their God-given duty to offer unwanted advice. He didn't care what other people thought. Sure, he valued Van's opinion—not that he'd seen much of Van since Zach, but still, Van was the only person he ever really listened to. He didn't need some random homo telling him what friends were for. No matter how fucking hot the guy was.

"You can go to hell," Nino told Brody before looking around at the other guys, who rolled their eyes. "And so can you."

He then turned and walked into the crowd of bears that surged around him. Jay called after him, but he didn't respond. He had to get out of there. He didn't belong with these guys. None of them were like him. He had to be somewhere where people understood him. And where he could understand himself.

IN A far corner of the deck, on the complete other side from where he had left Jay, Brody, and the bear crew, Nino spotted Van and Zach. The two lovebirds had their arms wrapped around each other, which wasn't unusual. They were typically glued together. He found it sickening. People didn't want to see all that sappy shit. Making out and fucking in public was fine. Because that was hot. And, well, sometimes exhibitionists let him join the fun.

But all that lovey-dovey crap? That was just publicly excluding others. It reminded everyone else of what they'd lost or didn't have. Who needed that?

"Why don't you get a room?" he asked as he leaned against the railing to their right. Their public displays of affection might make him queasy, but right now he needed to be with Van. He was the one person who could make him feel better.

"Nino," Zach said with a half smile. "Always a pleasure."

He and Zach weren't the best of friends. He still hadn't completely forgiven Zach for briefly breaking Van's heart last summer, but who was he to hold a grudge? Especially since Van had never been happier. As long as Zach kept that up, he'd allow Zach to keep his teeth.

"Tell me something I don't know, Rusthead," Nino retorted with a grin. Zach hated Nino's nickname for him. If he didn't like it, then he should dye the flaming red hair that danced atop his head some other, less irritating color. "Knowing me is an absolute delight."

"All right, you two," Van interjected. "I'm not in the mood to play referee. So how about we call a cease-fire for today?"

"Anything for you," Zach said with a kiss to Van's lips.

God. When did Van's life turn into some bad movie on the Hallmark channel? "Are you two finished grossing me out?"

"Never," Van replied. He moved around in Zach's arms so he stood in front with his back pressing into Zach's chest. "Now, why are you still in such a foul mood? I thought you went searching for a fuck to help cure you of that."

If they were alone, he'd be more likely to tell Van the truth. It might make him feel better and even understand just what the fuck was going on with him, but there was no way in hell that he'd open up in front of tall, white, and pasty. "I'm always in a bad mood during Bear Week."

"Then why come to tea?" Zach asked. "There's more bears here than in your apartment."

If he didn't love Van so much, he'd push him and Zach over the railing. Why did Van have to tell Zach about what he'd seen that morning? Oh, he forgot. Couples told each other everything. As if that tired old excuse made up for betraying his friend. What happened in Nino's bed was nobody's business. Unless Nino was the one doing the talking.

"Very funny," Nino finally said. "And you, why did you have to go and open your big mouth?"

"Are you kidding me?" Van asked. "A bear comes out of your room, and I'm expected to keep that to myself? That's front-page news, mister. Just be happy I haven't told Gary yet."

Nino bristled. Once Gary possessed information, the rest of the town was sure to follow. "And you better not tell Gary. I don't need him spreading his gossip. You know how he is."

"I do," Van agreed. "That's why I've only told Zach."

"And Tara," Zach added. His big, toothy grin told Nino he was quite pleased with himself for sharing that little tidbit.

"You told Tara?" He couldn't decide if he should kill them both now or later. Tara and Gary spread more gossip than TMZ. No, killing Van and Zach wasn't the answer. Suicide was.

"Unbunch your panties," Van said with a reassuring pat to his shoulder. "I made Tara promise to keep her mouth shut."

"Like that's gonna happen. You know how this town is. Once the rumor mill starts, there's no stopping it."

"So what?" Zach asked with a shrug. "Who cares if you fucked a bear? You've fucked more guys than I can count. And that's just in the past year that I've known you. Why do you care what people know?"

"I don't," he answered. Which was true. He'd never given one flying fuck what people thought about him. Most people called him an insatiable manslut. When had that ever bothered him? Hell, he prided himself on that reputation. It sure beat being the ugly, fat kid of his childhood.

"Look, I know you don't like bears," Van said. "You've gone on and on about that for years. But you obviously liked something about this guy enough to break your third rule."

"Third rule?" Zach asked. "What are you talking about?"

"Nino's got these six rules—" Van began, but Nino interrupted him.

"Do you have to divulge *every* secret to Zach? Is nothing sacred?"

Van briefly stared into Zach's eyes, and they shared an unspoken conversation. Couples often did that, telling each other shit with just a glance or a nod. Nino hated that. It was fucked up for someone to know another person so well that not even thoughts were sacred. He preferred for people to stay the fuck out of his head. Still, he wasn't stupid. Van had just told Zach he'd fill him in later.

Evidently, nothing between him and Van was private anymore.

That made him reevaluate their friendship. He'd come over here to feel better. To be with someone who understood him, unlike the judgmental bears he'd just left. But Van didn't really understand him anymore. He had Zach now, which left Nino out in the cold. Again.

"Nino, are you listening to me?"

Van's question pulled him from his thoughts. "What?"

"I said I've never known you to let a guy sleep over. Is that the problem? Do you like him?"

He was right. Van obviously didn't know him anymore. "Are you out of your fucking mind? This isn't high school, where I'm hiding some secret crush. You know me better than that. At least I thought you did. I don't invest in guys. I fuck them. End of story."

"Methinks the lady doth protest too much," Zach announced with a grin.

"I'm not even going to pretend to know what that means," Nino replied.

"All right, that's enough teasing," Van informed Zach. "I'm worried about you, Nino. You seem different. On the edge. That isn't like you."

"No shit!"

"Then tell me. What's going on?"

Nino shook his head. Maybe those guys were right. Maybe he didn't know how to be a friend. He couldn't even open up to the man he considered his brother. If he couldn't talk to Van, who could he talk to?

"I'll talk to you later," he said as he turned around and walked into the line of bears, heading away from Van and Zach.

Van called for him to come back, but he kept going.

Whatever he was searching for, he wasn't going to find it in Van.

Chapter Eight

AS SOON as Teddy stepped foot inside tea, a weight lifted off his shoulders. Maybe now that he was where he belonged, with other hairy men, he could stop thinking about what happened earlier. With Nino.

Why the hell was he being nice to Nino? Sure, he'd been relieved that Louie had been found. Even if it had been Nino who had found him. But still, that didn't require the playful way Teddy had joked around. He only did that with people he actually liked.

"Will you stop obsessing already?" Irene asked. Her blonde hair had been so excessively teased it made her a good two inches taller. And her bangs, well, they practically hung in front of her eyes. Her ensemble wouldn't have been complete without the five jelly bracelets that hung from her left wrist or the "Choose Life" shirt she wore in honor of the 1980s pop group Wham! Would she *ever* not embarrass him with her clothing choices?

"And just what am I obsessing about?" he asked, feigning ignorance.

"Nino," she said. She poked him in his chest with her press-on nails. They were a scarlet red that, unfortunately, matched the shade of her lipstick. Was she trying to look like a caricature?

"I'm not even thinking about that bastard," he lied as they walked through the crowd. As usual, they headed straight for Tara's station, where the line extended about fourteen people deep. Tara had been his bartender of choice for years, and like most of the other boys in P-town, he adored her.

"Denial doesn't suit you," Irene yelled, trying to be heard above the music and the din of the crowd. "You do better when you face problems head-on. You always have."

"What are you talking about?" he asked her as they bypassed the line of thirsty men waiting for their turn with Tara. When Tara saw him, she smiled and nodded. As usual, her wild mane of wavy hair lay flat from the perspiration of slinging cocktails on this sweltering day. As a good friend and a regular who tipped well, he enjoyed not having to wait in line. He had a standing order for two Planter's Punches. It was the drink of choice at tea after all.

"I saw the way you looked at Nino. And the way you talked to him. You were flirting."

"I was not," he told Irene. "I was just being nice because he'd found Louie."

"No," she added with a vigorous shake of her head. She had applied so much Aqua Net her hair didn't even move. Nothing short of a nuclear detonation would cause a dent in Irene's do. "You were flirting. I've seen you in action. Dozens of times. You were tossing barbs at him."

"I do that with everyone," he replied.

"Yes, but not with that twinkle in your eye. Or that crooked smile of yours. You only do that when you're flirting."

Had he been flirting with Nino? And if he was, why the hell had he been doing that? She had to be wrong.

Luckily, Tara interrupted them at just the right moment. "Here you go, sweetie," she said as she set the drinks in front of them and then leaned over the bar for her hug. He squeezed her tight, which seemed to irritate Irene. Why did she always act like a psychotic ex-girlfriend whenever he and Tara were together? Was Irene jealous of their relationship? He'd asked Irene about it before, but she never gave him a reasonable answer.

"How are you doing today?" Teddy asked once they'd released each other.

"I'm great. Just slammed," she said as she nodded to the line of men, who glared at Teddy for the interruption. "How are you, Irene?"

"Just great," she said. Why did Irene look so nervous?

"Awesome," Tara said as she went back to work. "You going to Gary and Quinn's party later?"

"I didn't know about it," he admitted.

"Well, it's not like it's very far from your condo. You should stop on by. You know the boys will be glad to see you."

"We just might," he announced as he threw forty dollars on the bar and then escorted Irene away. "You know, you could be friendly. She's a nice person."

Irene chuffed. Did she realize she was doing a Louie imitation? "Let's get back to you and Nino," she said after she took a big gulp of her drink.

He rolled his eyes at her as they wove through the crowd. "There is no me and Nino."

"Uh-huh," she said, apparently unconvinced. "You two hooked up. That's something in my book."

"Not if I don't even remember it," he admitted.

Irene stopped him by grabbing his hand. She led him over to the side railing and then gazed into his eyes. "You need to stop this," she said. "Now. Before it gets out of hand."

What the hell was she going on about now? Perhaps she had sunstroke and was delirious. "I don't know what you're talking about."

"Yes, you do. You're just acting dumb."

"Don't call me that," he warned Irene. Those were fighting words. He hated being called dumb. Especially since that had been the way his mother often referred to him.

"Right," she added with a nod. "Sorry. But you're not seeing things clearly. And you need to."

"And what is that?" he asked. "Enlighten me with your wisdom."

"You talk a big talk about the bears and how much you love them. But I know better. Like I was telling you earlier on the beach. You may have fun playing with the bears, but you really want what you're most afraid of having."

"And that would be?"

"The hot all-American boy."

"That's ridiculous!"

"Is it?" she asked. "You've only been in love once. With Br—" She stopped when he arched his eyebrow in warning. Saying his name was taboo. "With He-Who-Must-Not-Be-Named. You've never been in love since. Coincidence? I think not."

"You're crazy," he told her as he grabbed her hand. They once again worked their way through the packs of bears.

"I am not. I've seen the porn on your computer," she revealed. He stopped and turned to face her. How could she have invaded his privacy like that? "No bears. Just the hairless pups, as you call them."

"What right do you have to be going through my shit?" he said. The heat of his words caused some of the guys closest to them to glance at them sideways. "How dare you do that, Irene!"

"Bitch at me about it later," she said, waving away his anger as if it weren't justified. "Right now, let's deal with Nino. You like him. I know it. Now you just need to admit it to yourself."

If he had his way, he'd leave Irene here alone. Snooping around his stuff was unforgiveable, but it didn't erase the truth. He did get off to nonbear porn. Nasty Boy Studios had been his masturbation theater of choice, and they never featured bears. Their models tended to be hairless, young, and similar in physical characteristics to Nino.

He'd always written off the videos as a perversion. Those guys got him off because they weren't the types of men he typically let in his cave. But was there some truth to what Irene was saying?

Did he secretly lust after the pretty boys? Was he really *that* screwed up?

THANKFULLY, TEDDY didn't have time to ponder some hidden attraction to guys he'd complained about hating for most of his life. Who had time to think around his good friend Jay?

"Teddy!" the big guy hollered as he stampeded across the deck to reach him. Bringing up the rear were Carl, Rick, Dave, Brad, Steve, and some random gym twink. It wasn't hard to pick out who didn't belong in that group.

"How are you, Jay?" he asked. In reply, Jay wrapped his huge arms around Teddy and almost squeezed the life right out of his body. He was glad he'd finished his Planter's Punch just moments before. The drink would not have survived such a greeting.

"I'm great!" Jay said after he released Teddy. He'd met Jay and the rest of these guys a few years ago at tea. They all hit it off and became good friends. Since then, they tried to arrange their P-town vacations so they could see each other at least once a year. "I was hoping we'd run into you again. Especially since you ditched me for lunch today."

"Sorry about that," he said as he hugged the remaining guys in the group. "But I was hungover and needed a shower."

"Yeah, to wash all the cum out of your belly hair," Jay added with a wink.

"Ooh, do tell," Brad urged. He always enjoyed a good trick story.

"Not much to tell," he told the guys.

Irene snorted. Could she be any more like Louie? "Guys, you all remember Irene, right?" He hoped switching the subject might deter Irene from launching into another tirade about Nino and his secret yearning for the nonbearish guy.

"How are you, Irene?" Jay asked.

"I'm good," she told Jay with a big smile. "I'm surrounded by gay men. What else would I be?"

Her comment obviously startled his friends, since they took a step back. They had all been on the receiving end of Irene's flirtations. She'd hit on each of them at least twice this week, and they all evidently feared a repeat performance.

Jay, however, looked immune to Irene. He wrapped his arm around the shoulders of the twink. Unlike most other bears, Jay preferred his men young and hairless. Maybe he and Jay had more in common than he had once thought. No, he couldn't go there. He liked bears, and if he had to fuck every last one of them at tea to prove it to Irene and himself, he would.

"So who's this?" he asked, attempting to slice through the tension.

"This is Terry," Jay announced. "We met at lunch today."

"Nice to meet you, Terry," he said as he shook the younger man's hand. "I see you didn't miss me at lunch after all."

"Of course I did, you silly little bear." Jay always called him that. Not just because of his height but because his belly wasn't as round as most everyone else's. Jay referred to his stomach as a baby bump. "But I did make a fantastic new friend."

"I can see that," he said with an eyebrow wiggle.

Jay chuckled and whacked him on the shoulder. Damn, his big hand hurt. When was he going to learn to pull his punches?

"I'm not talking about Terry, you goof!"

The other men in the group moaned collectively. Evidently, they didn't think much of Jay's new friend. Only Terry remained quiet. He was too busy gazing up into Jay's face like a baby bird waiting to be fed.

"Then who?"

"Let's not talk about him," Steve commented. "He's a jerk."

"No, he's not," Jay said, defending his new friend. "He's really a nice guy. You just haven't gotten to know him yet."

"I'm okay with that," Rick added. The others nodded in agreement.

"Damn," Teddy said. "Tough crowd."

"Too tough," Jay chided. "You all can't see the hurt little boy, but I can. He's obviously not used to making friends. That's just awful and rather telling about the life he's led."

Teddy smiled at Jay. He had a heart bigger than the body that housed it. That was one of the reasons he liked Jay so much.

"Well, I promise to give him the benefit of the doubt if I ever meet him."

"Thank you, honey," Jay said. He leaned over and kissed the top of Teddy's head. "Now, I can't wait for you to meet my roommate." He scanned the crowd in search of his missing friend. "We met last year, you know, the year you *didn't* come for Bear Week."

Teddy rolled his eyes and nodded. "I think you've berated me enough for that."

"Not quite." Jay grinned. "But my roomie's such a sweet guy. Lives in Boston too. Maybe you know him."

"Boston isn't exactly a sleepy little town," he reminded Jay.

"I know that, but you know how the gay world is. Most guys we meet usually end up connected to us by one trick or another."

Teddy nodded. That much was true. The gay community was surprisingly incestuous at times.

"What's his name?" he asked. "Maybe we've already hooked up."

Everyone laughed.

"There he is!" Jay shouted as he waved his friend over. Since he was so short, Teddy couldn't see above the mass of fur that surrounded them. He also couldn't turn around. During their conversation, he had managed to get wedged between the canopy covering the front part of the deck and the railing behind him.

"Teddy," Jay said as he beamed. He loved few things more than introducing friends to his friends. "This is Brody O'Shea."

His world suddenly turned fuzzy and out of focus. Did he hear Jay right? Did he just utter the name Brody O'Shea? It couldn't be him. Could it?

The gasp of surprise that escaped Irene's throat gave Teddy his answer.

It was Brody. Or, as he and Irene referred to him, He-Who-Must-Not-Be-Named.

WHEN DID he enter the Twilight Zone? Because that had to be where Teddy was. There was no way in hell he could be staring into the green eyes of the man who had broken his heart in college.

He'd spent his entire junior year of college trying to get Brody to notice him. When Brody finally did, he couldn't believe someone as perfect as Brody would date, much less start a relationship with, someone like him. His mother had called him a short, hairy, worthless piece of shit, and that was what he'd always seen himself as. Until Brody.

Being with Brody made him feel as if perhaps he was worth something after all. That maybe he wasn't a big loser. All the happiness he never had in his life had suddenly been found, and Brody had been the reason. When he lost Brody, well, he no longer had a reason to be happy. And he hadn't really found one since.

"Teddy?" Brody said. His gorgeous face spread into a huge grin. He half expected to see a lens flare reflect off those perfect teeth. "Jesus! How are you? It's been what? Ten years?"

"Eleven," he replied. "But who's counting?"

"It's good to see you," Brody said. The golden flecks in Brody's green eyes sparkled. Whenever they did that in college, he used to fall on his back and spread his legs in response. He hoped he didn't embarrass himself by doing that now. "And Irene?" Brody asked as he suddenly noticed her scowling. "My God! You haven't changed one bit."

"Apparently, neither have you," she said coolly. "Ever the charmer."

Brody shrugged. His smile hooked up on the right. If Teddy didn't have self-control, he'd have hopped onto Brody right there in front of everyone. That damned crooked smile had always driven him crazy. "Me? Charming?"

Everyone busted out laughing. Teddy had completely forgotten that Jay and the others were there. Once he laid eyes on Brody, the rest of the world disappeared. Just like it had been in college.

"You could out-charm all the Disney princes with one grin," Jay commented.

"Amen to that!" Dave said. "I'd even bottom for you." Brad and Steve smacked their husband upside his head.

"I've wanted to fuck you all week," Steve complained.

"And if anyone's getting in that ass, it's us," Brad added.

Dave sighed in fake exasperation. "Why did I want two husbands again?" His comment earned him two more smacks.

"Ladies, please," Jay said, shushing the bear trio into silence. "We've got more pressing matters to attend to than who's getting inside Dave's old, hairy hole."

"Hey!" Dave complained.

Jay ignored Dave and turned back to face Teddy and Brody. "So, how do you two know each other?"

"We dated in college," Brody answered.

Dated? They'd been in love. Well, at least Teddy had been. Had Brody never really felt the same way?

"What a small world!" Jay exclaimed. Why did Jay's words sound more like concern than joy? Did he somehow realize Teddy was freaking out about this?

"Isn't it, though?" Brody asked as he wrapped his arm around Teddy's neck. Brody's touch spread like a wildfire from his shoulder down to his cock, where it blazed into a scorching inferno. His dick stiffened almost immediately. When he inhaled and caught that familiar scent of sage and lavender, his knees almost buckled. Luckily, he'd been leaning against the railing, which kept him from falling over. "We haven't seen each other since before graduation."

The *night* before graduation, but he didn't want to say that out loud. The memory of that night had haunted him for years. He promised himself he'd never fall in love again, and to this day, he hadn't gone back on that.

"You've obviously got a lot of catching up to do," Carl said. A devilish grin fluttered across his lips.

"Maybe," Brody teased as he absently ran the hand that dangled over his left shoulder up and down Teddy's chest. He used to do that whenever they snuggled in bed together.

What the hell was going on? Brody had dumped him. Tossed him by the side of the road like an unwanted candy wrapper. They had nothing left to catch up on.

Those were the words he tried to force from his lips, but they'd apparently been paralyzed by Brody's flirty behavior. His mind screamed at him to take a stand, but his heart and his cock longed for just one more taste. He was behaving like some lovesick crackhead presented with a pipe after years of sobriety. He needed to get a grip. And fast.

"Maybe not," Irene declared. She knocked Brody's arm from around Teddy's shoulder. "Teddy here might be too much of a pussy to say anything, but I'm not."

Brody stared at Irene as if she was crazy. Everyone else appeared mortified. They obviously wanted to flee, but their fascination with the unfolding train wreck kept their feet glued in place.

As they stood there, a small pocket of impending discord amid the swirling celebration that was tea, the first notes of Gloria Gaynor's "I Will Survive" blared through the speakers. Just like Gloria, Teddy was afraid *and* petrified.

"Reenie, please," he begged. Although he didn't really want her to stop. She was able to voice what he couldn't.

"You break Teddy's heart and then you have the gall to pretend like none of that happened. Why don't you take a flying jump into a pit of dirty needles?"

"Irene, that was ages ago," Brody said. Yes, but now he was back. From outer space. Just like Gloria sang it. Except there was no sad look upon Brody's face. His standard cavalier grin lingered on his lips. Just like it always had. Brody met Irene's anger with an air of nonchalance. Did anything ever upset him? Ending their relationship sure hadn't. Brody had taken that in stride, as if he were simply stepping over a puddle in the street. But that had always been Brody's way. Teddy had fallen in love with him regardless. Could he really blame Brody for being who he'd always been?

"That doesn't change the fact that you're an asswipe," Irene responded as she stood between him and Brody. The move was perfectly choreographed with the line from the song "go on now go." Did anyone else notice that? From his friends' astonished expressions, they apparently did not. Their eyes were glued to the crap storm that suddenly swirled about them. He'd find all this humorous if he weren't about to hurl.

"I'm not about to let you walk on over here. Take the hint. You're not welcome anymore." Now Irene was just directly quoting the lyrics. Was that on purpose? "Do you ever deal with the path of destruction you leave behind you?" she asked in disgust.

"Teddy doesn't look destroyed to me," Brody pointed out. He winked at Teddy in an attempt to defuse the situation. After all this time, he still read Brody's body language as if they'd never broken up, and Brody had just signaled Teddy to come to his defense. As if interpreting Brody's wink wasn't sad enough, he actually had to fight the desire to do as requested. Why did Brody still have that power over him?

Luckily, Irene continued her tirade before Teddy embarrassed himself by doing what Brody wanted. "That's because you haven't had to deal with the consequences," she said. "But when have you ever? You were always like that in college. Using your charm to get what you want. Well, your spell doesn't work on me."

"Irene, please," he said. This time, he *did* want her to stop. He couldn't deal with this. Not here. Not now. She was causing a scene. As it was, Jay and the gang were watching them as if this were an episode of *The Young and the Restless*. This was tea in Provincetown, and Gloria Gaynor was singing a gay anthem. Now was the time for dancing, not drama.

"What I'd like for you to do," she continued as if he hadn't spoken, "is turn around and walk away. That's what you do the best."

"First of all," Brody said as he held up his index finger. That was something Brody did whenever he counted out a list of reasons. "I don't take orders. From anyone." Holding up two fingers, he continued. "Secondly, Teddy's a big boy. He can speak for himself. Something *you'd* never let him do in college. You were always mouthing off, talking for him as if Teddy was some puppet and you were the puppeteer with your hand up his ass. Looks like that hasn't changed any." Brody glanced from Irene to Teddy when he held up his third finger. "And last, don't pretend your concern for Teddy has anything to do with trying to protect him. We both know why you're acting this way. It isn't anger. You're terrified because you've never told him about our little discussion. Am I right?"

Irene gasped as if Brody had struck her.

"What discussion?" Teddy asked as he gazed back and forth between Brody and Irene.

"I thought so," Brody said. His grin returned as he shook his head in disappointment. Even after all that, he didn't look angry. How did Brody manage to remain so composed after dealing with Irene's wrath?

"Now's not the time," Irene said as she grabbed Teddy's hand. "Come on. Let's go."

Gloria apparently agreed, as she told her lover in her song to walk out the door. He, however, was going nowhere. He withdrew his hand from her grasp. He'd spent so many years running from his past with Brody that he couldn't hide from it anymore. He had to deal with it, starting right now. Especially if he didn't have all the pieces to the puzzle. "I'm not going anywhere. At least not till I know what's going on."

Irene glared at Brody. "He's just trying to start trouble. As always."

"Then don't let him," he said. "You know what I went through when Brody dumped me. You helped me through it. But if there's something I don't know, I think I deserve to know the truth."

"Yes, you do," Brody said. "You think we broke up because of what you asked me, right?"

He nodded. He'd always thought the reason Brody left was because Teddy had proposed. It wouldn't have been legal. Same-sex marriage hadn't yet been recognized in Massachusetts. But it wasn't about the legality. It had been more symbolic for Teddy. A way to show they were committed to a lifetime together. When Brody rejected him with no explanation and then left, he'd always assumed he just wasn't good enough for Brody and that Brody had finally figured that out for himself.

"That's not the whole reason," Brody told him. "Sure, I wasn't ready, but neither were you."

"But why didn't you just say that instead of just saying no and walking out of my dorm room?" If this conversation continued in synch with the song, he was going to rip the speakers out of the wall.

"Irene thought it was best that way," Brody replied as he glanced over at Teddy's best friend.

"She what?" he asked as he turned to face her. "You told him to dump me?"

She inhaled deeply and ran her fingers through her rock-hard hair. That was Irene's way of admitting she'd done something wrong. How could she do that to him? He'd been destroyed, or as Gloria so aptly put it, he had crumbled and wanted to lay down and die.

"It was for your own good," she finally said. "Brody wasn't ready for marriage. Neither were you."

"That wasn't your decision to make," he said.

"It wasn't," Brody admitted. "That didn't matter, though. I still wouldn't have said yes to your proposal."

"Can you finally tell me why?"

"Teddy, you're a good man. And I cared for you a great deal. But you lost yourself in our relationship. I became the reason for your happiness. Not only is that unhealthy, but that's a lot to place on one person's shoulders. Especially at that age. I was still trying to figure out my life. I couldn't be in charge of your happiness. And mine. So I had to choose. You or me. It might have been a chickenshit thing to do, but I thought you'd be better off if I just left. That's why I didn't give you the explanation you wanted. I figured if you hated me, you'd have no choice but to move on."

That was where he and Ms. Gaynor's song parted ways. Sure, he'd gone on living after the breakup, but he hadn't really been alive. He'd hopped from one hairy pair of arms to another. Because it was safe. He'd completely forgotten how to love, but could he learn how to again?

He didn't have the answers. Especially not with everyone staring at him and waiting for him to react. He needed to do that alone, so he walked right past Brody, Irene, and his friends and headed out of tea.

Maybe now, he would survive.

Chapter Nine

TEDDY HADN'T realized how far he'd walked until he stood before the breakwater. He'd traveled at least a mile from the Boatslip. Had he really walked that far? He didn't even remember passing the Coast Guard station or Relish, one of P-town's most popular bakeries. If he'd been paying attention, he might have stopped in and purchased a donut or three.

Still, he couldn't complain. He loved the breakwater. It was one of the best places to visit in Provincetown, and he hadn't been there in years. Partly because it was so out of the way and partly because he usually spent his time on the Cape drinking or tricking.

Who had time for anything else?

But he was here now, so he planned on enjoying it.

The rock structure had always amazed him. It extended from the end of Commercial Street all the way across the bay to the outermost finger of the jutting Cape. He'd made the journey across to the Long Point Lighthouse a few years ago. It took him about two hours to scramble across the uneven rocks, and halfway out a dense fog had enveloped the Cape. It made for a slow, cold journey. Once he'd reached the other side, though, and the fog had lifted, he had forgotten all about his damp clothes and his chattering teeth.

The quiet beaches on the other side had been a nice respite from the crowds of people, and right now that was exactly what he needed. Some alone time away from everything and everyone.

Maybe then he could stop thinking about Irene and Brody. How his best friend had secretly worked behind the scenes to secure his breakup with the only man he'd ever loved. And how Brody had just let it all happen. Without an explanation.

Had they been blind to his devastation? Did they really believe they had been helping him?

No, he had to stop thinking about it. If he didn't, he might leap right into the open water. What he needed was a distraction.

So he stepped up onto the rocky path and started to cross.

When he was a quarter way over the breakwater, with the cold Atlantic slapping against the rocks, he spotted a lone figure walking back down the path toward him. The man appeared to be walking at a fast clip, leaping from one rock to another. Was he stupid? The rocks were slippery from the sea mist. One misstep and that dumbass would find himself head over heels in the Atlantic.

Maybe the guy had a death wish. Maybe he'd had a crappy day just like Teddy.

Or maybe he was just a complete and utter idiot.

Who else but a dumbass jogged across the breakwater? Especially when the sun had already begun its descent into the ocean.

Of course, how much of a dumbass was he? Crossing the breakwater at this time of day wasn't exactly the smartest move. If he continued, he'd have to cross back in pitch-dark.

That was just tragedy waiting to happen.

He wasn't exactly a great swimmer. He couldn't even float. Whenever he tried, he'd always sink to the bottom of the swimming pool. And this was no five-foot-deep in-ground pool in someone's backyard. Just how deep was it out there? He crossed over to the edge of the breakwater and peered into the ocean. The fading sunlight turned the water black instead of its customary blue. Staring out at the ocean had always had a calming effect. But that was when he was safe on shore, not standing on the slick, rocky path with night on its way.

Who was the dumbass now?

When he gazed back down the path, the man who'd been practically parkouring his way to where Teddy stood was nowhere to be seen.

Shit! Had he tumbled into the ocean?

Teddy turned around to see if the guy had somehow passed him, but no one else was on the breakwater but him. He fumbled his phone out of his pocket as he scuttled across the uneven path to the spot where he'd last seen the fool rushing across the rocks. If the guy had fallen, he would need help.

Why wasn't his phone connecting? A glance at his cell phone screen told him he had no bars. Fuck, there was no service out in the middle of the ocean!

He picked up his pace, traversing the distance with less caution than he was accustomed to taking. What choice did he have? If the guy was in trouble, it was up to Teddy to save the day.

After a few scary moments, one where he almost skidded off the breakwater and into the ocean, he noticed someone lying on his back in the middle of the path. The guy hadn't tumbled into the water after all. He'd apparently just fallen flat on his ass.

Stupid jerk. It would serve him right to have a broken tailbone.

He entertained the idea of turning back, but he'd already come all this way. Besides, the idiot might have hit his head. With his luck, the guy would have a concussion and Teddy would not only have to escort him off the breakwater but to some urgent care center on the Cape.

Wouldn't that just be the cherry on top of this crap sundae?

"Hey, man," he called out as he drew closer. The guy was still on his back. "You okay?"

When the man sat up, he glimpsed dark, curly hair whipping in the wind. No, it couldn't be. Not all the way out there in the middle of the ocean. But he couldn't be certain. Dusk had hidden the man's face in shadow.

"Are you kidding me right now?" the man asked from where he sat. "What the hell are you doing out here?"

Teddy halted his progress. There was no doubt about it. The idiot he'd come out here to save was Nino.

Looked like his crap sundae had just turned into a crap sandwich.

FUCK! AS if falling on his ass didn't sting enough, now Nino had to deal with Teddy the bear. Just great. How much more could this day suck?

"Did you somehow think the laws of physics wouldn't apply to you?" Teddy asked. He slowly made his way over a precarious part of the breakwater.

Did the furry fuck have to look as if he was enjoying this so much?

"I don't follow rules," he announced. "I break them." Although right now, his ass was in so much pain he did wish he'd been a little more careful. But outrunning the monster had been too tempting. It was something he'd done since childhood. Whenever life got too rough, no matter where he was, a sudden desire to run as fast as he could took control of his legs, and he'd take off until he couldn't run anymore.

It had always made him feel better. But today, not so much.

"How's that working out for you?" Teddy asked as he slid to a stop just a few feet from where Nino still sat.

"Just great," he replied. "Till you showed up."

"Uh-huh," Teddy said. A knowing grin slowly stretched across his lips. He could obviously tell Nino was in excruciating pain. "You're in pain and you need help. Just admit it."

He snorted. "I don't need nothing from nobody."

"Well, for one thing, you need to brush up on proper grammar," Teddy said as he peered down at Nino. "Your annoying use of a double negative reveals that about as much as the tears in your eyes tell me that you're in pain."

What the fuck did he say? Tears? He didn't cry, but when he wiped his eyes with his left hand, it came away moist. He was officially falling apart now. He hadn't cried in years. Not since his older sister had called him a *bicha*. Now that had hurt. It was the first time anyone in his family had ever called him a faggot. Unfortunately, it wasn't the last.

"It's sea spray," he told Teddy. "Nothing more."

For a few minutes the little bear stood over him, beaming. He evidently enjoyed finally being taller than someone else. When Nino was standing, the top of Teddy's head just barely made it to Nino's chin. So if he was getting such a big kick out of this, then why did

Teddy's shit-eating grin disappear so quickly? His high spirits suddenly and rather inexplicably crashed.

What was that about?

"I can see you've had a shitty day too, huh?" Teddy asked before sitting down next to Nino. He pulled his knees up to his chest and hugged them close to his body. He reminded Nino of the scared little boy he'd once been.

Obviously, a deep pain bit away inside Teddy, and he almost reached out to put his arm around Teddy's shoulder for comfort. Luckily, he remembered he didn't do that kind of shit. They weren't friends. Hell, they didn't even really like each other. What did he care if Teddy looked like someone had kicked him in the face and stole his lunch money? No one had been there for him when that had actually happened to him.

He had survived. Chances were Teddy would too.

"So, what happened to you?" Teddy asked him.

"Look, let's not pretend we're buddies, okay? You don't like me. I don't like you."

Teddy nodded. He wiped something away from his eyes. It had to have been the sea mist, right? There was just no way this dude was sitting next to him and crying.

"You're right," Teddy agreed. He cleared his throat and released his knees. Instead of standing, though, he sat cross-legged next to him and continued to peer into the bay.

Why wouldn't Teddy just leave him to suffer in silence?

"Maybe that's what I need, though. Maybe I need some heartless prick like you to tell me to just get over myself. To pull up my big-boy undies and move on."

What was he going on about now? "Why would you need anyone to tell you that?" Nino asked. "If you know that's what you've got to do, then just do it. Don't wait around for someone to give you permission. You can't live your life by other people's rules. I sure as hell don't. I've been there and done that. That got me absofuckinglutely nowhere. People just don't give a shit. The sooner you accept that, the better off you'll be."

"But how can you live that way?" Teddy asked. "I get that some people don't give a shit. I'm fine with that. I don't need everyone to like me. But based on what you've said, you go through life thinking that *no one* cares."

"They don't," he said matter-of-factly.

"God, your family must be even worse than mine!"

His body stiffened, and a frost settled across his skin. That typically happened whenever anyone brought up his family. He made it a point *not* to discuss them. With anyone. Not even Van. "Don't go there," he warned.

Teddy nodded. "Yeah, me too. I think I've lived my life in reaction to my mother. To prove her wrong. To show her that I have worth."

Oh God. He didn't need this. The last thing he wanted was to hear Teddy's life story. If he could, he'd get up and walk away, but whenever he moved, pain shot through his ass and down his leg. Whether he liked it or not, he was going nowhere.

"You know, you reminded me of her this morning."

"Why?" he asked. "Did you often get drunk at birthday parties and wake up naked next to her?"

"No, you jerk!" Teddy laughed.

He playfully smacked Nino's shoulder. When the hell did they cross the no-touching threshold?

"It's just that when I woke up and saw the look of disgust on your face, well, let's just say that my dear old mother has pretty much looked at me that way my whole life. Maybe I look like my father, who dumped her ass before I was born. Who knows? But she's never had a kind word to say to me for most of my life. So when you were standing there, judging me like she so often did, I kinda lost it and was a complete ass to you." He inhaled as if the next words out of his mouth would be extremely painful. "And even though you were a complete ass hat, I shouldn't have been so ugly to you."

"That sounds like an apology," Nino said.

Teddy turned to him and grinned. It was the first time they'd stared into each other's eyes since Teddy sat beside him. The hardness he'd seen that morning had softened. They no longer pierced through him like the barbs Teddy so often shot his way. They were now soft and inviting, and he had a strong desire to dive into the warm, welcoming pools.

"Like you told me, you don't need anyone to give you permission," Teddy told him. His voice jarred Nino from his thoughts. He'd almost leaned over to Teddy and, well, embarrassed himself. "If that's what you hear, then that's what you hear. I'm not going to tell you otherwise."

"An apology it is, then," Nino said. Why did he have to follow the statement with a smile? If he continued to do that, then Teddy was going to get the wrong idea and think they might actually be friends or something.

"Whatever you say, Curly."

Nino frowned. "I don't like that name. In fact, I don't like nicknames period." Teddy's grin widened into a full-blown smile. It lightened up his usually serious face and made him quite handsome, even surrounded by his stubble. In fact, Nino doubted Teddy's face would be as attractive without the scruff. He'd never thought that of anyone before.

"Curly it is, then," Teddy said with a nod.

Nino groaned. "You know I'm going to push you off the breakwater for that, don't you?"

Teddy's grin hooked up to the left. "You'd have to be able to stand first, and I don't think you're quite ready for that yet."

"Fuck you," he cursed, but his typical biting tone had gone the way of Teddy's stern expression. It actually came across as good-natured. He only did that with Van. Just what was going on with him now?

"You've already had the pleasure," Teddy reminded him with a wink.

"Yeah, it was so good I don't remember it."

"Same here, Curly. You didn't exactly make it one to remember for me either."

For a few moments, silence settled between them. It was different from before, though. When Teddy first arrived, it had hung around them like an oppressive fog. Now it reminded Nino more of sitting before a roaring fire on a cold New England day.

He'd never been this comfortable with anyone before.

HOW LONG had they been out there? The sun had disappeared entirely and taken the air it warmed with it. A chilly breeze swirled all around them, and the moon's reflection now shimmered on the ocean. Teddy pulled his phone out of his shorts and clicked it on. It was almost nine o'clock. They'd been sitting out on the breakwater together for almost two hours.

Who would have ever thought that possible? They couldn't get away from each other fast enough that morning. Now they were chatting as if they were friends.

Provincetown was obviously to blame. She often did that. Bring two people together who'd never cross paths under ordinary circumstances. How else could he explain the fact that he and a man he'd thought he'd hate until the end of time would be sitting in the middle of the ocean, sharing details about their lives?

"Sounds like you and I are a lot alike," he admitted to Nino. "We've both been trying to escape our families."

Nino nodded reluctantly. Much of their conversation had gone the same way, with hesitance on Nino's part. He obviously detested talking about his past. It had been like pulling teeth to get Nino to admit why he believed no one cared. That he had been born into a family that ostracized Nino almost as cruelly as Amanda Miller had treated him.

Except in Nino's case, he suffered not only at the hands of bullies but from the cutting tongues of his older sisters, who terrorized him on a daily basis. The poor guy had no safe haven. At least Teddy had the apartment where he grew up to himself most of the time. While his mother was stripping the night away, he could prepare himself for the eventual onslaught of abuse when she got home.

Nino didn't have that. He went straight from the bullies at school to the ones who waited for him at home.

"I take it that's why you became a model," he added.

"Yeah. I wanted to shove it in everyone's face. I wanted them to see that their ugly duckling had turned into a swan and flown as far away from them as possible. But I also didn't want them to forget."

"What do you mean?"

A devilish twinkle lit up Nino's eyes. God, whenever Nino did that, Teddy wanted to jump his bones. Had he not already learned his lesson with Brody?

"Well, I'm on the cover of many magazines," Nino said as he shifted position so that his body faced Teddy. "The way I look at it, they see my face everywhere they go. In the grocery store. The doctor's office. Their friends' houses. I'm there. And they have to deal with the fact that, yes, I may have been fat and ugly when I was a kid, but look at me now." Nino delighted in flexing his muscles. He even pulled up his shirt and punched his flat, smooth stomach. "Not a trace of fat anywhere. They, on the other hand, have turned into ugly hags. I know it. I've seen pictures."

Teddy couldn't help but laugh. The sheer joy that radiated from Nino's smile was infectious. It made him want to do anything to see that smile again. "Success is the best revenge," he agreed. After all, that was what helped him survive his mother. He'd made something of himself and escaped her clutches as soon as he could. Amanda Miller couldn't escape herself, though. She had most recently divorced loser husband number four, and she had nothing to fall back on.

Her good looks were gone, pissed away by a life of hard living, alcohol, and drugs, and she often had to humble herself by asking Teddy for money to make ends meet. He'd give it to her. Within reason. She was his mother after all, but the fact that it upset her to have to crawl to the son she'd never appreciated somehow made his victory sweet.

"I just hope the success continues," Nino mumbled.

The sadness and worry in Nino's voice was unmistakable. Evidently, there were more recent troubles that weighed heavily upon his mind. "What do you mean?"

Nino exhaled and then sat in silence. Teddy had half convinced himself Nino would say no more. Although he wanted to know, he didn't want to push. He'd nudged Nino enough for one night. That was why he was so surprised Nino continued with no further urging. "I haven't worked since before Christmas," he admitted. "And I'm running out of money."

What was he supposed to say to that? Sorry you're out of work and penniless? No, that was trite and unfeeling. All he could think to say was, "Do you know why?"

"Yeah."

"What is it? Maybe it can be fixed."

Nino turned away. Why did he look embarrassed? From what he'd come to know about Nino, he was incapable of being mortified.

"Tell me."

"I haven't told anyone. Not even my best friend."

Teddy nodded. "Well, we're not friends, remember? We hate each other. So you can tell me."

Nino faced him once again. The melancholy that had darkened his face lifted for a moment and was replaced by the grin Teddy had come to appreciate. "I fucked up," he admitted, and the sadness once again returned.

"How so?"

"I accidentally tricked with the partner of one of the fashion designers."

Ouch! No wonder Nino hadn't been getting called out for modeling assignments. His cock had gotten him in trouble. "I'm not certain how you can accidentally trick with someone."

Nino rolled his eyes. "I didn't know the guy was involved with Ford Michaels."

Ford Michaels was one of the premier male fashion designers. Even Teddy knew that. His clothes were the envy of most on the runway. To work for him made people stars. Evidently, crossing him unmade a career just as quickly.

"We met at a club in New York when I was on assignment," Nino continued. "He flirted with me. I flirted back. Then we headed back to my hotel room. We fucked. Then, like usual, I kicked him out. Apparently he didn't like that. He tattled to Ford about me, saying that I should never work for him again."

"Wait a minute," Teddy said. "He was the one who cheated."

Nino rolled his eyes. His exasperation with Teddy's comment was apparent. "You know how gays are. They had an open relationship. They can fuck whomever they want as long as they tell each other about it."

Teddy nodded. "Ah, yes, the open relationship. I don't understand them, but go on."

"Don't understand them?" Nino asked. "That's because they're stupid. Why be in a relationship if you're just gonna fuck around? You might as well just stay single. Then you can get all the cock or ass you want and not have to worry about screwing up a relationship."

"Can't argue with that."

"Now, because of their stupid arrangement, my career is in limbo."

Of course, Nino was completely overlooking the fact that his need to constantly hook up was partially to blame, but Teddy saw no reason to point out the obvious. "Would you like my advice? And before you answer, you should know I'm a lawyer."

"If I say no, will that stop you from giving it?" Nino asked. The playfulness had returned. Teddy liked that. He also couldn't help but notice how Nino didn't seem quite as stressed as he had been. Evidently, this had been weighing heavily on his shoulders, and his inability to talk to his friends had only compounded the problem.

"Fine," he said as he rose to stand. "I'll just be on my way."

"Oh, shut it and sit your ass back down," Nino snorted. He reached out and grabbed Teddy's hand to pull him back onto the rock they shared. The move unbalanced Teddy, and when he landed, he fell right in Nino's lap. He had to wrap his left arm around Nino's shoulder to catch himself and use his right arm to prop them up. Otherwise, they both might have tumbled off the breakwater.

When they realized they wouldn't be going for a late-night dip, they broke into laughter. It was good for Teddy's soul. For both of theirs, obviously. Nino's body convulsed with such sheer joy that he found it hard not to stare. It seemed as if Nino rarely let himself express such happiness. As if he lived too guardedly and refused to let others see what lay beneath the tough exterior.

Teddy could relate to that. But as they both gasped for air, lost in their merriment, Teddy rested his forehead against Nino's shoulder, and the warmth of Nino's skin caused another emotion to surge through him.

His skin was as smooth as milk and smelled like honey. No doubt a result of some lotion Nino religiously applied. If he weren't careful, Nino would notice the obvious bulge in his shorts.

That wouldn't do either of them any good, so he scrambled out of Nino's lap. Luckily, Nino's constant giggling and the soft moonlight managed to hide how their brief contact affected him.

"If you wanted me to sit in your lap, you could have just asked," he finally said, hoping he sounded nonchalant. Instead, his words came out in a low rasp.

"You should have seen the look on your face," Nino said with a chuckle. "You looked like a cat about to be tossed in the water."

"Well, I was a bear about to fall in the ocean," he admitted. "I think my reaction was quite normal, thank you very much."

Nino wiped his eyes. "God, that was so funny!"

"I see you're easily amused."

"I wish that had been captured on video."

"I bet you say that to a lot of guys."

Nino winked. "I do. And I've got the sex tapes to prove it."

He smacked Nino on the shoulder. "Are you done? Can I say what I was going to say before you almost killed us both?"

Nino took three deep breaths to calm down. "Fine," he said. "What's your advice? And you better make it good. I don't usually listen to what other people have to say. *Especially* lawyers."

"I think you need to confront Ford Michaels and his partner."

Nino's face turned serious. "Is that what they teach you in law school? To confront someone? I thought a lawyer's answer to every problem was to sue for damages." When Teddy glared at Nino, Nino rolled his eyes. "Fine. What good will confronting him do?"

"It's my experience that men respond well to settling grievances. Besides, it's not like you were trying to break up Ford and his partner. They do have an open relationship, and you did nothing wrong. If that doesn't work, you can always threaten to go to the tabloids or TMZ. Drag their names through the mud for a bit. That ought to get their attention. I think if you show them you've got the balls to stand up to them, that it will go a long way to saving your career *without* incurring legal expense." He paused and studied Nino's response. "What have you got to lose?"

"Pissing them off and being blackballed forever," Nino pointed out.

"Looks to me like that's already happening. Wouldn't you say?"

Nino nodded as he gave Teddy's suggestion some thought. His devilish grin returned in full force. "You're right. If I'm going down, I might as well go down swinging. I've never run from a challenge before."

"There you go, then."

Nino stood up and held out his hand. Teddy grabbed it, and Nino pulled him up. "Thanks."

Teddy looked up into Nino's eyes, which were ablaze like one of the stars in the night sky. Apparently, he'd once again found hope. Teddy was glad he could reignite the spark.

"Now let's get out of here," Nino said. "It's been a long-ass day."

Teddy nodded without saying a word as he followed Nino back the way he'd come. When he first came out here, he'd been distraught and angry. He hadn't been that unhappy in a long time. But now, after a few hours with Nino, his issues with Irene and Brody just didn't seem to be as big of a deal.

What exactly had changed out there on the breakwater between him and Nino?

Chapter Ten

WHEN TEDDY suggested they grab something to eat, Nino surprised himself by agreeing. The yes had come out of his mouth before he had time to think. It wasn't that he didn't want to eat. He was hungry. He hadn't had anything in his stomach since lunch with Jay at Bubala's.

What was the problem, then?

The furry little bastard wasn't as much of an asshole as he'd once thought. Teddy had even apologized. Even though he didn't want to admit it, the apology meant a lot to him. People who'd been cruel to him in the past had never been sorry. Especially not his sisters.

So it wasn't that he hated Teddy. At least not anymore.

He just didn't like that he continued to do things he'd never done before. Eating dinner with a guy he'd just spent a couple of hours getting to know was entirely unlike him. It also seemed to break his sixth rule—don't give a fuck.

If he truly didn't give a fuck, he wouldn't have shared his past or agreed to share a meal. He wouldn't have divulged his problems with his modeling career or taken Teddy's advice. All of that showed he apparently gave a fuck. That was very unnerving.

How was he supposed to protect himself if he actually cared?

"Oooh, let's have Spiritus," Teddy said from his right. "I'm craving some pizza."

What had he been thinking? Of course, dinner with a bear meant eating carbs. He did *not* consume such useless calories. "Try again," Nino said. "How about Jimmy's HideAway? I can get a salad there."

"A salad?" Teddy scrunched up his face and stuck out his tongue. Apparently, consuming healthy food was both distasteful and unusual. What else could he expect from a bear?

"Yes, a salad," he replied. "It's healthy, and this late at night, it's not as bad for your digestive system."

Teddy gave him a raspberry. "Who cares about that? Haven't you ever just been bad once?" Before he could reply, Teddy cut him off. "And I'm not talking about your sexual escapades, so don't even start. I'm talking about throwing caution to the wind, and instead of eating right and counting calories, just eat something because it's really, *really*, bad for you."

"I wouldn't look the way I do if I did that," he announced. Teddy peered at him out of the corners of his eyes. He obviously was trying to determine if he was joking or not, so he added an eyebrow wiggle for Teddy's benefit. He didn't want Teddy to take his comment the wrong way. Oh God, now *that* sounded like he gave a fuck. Well, shit!

"Well, for that, Curly, I'm gonna buy you a slice of pizza, and you're going to eat it."

"No, I'm not," he said with a shake of his head. "And don't call me Curly."

"Oh, yes you are," Teddy sang as he grabbed Nino's hand and tugged him toward Spiritus, which apparently had been mobbed by bears. The big guys were everywhere. Some sat on the curb out front with pizza dripping grease onto their paper plates. Others didn't even bother with the plates. They folded the pizza long-ways and chomped down half the slice in one bite. He could hear their arteries clogging from here.

"You wait here," Teddy said as he stood Nino by the tree to the left of the building. "I'm going to wade through the crowd and get us a couple of slices."

"I'll wait here," he agreed. "But I won't eat the pizza."

"You'll eat what I give you," Teddy said, his words made even more suggestive by the sudden twinkle in his eyes. "And you'll like it."

The bears in their immediate vicinity echoed their appreciation of Teddy's comment by growling. Ordinarily, their bearspeak irritated him. Tonight, though, he just laughed and shrugged at them.

"All right, boys," Teddy told the bears sitting on the bench by the tree. "Watch Curly here. Make sure he doesn't get away, because this bitch needs to eat."

"We'll watch him for you, daddy," one of the younger bears replied. "You go get your pup some chow."

His pup? When did he become Teddy's pup? He opened his mouth to correct the man, but when Teddy nodded and told them thank you, he couldn't speak. Did Teddy not hear what the man said? If he did, did he not care that these guys obviously thought they were together?

He couldn't ask any of those questions, though, because by the time his ability to speak had returned, Teddy had disappeared into Spiritus.

"What's your name?" asked the older gentleman who sat next to the younger bear. "I don't plan on calling you Curly."

He laughed. "It's Nino," he replied and extended his hand. Since when did he become so damn friendly? "And I hate that nickname too."

"I bet," he said with a wink. "I'm Ron, and this here's Andy. My pup."

Andy shook Nino's offered hand with a smile bigger than the belly that stuck out from under his shirt. "Nice to meet you, Nino."

"Same here." Did he really mean that? He might have actually been sincere. Well, wasn't that unusual as fuck.

"You really do need to eat," Ron said. He tossed his and Andy's empty plates into the trash can behind them. "It's not good to starve yourself."

"Why do people always think that?" he asked. "I just eat healthy."

"You're too skinny," Andy agreed. "Bones are meant to have meat on them."

The crowd around him cheered the statement. When Nino turned around, most of the bears were staring at him. They weren't being judgmental. They appeared more concerned than anything else. As if they were watching someone waste away in front of their eyes.

"I'm not *that* skinny."

"Honey," one of the bears on the curb said. "About three of you could fit in my shirt."

That was no understatement. The guy was pretty damn big, maybe even bigger than Jay. Normally, he would have reminded them all that perhaps he wasn't too skinny. They could just be too fat. He just didn't have the heart to be such an ass.

Where was that kindhearted approach coming from?

"All right, here's your pizza," Teddy said from his left. He handed Nino a big slice. It had pepperoni and what appeared to be more grease than cheese. If he ate this, he'd have heartburn all night.

Teddy took a big bite of his pizza. His eyes rolled back in his head. If he didn't know better, Nino would've guessed Teddy had just jizzed in his shorts. There was no way the pizza was that good. Was there?

"Well, eat it," Teddy mumbled through a mouthful of pizza.

"I said I wouldn't," he reminded Teddy.

"Aw, come on," Andy said to his left. "He bought it for you. You have to eat it now."

Ron nodded. "You don't want to be rude, right?"

"Eat it, honey," the bear by the curb said. "You just might like it."

"That's right," another bear said. "Besides, what gay man doesn't like a good piece of meat in his mouth?"

At that, all the bears growled. Even Teddy. Nino was starting to feel like Goldilocks. When they all started chanting "Eat it," Nino gave in. He opened his mouth and closed his eyes. There was no way he was going to watch himself ingest this calorie bomb.

After he bit into the pizza, he couldn't help the low groan that came out of his throat. This pizza *was* good. A little spicy. But good. He'd grown so accustomed to salads and protein shakes that he'd almost forgotten how regular food tasted.

It was actually pretty fucking delicious, and his body craved more. This time, he bit off a bigger piece and nodded at Teddy, who beamed before him. He was obviously pleased with himself.

"It's good," he said. Now it was his turn to speak with a full mouth.

"See what happens when you live a little," Teddy told him. "You never know what you might like if you don't give it a try."

He couldn't argue with that. He hadn't realized how much he'd been denying himself. Sure, he jetted around the world and fucked more guys than he could count, but that was what his world had become. Modeling and fucking. He'd thought those things had made him happy before.

But did they really? Were there not more things out there that might do a better job? That might fill the hole that sometimes opened up in the pit of his stomach?

Maybe it was time to test out a few of those things. But first, he needed more pizza.

"I CAN'T believe you had three pieces!" Teddy exclaimed while they continued down Commercial Street. "You out-ate me!"

Nino wanted to comment, but his belly hurt. He hadn't consumed that much food in years. He'd be regretting it later when he was downing antacids and farting up a storm.

Why had he done that?

The simple answer was it had been nice to indulge. The answer he'd admit to was he'd been forced by a bunch of bears. That was what he'd go to his grave saying to anyone who'd listen.

"Stop gloating," he said to Teddy, who wouldn't stop smiling. He then let out a big burp that earned him applause from passing bears. He thanked his admirers and patted his bloated belly. Releasing the built-up pressure had lessened his discomfort.

"You ate like a bear, and now you sound like one too. You just need to look like one to complete the package."

"That's not gonna happen," he announced. "I work hard to look this fine. I'm not about to grow a beer belly or fur."

"I think you'd look cute," Teddy said. He immediately grew quiet. He also shoved his hands in his pockets and starting looking around. Although Teddy was trying to look nonchalant, there was no way he could recover from what he'd revealed.

Teddy found him attractive after all. It was nice to know he still had it. After what happened this morning, he had doubted himself. He didn't anymore.

Why did that make him so happy? So what if Teddy wanted in his pants? Lots of guys wanted the chance to ride the Nino express. What made Teddy so different?

"And for your information, I'd be the hottest bear there ever was."

Teddy didn't reply. He just smiled and continued to walk beside him in silence.

Why did he find Teddy's obvious mortification so damn cute? He'd never been guilty of that before either. He didn't ooh or ah over facial expressions. Or any other lame-ass shit that most people found so adorable they just had to share with everyone. Why the change now? And why did he feel responsible for saving Teddy from humiliation?

"Can I ask you something?" he asked. He hoped the subject change would be the distraction Teddy apparently needed.

"Sure," Teddy replied as they strolled past WA, a local home interior store, and Seamen's Bank.

The name always made Nino chuckle. He'd once made a deposit there, down the throat of one of the tellers who had been on lunch break. That had been a good day.

"Why were you on the breakwater?"

Teddy sighed and stared up at the stars. He was either searching for a lie or deciding whether to tell the truth. Surprisingly, Nino hoped it was the latter. He actually wanted to know what had been bothering Teddy.

How weird was that?

"I ran into my ex at tea," Teddy finally admitted with a long exhalation.

"Ah, the dreaded ex," Nino said with a nod. "I've never had one. But from what I know, they are a pain in the ass."

Teddy stared up at him as if he'd somehow grown a third head. "You've *never* had a boyfriend?"

He wagged his finger at Teddy. "Uh-uh, no switching subjects. We were talking about you. Not me."

Teddy scowled at him and turned away.

"So, you ran into your ex-boyfriend. Are you still in love with him?" Teddy fell silent again. The answer was obviously yes, but he apparently didn't want to admit it. "How long has it been since you broke up?"

"Eleven years."

Damn! Talk about carrying a torch. This guy must either be wicked hot and a wiz in the sack or Teddy was just incapable of moving on. Somehow, Nino believed it was a combination of the two. "That's a long time to still be in love with someone."

"How would you know?" Teddy asked. His demeanor had changed. His shoulders were tense, and his stride quickened. What had he said that pissed Teddy off? "You've never had a boyfriend, remember?"

"True, but that doesn't change the fact that you've been in love with someone for longer than the two of you were probably together. That seems odd."

"Yeah, well, I think it's odd that you've never been in a relationship. So there!"

"Okay, I'm not sure where the attitude's coming from, but I'm just saying that there must be a reason you're still in love with him."

"He was my first love," Teddy announced, as if that explained everything. And maybe it would. To someone who'd been in love before. To Nino, it came off as pathetic. How ridiculous was it to be in love with someone who obviously didn't feel the same way?

"I also found out that my best friend was partly to blame for our breakup."

Now that pissed Nino off. The one person he did trust in this world was Van. If Van ever betrayed him, he doubted he'd ever recover from that. "That bastard! How could he do that to you? What did he do? Did he sleep with your ex?"

Teddy chuckled. "My best friend's name is Irene, and no, she didn't sleep with him. She just helped him see that we weren't ready for the kind of commitment I wanted."

Nino grabbed Teddy's hand and led him through the black iron gate of the Unitarian Church on Commercial Street.

"What? Are we going to church?" Teddy asked.

He shook his head and led Teddy over to the small, manicured grounds and sat down. "You helped me with my modeling stuff. Now let me help you." Was this really happening? Apparently it was, as he tugged Teddy down to the ground and said, "Let's hear it."

After Teddy brought him up to speed, he sat in silence. What was he supposed to do now? He didn't have any real experience with helping people sort out their own shit. Sure, he'd been there for Van during his low points, but it had just been as a sounding board or to provide an escape. He'd never offered Van advice, and Van had never really sought it. It wasn't that he and Van didn't value each other's opinions. It was just that the two of them preferred to work things out on their own.

But now he'd made this grand gesture to Teddy, and he had to follow through. But what the hell was he supposed to do?

"This is where you talk now," Teddy said as he nudged him in the knee with his foot.

"I'm thinking," he announced. "This is new to me, you know?"

"What is?"

"Giving advice. I usually don't give a fuck."

A smile slowly rolled across Teddy's lips. What the hell was that for?

"Well, I feel honored," Teddy said, even though he was still grinning like an idiot.

If he had to say something, he might as well just say what was on his mind. That had to count for something, right? "It sounds to me like Irene was just trying to protect you. She obviously saw something in your relationship that you didn't or couldn't see. She didn't want you to get hurt. Did she go about it the right way? No. She seriously screwed the pooch on that one. She should have told you what she'd done and not kept it from you all these years. As for your ex, well, it sounds like he didn't want to hurt you either. From what you said he said, he was trying to spare your feelings. That was actually pretty decent. No one's ever done that for me before. Most people in my life have told me what they thought whether it hurt or not. Your guy didn't do that. He could've done a better job at protecting you. Like telling you the truth. But he was young. You were young. How smart were any of us back then? I think you should cut them some slack and hear them out."

When he stopped speaking, Teddy stared at him with mouth agape. He'd evidently stuck his Prada-wearing feet in his mouth. Where did he go wrong? All he did was speak from his gut. Maybe that was not what he should have done. He'd never been any good at this anyway.

"Look, I'm sorry. Like I said before, I'm not good at the advice crap. I didn't mean to piss you off or anything. Maybe what you need to do is talk to one of your other friends. They'd probably do a better job."

He tried to stand, but Teddy leaped into Nino's arms. The force of the collision knocked him over. Nino landed with his back in the grass and Teddy on top of him. A huge grin drew across Teddy's face.

"What the hell are you talking about?" Teddy asked. "That was awesome advice." He didn't get off Nino. He simply adjusted his position until he straddled Nino's stomach and gazed down into his eyes. Teddy's cock, which apparently wasn't confined by underwear, rested snugly against his abdominals and started to come to life. Did Teddy even realize he was sporting wood right now?

"It was?" Nino asked, although all he could focus on was the weight of Teddy's cock. He even pushed out his stomach a bit more to feel the entire length. If he had to guess, it was a nice seven inches and perhaps thicker around the middle than at the base. That was pretty impressive.

"Yes, Curly. It was!"

"Please stop calling me that."

Teddy ignored him. "You're right. They were trying to protect me. I was too caught up in my own pity party to realize that. They did fuck up. Irene mostly. But neither of them did it to hurt me. They did it because they loved me." A hopeful look flashed across Teddy's eyes. "Do you think he still loves me?"

Was that why Teddy was hard? He was excited over the possibility of getting his ex-boyfriend back. For a minute there, he'd... well, that wasn't important. It was time for Teddy to get off him, though, so he slid to his side and Teddy dropped off onto the grass beside him. As Teddy gazed back at him, waiting for an answer, Nino adjusted his cock in his shorts. It had unexpectedly stiffened, and it needed to go back to sleep.

There was no reason for it to be awake. It had been a false alarm.

"So, do you think he might still love me?" Teddy repeated. "Do you think that's why I met him here after all these years? Is fate trying to get us back together?"

Nino shrugged. "What I think doesn't matter. Remember what I told you on the breakwater?"

Teddy nodded. "Don't wait around for someone to give me permission. If it's what I feel, then I should just go with it."

"Exactly." His tone wasn't as enthusiastic as he wanted it to be. Why did it ring hollow? Maybe it was the uncomfortable sensation in his stomach. That had to have been from eating too much pizza.

"I know just what to do," Teddy announced as he sprung from the ground. "I can't thank you enough."

Nino stood next to him, wiping the grass from his shorts. "No problem. It was the least I could do."

"I think I'm gonna head back to my condo now. I want to get my thoughts straight before I.... Well, you know."

Nino nodded. He was smiling, but he didn't feel happy. What was going on with him now? Had he suddenly developed a bipolar disorder? "Get going," he finally said. "I've had all I can stomach of you today."

Teddy laughed. "Okay," he said as he opened the gate that separated Commercial Street from the churchyard. "I really can't thank you enough."

"The only thanks I need is to be rid of your hairy ass for a while."

"Fuck you too," Teddy said with a smile. He then sprinted off into the night.

NINO DIDN'T head back to his apartment after Teddy left him standing in front of the church. Why didn't he want to be alone right now? Being by himself had never bothered him before. But now, just the idea of it gave him the cold pricklies. He hadn't reacted that way since he had lived at home. Whenever that used to happen, he would crawl into bed and snuggle with Teo. But Teo no longer lived with him.

He'd lost his teddy bear best friend years ago.

Maybe that was part of his problem. For a few moments there, with Teddy, that old feeling had returned. He hadn't felt that comfortable or safe in years, and it made him miss Teo real bad.

What could he do about it now, though? Well, he could always go to Van and Zach's. Van wouldn't turn him away, and Van might even let him sleep on the couch. Was that why he was headed back toward the west end? Van lived past the Boatslip and much farther down Commercial, where Van and Zach had purchased the condo above Relish.

But as the Boatslip came into view, his feet led him toward a path he'd never taken before, yet one that called to him. It was the trail that led to the dick dock. If he followed the gravel drive just past the hotel down to the beach, he'd be underneath the deck where tea was held. There, he'd find other lonely souls reaching around in the dark for another loser to hold onto.

Among the naked, writhing bodies on the beach, he just might find the connection he seemed to need so badly right now.

He stopped at the head of the path. Was he really going to do this? Was he going to head down into the blackness and have anonymous sex with some troll who couldn't get lucky with the lights on? Had he fallen that far? And how the hell had that happened?

That didn't really matter, though. Did it? He was here. He'd been doing crap all day that he'd never done before. Why not just add another to the list?

"I didn't take you for a dick dock connoisseur."

He whipped around, stunned to suddenly hear someone talking right behind him. Had he been so zoned out that the crunch of gravel underneath the newcomer's feet had gone unnoticed? When he gazed into Brody's green eyes, he wanted to crawl away and hide under a rock. The last thing he needed right now was to be judged. Especially by the apparently perfect Brody with the dazzling smile and lush green eyes.

Why did Brody make him feel less than what he'd always believed himself to be?

"I'm not," he said. "But I was thinking about it." Why the hell did he just admit that? He should have lied about staring at the moon or some other crap. That was what he'd always done in the past whenever he was confronted with something he didn't want to confess to.

"Interesting," Brody replied. Why did he sound impressed? What was so awe-inspiring about Nino's frank admission?

"Why's that?" he asked.

"You just surprised me, is all. You struck me as someone who'd rather lie than leave yourself vulnerable to criticism."

No shit! "Yeah, well, it surprised me too."

"Maybe I misjudged you," Brody admitted. "And I may have been a bit harsh on you at tea today. I'm sorry about that. I tend to speak before I think sometimes. It's not very endearing."

"Don't worry about it," he replied as he turned back to look down the dark passageway. "I'm a big boy."

"Yes," Brody replied. "You are."

The tone in his voice had changed. Was Brody flirting with him now? If he'd been on a Tilt-A-Whirl at a carnival, he couldn't be more disoriented. This had to have been one of the most confusing days of his life.

"Well, I'll be seeing you," he said as he started down the path to the dick dock. "I apparently have a date with someone I'll never be able to pick out of a lineup."

"Or you could come back to my room with me," Brody announced.

Nino stopped and peered back over his shoulder. "Are you serious? I thought you hated me."

Brody shook his head. "Not at all. Like I said, I was an idiot at tea." Brody stood there, smiling at him under the moonlight. The silvery light transformed his blond hair into platinum. He resembled a chiseled work of art, someone more reminiscent of the men Nino had grown accustomed to entertaining over the years.

Then why could he only think about Teddy right now? The way they laughed together on the breakwater. Or the warm weight of

Teddy's body on top of him and the hard cock that had snaked across Nino's belly.

But the hard-on hadn't been for him. It had been for Teddy's ex-boyfriend.

Teddy wasn't here. Brody was.

Why should he waste this opportunity?

"Let's do it," Nino said as he strolled back toward where Brody stood.

"Excellent," Brody replied. "I've still got the rubber sheets on my bed, and my roommate is spending the night over at his new boy toy's place. We'll have the whole night to do what gay men do best."

"Sounds perfect," he replied. But it didn't feel perfect at all.

Chapter Eleven

COULD HE be happier right now? Teddy didn't think so. Not only was it another beautiful day in Provincetown, but hope had wrapped its comforting arms around him once again. He'd lived too long without anything to truly look forward to. Now, when he considered life after Provincetown, it didn't seem more of the same old routine. How kick-ass awesome was that?

His life hadn't been awful or anything. He hadn't been living under a rock. He had enjoyed himself. He also had a good job and some decent friends. Plus, he'd had tons of hairy guys and their furry loving to keep him occupied. But that hadn't been very fulfilling, had it?

He'd been chasing bears to keep himself from thinking about what he really wanted. And that was Brody. Maybe that was lame and pathetic after all these years. What did he care? Oh God, now he sounded like Nino. But Nino had been right. What did it matter what everyone else thought? The only person's opinion that mattered in his life was his.

He'd remember that from now on.

What he did know, though, was this: he still loved Brody. And just the idea of Brody perhaps still feeling the same way, well, that was enough of a wind current to keep him afloat on his current flight of happiness.

And who did he have to thank for this? Nino, of all people. Wasn't that just a kick to the nuts?

He sure never saw that one coming. He'd figured they'd scowl at each other till the end of time, but Nino had surprised him. He was actually a pretty good guy. Once he'd gotten past the vain, self-absorbed-prick persona he presented to the world. It turned out that wasn't who Nino was at all.

Beneath that mask of perfection actually hid a wealth of insecurities that would make Woody Allen look like the most stable of individuals. The real Nino was a person he could handle and perhaps call a friend.

No, that wasn't right. After last night, Nino *was* his friend. How weird was that?

That was just one more miracle chalked up to the magic of Provincetown.

The clicking of tiny toenails echoed down the stairwell. Louie had apparently decided to finally get out of bed. The lazy little stinker butt.

"How's my handsome man?" he asked. Louie bounded off the last step and rocketed toward him. He leaped up on Teddy's leg, his ears pinned back and the most adorable doggie grin on his muzzle. God, how he loved this dog!

He bent down to scratch Louie's sweet spot, and Louie responded by gently licking Teddy's leg while he scratched. It was how they told each other good morning.

"How'd you sleep?" he asked. Louie replied with an arf and a snort. "That good, huh? Me too, boy. Me too."

Louie's wagging butt meant he was pleased to hear it. "Thank you," he told Louie as he stood back up to finish making breakfast, but Louie wouldn't crawl down from his leg. He was too busy sniffing and snorting across Teddy's skin.

"All right, cut that out," he said. "It tickles!"

Louie didn't care. He said as much by continuing to sniff. Louie then looked up at him and arfed twice.

Teddy rolled his eyes. "Yes, I was with Nino again." His reply was met with a wagging butt. "You like him, don't you?"

Again, Louie arfed twice.

"Well, we didn't do anything, if you must know," he announced as he scooped the scrambled eggs onto three plates. "We just talked."

Louie chuffed.

"We're friends, Louie. That's all."

He chuffed again.

He peered down at the cutest little face in the world. "What? You think you're my pimp or something?"

Louie snorted.

"Yeah, well, you're not!"

"Why do you hold conversations with that mutt as if he actually understood you?" Irene asked as she exited the stairwell. Today, she wore a shredded pink T-shirt that could have stepped out of a Poison music video, and her hair was once again teased to new heights.

Louie turned his butt toward Irene and passed gas.

"You little fucker!" she scolded as she waved the air before her. "That's gross!"

"I think that's his way of telling you that he *does* understand," he told Irene. He couldn't help but laugh at the look of disgust on her face. Louie's farts did stink to high heaven, but after years of sleeping with his gassy boy, he'd grown accustomed to the stench.

Not Irene, though. She attempted to shoo Louie out of the kitchen, but he sat on his haunches and snuffed. He was going nowhere, and he was making that quite clear.

"Why doesn't he ever listen to me?"

"Because you're so mean to him," he pointed out.

"Are you kidding me?" she asked, glaring down at Louie, who refused to look her in the eye. Not because he feared Irene but because he rarely dignified her outbursts with any acknowledgement. "He pisses on my shoes. He farts in my face, and he only jumps on me when he's dirty. *He's* the one that hates *me*!"

"How about we go outside and eat?" he asked as he picked up their breakfast. He didn't want to argue with Irene. They'd never agree about Louie, and for him, Louie would always win anyway. "It's a gorgeous day out."

"Why are you in such a good mood?" she asked as she grabbed the juice glasses and followed him to the deck. She'd obviously noticed the grin he couldn't wipe off his face. Not that he really wanted to. "You not mad at me anymore?"

After they sat down and he placed Louie's plate of food on the deck, he finally replied. "No. I'm not."

She eyed him suspiciously as she munched on her eggs. "That's not like you. You can carry a grudge for days."

He supposed that was true. But there was no reason for resentment. He wasn't happy Irene had taken it upon herself to decide his life for him, but it hadn't been out of malice. It had been out of friendship. "No grudge," he announced with a shake of his head.

"Then why did you leave so abruptly after tea?"

"I needed to think," he told her after swallowing his food. "That was a lot of information to process. I had to be alone."

"And?" she asked. Her eyes were wide and hopeful. She'd obviously been worried he'd never forgive her.

"Well, after thinking it through, I realized that even though what you and Brody did was pretty shitty, you were only trying to keep me safe."

"I was," she admitted. "I know you don't want to hear it, sweetie, but you were headed for a serious heartbreak. Brody wasn't ready for that commitment, and if he'd walked into your marriage proposal without knowing what was going on, I don't even want to imagine what would have happened."

Why did her comment bother him? It was like she still saw something he couldn't.

"One thing I didn't tell you was that Brody and I had a talk a few weeks before you dropped your marriage bomb on me. I'd kinda guessed that's where you were headed, and I wanted to see where his head was. During our talk, I learned he wasn't a big believer in the institution of marriage. Probably because of his fucked-up mother and her many public scandals."

He nodded. Brody's mother, Joy—who was, ironically, the most unjoyful person he'd ever met—had once been in a pretty popular grunge band in the early nineties. Now the only gigs she could get were on *Celebrity Rehab* or VH1's *Where Are They Now?* Her star had fizzled out. Did that matter to Joy O'Shea? Not one bit. She continued to live the life of a rocker, even though she had no star power and was in reality a fame-obsessed alcoholic.

Brody had been battling against his mother's reputation his entire life. Maybe that was why he didn't do commitment. Like Amanda Miller, Joy had no concept of what a real relationship was. But Teddy had confidence he and Brody could figure that one out together.

"Are you even listening to me?"

"Sorry. I was thinking about Brody's mom."

Irene scrunched up her nose. She really did do a good Louie impersonation. "Please, don't. That woman's insane. But as I was saying, he told me he never wanted to get married. And that he'd never want kids."

No kids? That was news to Teddy. He eventually wanted children. He always had.

"I know," Irene said, as if she read his thoughts. "Being a dad has always been something you've wanted. To make up for your own fucked-up childhood."

He couldn't argue with that.

"He told me he didn't really like kids. That they made him nervous and that the only good kid was one that was asleep."

Would Brody really have said that? They'd never discussed children when they were together. But that had also been a long time ago. They'd both changed since then. It was likely that Brody's perspective on kids had changed as well.

"So when you told me you wanted to marry him," Irene continued. "I just had to let him know what you were planning. I wanted him to think about that proposal. To really give it some thought beforehand. Because if he didn't really want to do it, I wanted him to find a way to break it off with you so that you weren't destroyed."

"The only problem with that was it devastated me," he reminded her. "You know that."

"I know," she admitted apologetically. "Why do you think I've made it my life's mission to make you happy? I've just never figured out how to do that."

Was that why she'd been such a constant influence in his life? Had she been trying to atone for what she'd done in college? Teddy reached over and held her hand. "You can't make me happy. I'm the only one that can do that. And I think I know how."

"Really?" She didn't need to look so surprised.

"Yes, really."

"Tell me."

With his breakfast finished, he scooped Louie into his lap and told her what he and Nino talked about last night.

"I don't get it," she revealed after he'd finished. "What exactly is going to make you happy now?"

"Brody," he announced. If she looked any more apprehensive, she'd be attached to a bungee cord and staring off the edge of a cliff. "I love him, Reenie. I always have. That's why I've been unable to move on and find another relationship. How could I when it's always been Brody?"

"Are you serious?"

He nodded.

"But it's been eleven years," she reminded him. "Up until yesterday, we couldn't even say his name without invoking your wrath. How could you still possibly be in love with him?"

That was a fair question. "Because I'd always believed that I wasn't good enough for Brody. That's why I thought he'd broken up with me. But he didn't. He did it to protect me. That means he really did love me. That I was worthy to be with him. You have no idea how much better that makes me feel after all these years. It's like a giant weight has been lifted off my shoulders. He wasn't the monster I made him out to be and definitely not the one you made him out to be either."

"True," she agreed. "I only did that to help you move on. But I still don't understand."

"There's nothing for you to understand," he announced. "I'm not looking for your approval or your advice. I love Brody, and I'm going to tell him that. I'm going to help him see that we have a future together. If he wants it."

"But—"

He shushed her into silence. "I don't want to hear it," he said. "I'm doing this, and nothing you say is going to stop me."

He then grabbed their dirty dishes in one hand and held Louie in the other as he stood. "Now I'm gonna clean up and then get going. I'm a man on a mission."

He closed the patio door behind him to drown out Irene if she decided to pursue the matter further. He didn't have time to deal with her concerns. He had something far more important to attend to.

Because, hopefully, by this time tomorrow he'd be happier than he'd been in years.

TWO HOURS and one nice hot shower later, Teddy stood outside Brody's room at the Boatslip. He hadn't been there before, but prior to learning that Jay and Brody were roommates, Jay had given him his room number. Jay liked his friends to be able to find him. Right now, Teddy couldn't have been happier with that.

On the other side of the door, the man he loved waited. Well, not that he in any way thought Brody was lying around waiting on him, but he was inside the room. Or at least he hoped he was. If Teddy was lucky, he might even be lounging around naked. Brody had always preferred to be *au naturel* behind closed doors. He'd certainly never minded that when they'd been together. It meant he could suck on Brody's gorgeous cock whenever he wanted, and Brody loved being sucked off.

Damn, was he hard already? All it took was one thought of Brody's dick and *bam!* Insta-boner. Brody had always had that effect on him.

The snort coming from the direction of his feet reminded him Louie was impatiently waiting for him to knock on the door. It had been a long, hot walk down Commercial Street, and his little bully was ready to be in the air-conditioned indoors. He'd debated leaving Louie behind, but he needed the kind of moral support only Louie could give.

"Just give me a minute," he said. "I'm working up my nerve here."

Louie snuffed and then yawned. It was his way of saying just knock on the fucking door already.

When Teddy finally did as Louie demanded, his heart stopped beating. This was it. Once the door opened, there'd be no turning back. Feet shuffled on the other side and then stopped at the door. He held his breath and waited. After what seemed like an agonizing millennia, the door swung inward.

"Well, look who we've got there," Jay said. His face practically sparkled with delight. He then grabbed Teddy and almost squeezed the life out of him once again. "And looky who you brought with you. How are you doing, Louie Louie?"

Louie detested having his name repeated. He showed his disdain for the greeting by turning up his nose and walking into the room uninvited.

"Not one for manners, is he?" Jay asked.

"He's just hot," he replied. "We both are."

"Speaking of manners," Jay said as he waved Teddy inside. "Come on in. There's beer in the fridge and alcohol on the dresser. Make yourself whatever you'd like."

Even in P-town, noon was too early for a cocktail. At least for Teddy. The same couldn't be said for Terry, who grinned at him from what had to be Jay's bed. He was sprawled across it with a margarita in his left hand.

"Heya, Teddy," Terry said. If Terry were any happier, he'd be a kid on Christmas morning. The younger man obviously enjoyed spending all his time with Jay. While he was happy for Jay, he was disappointed Brody wasn't home.

"Where'd you get off to after that horrible scene at tea?" Jay asked. The concern on his friend's face was apparent. Jay hated it when his friends were unhappy, and he typically did whatever he could to turn that around. Right now what Teddy needed was to talk to Brody, so if Jay would produce him out of his back pocket, that would be great.

"I had to think," he told Jay as he surveyed the room. He hoped to find some clue as to where Brody had gone off to. All he saw were empty liquor bottles, dirty clothes lying in the corner, and two discarded condom wrappers. Apparently, some people had a good time last night. Good for Jay and Terry.

"You doing okay?" Jay asked as he sat on the bed next to his new boyfriend. "You seem distracted."

"Sorry. I guess I am." What distracted him even more was how intently Louie was sniffing around the room. He had his nose glued to the floor. He followed some unseen trail from the door to the dresser. He then stopped, walked in a circle, and then proceeded to the bed opposite where Jay and Terry sat.

"That's a cute little pooch," Terry said. "What's he doing, though?"

"I'm not sure," Teddy replied. "He obviously found a smell he liked."

Louie chased the scent up onto the bed and then snuffed vigorously around the sheets and pillows.

"Louie!" he called out. "That's not your bed." He moved to fetch his ill-mannered dog from Brody's sheets, but Jay waved him off.

"Leave him be. Brody likes dogs. But I'm sure you know that already."

He nodded. Brody adored dogs. Although he preferred larger breeds like boxers or bullmastiffs. Teddy had never understood that. Who wanted to deal with the shit of a big-ass dog? And he meant that quite literally. Picking up Louie's poop was gross enough without the turd being bigger than his hand. No thank you.

"He must really like the way Brody smells," Terry commented.

He nodded. Apparently Louie did. The only other person he'd sniffed around that intently for had been Nino, and there was no way Louie had picked up Nino's trail here. If Louie liked Brody half as much as he liked Nino, well, that had to be a good sign. Right? After all, his handsome little man hadn't taken a liking to anyone but him in years. With the recent exception of Nino.

"So tell me," Jay said. "What's going on?"

"What do you mean?" he asked. Louie had apparently found the spot where Brody's smell was the strongest, because he walked around the area, lay down, and then promptly fell asleep.

"I assume you're here for some other reason than to watch Louie snort Brody's sheets as if it were a line of coke. Did you need to talk about what happened yesterday?"

He shook his head. "No. I've worked past that."

"Really? You were quite upset when you left tea."

"I was," he admitted. "But I've gained perspective since then. And that's why I'm here. To talk to Brody."

"Well, as you can see, he's not here. But I do know where he'll be later."

Yes! That was the kind of information he needed. "Where?" he asked, hoping he didn't come across quite as eager as he appeared.

"A bunch of us are getting together at Herring Cove later this afternoon."

"Really? Where?"

Jay grinned. What was that for? Did he suspect how truly anxious he was to see Brody? God, if Jay did, then he was going to have to work on calming the fuck down.

"The same spot where Gary and Quinn had their beach party a couple of days ago. I just didn't know if you'd remember. Considering how wasted you got that night."

He might not remember what happened at the party or how exactly he and Nino ended up in bed together the next morning, but he recalled exactly where the celebration had taken place that night. "I remember," he announced. He even smugly jutted out his chin in defiance of Jay's playful ribbing.

"Good. I'm glad you remember something from that night."

"What time are you guys meeting up?"

"Two thirty, I think," he glanced over his shoulder at Terry, who nodded in agreement.

"Mind if I join you?"

Jay rolled his eyes at the comment. "Of course I don't mind. We'd all love to hang out with you more than we have been."

"Who else is going to be there?"

"Carl and Rick. And Dave, Brad, and Steve, of course. I think Gary and Quinn are also coming. It's Tara's day off, so she might join us. They've also invited a couple I haven't met yet. Some guys named Van and Zach. Do you know them?"

He shook his head. He had no clue who they were, and he really didn't care. All that mattered to him was if Brody would be there. "And Brody, right?"

Jay grinned. "Yes, I already told you that."

"Then I'll be there."

"Will you be bringing the ever-delightful Irene?"

"Well, I can't just leave her at home."

"That's a pity," Jay commented as he settled back against the headboard. Like a mewling kitten, Terry curled up on Jay's stomach and sighed contently. If he didn't know better, he'd swear Terry was actually purring.

Teddy crossed the room and snatched Louie from his snore-filled slumber. In typical Louie fashion, he chuffed at being disturbed. "Then I'll see you at two thirty at Herring Cove," he said to Jay and Terry. He then walked out the door and out of the Boatslip.

In a few hours, he'd be with Brody, and with any luck, they'd be naked in each other's arms later that evening.

What more could he possibly hope for right now?

Chapter Twelve

IF NINO could scream, he would. Typically a good fuck made his troubles go bye-bye. And last night had been one of the best screws he'd had in a long time. Brody had some mighty fine skills and almost complete control over his ass muscles. Had his cock ever been gripped that tightly by someone's butt before? Not that he could remember.

They'd gone at it for hours and even had to use two condoms, since the first had developed a small tear from the relentless pounding he'd been giving Brody. Once he finally busted his nut, some of his frustration had been relieved. Until Brody unexpectedly flipped him on his back and started to lube up Nino's ass. Talk about a "what the *fuck* are you doing?" moment.

No one had ever entered his back door, much less knocked at it the way Brody had. Sure, he'd let guys make out with his ass if they liked. That was hot as shit. But it never went beyond that. He was a top. Exclusively. In fact, his second rule was never to bottom. He'd seen how messed up bottoms got. They sometimes turned into women and expected love and commitment once they let some guy stick his cock up their ass. What was up with that?

Just because some guy settled up inside a butt for the night didn't mean he planned on staying past the cum dump. That was why he promised himself to never *ever* let some guy fuck him. Not only did it leave the dude getting plowed vulnerable, which he didn't do at all, but it was also too intimate. He preferred to keep his encounters as superficial as possible.

When he told Brody there would be no flip fucking, Brody hadn't taken the news very well. He had reminded Nino of someone who'd just been told the roller coaster ride he'd been waiting in line for had been shut down.

He'd managed to deflect some of Brody's wrath with a good blowjob. At first, Brody had been resistant, but when Brody realized that he sucked as well as he fucked, well, he lay back and let Nino's mouth finish the job.

But shortly after he'd left Brody's, an uneasy feeling slowly crept over him. It started as an emptiness in his belly. It was like he hadn't eaten in days. That wasn't the case. He'd just eaten three slices of pizza. When he had recalled his evening with Teddy, the sensation had then spread to his chest. His heart had suddenly seemed to weigh a ton. He'd chalked it up to indigestion. He came home, popped four antacids, and went to sleep.

This morning, though, it was still there. What was wrong with him?

Was this the beginning of some heart disease? His father did have a heart attack at an early age. Maybe that was what was happening to him.

A knock at his front door dragged him out of his descent into hypochondria. He really didn't want a visitor right now. When he opened the door, he was surprised to see Van standing on the other side. He was dressed in a square-cut swimsuit and white muscle shirt. A beach towel had also been tucked under his left arm. Evidently, his best friend was headed to the dunes for an afternoon romp in the sand.

"Since when do you knock?" he asked. He opened the door and stood aside to let Van enter.

"Since you've been acting like an asshole for no apparent reason."

He sighed as he shut the door. From the determined expression on Van's face, he wasn't getting out of this apartment without hearing everything Van had to say. "All right, let me have it."

Van stood in silence with his arms crossed over his chest. If Van studied him any more intently, he'd need a microscope.

"Will you just say it already?" he asked. If he had to endure Van's pissiness, he'd rather just get it over with.

Instead of the full-on verbal onslaught he'd been expecting, Van dropped his towel on the table. He then crossed over to Nino and hugged him. Van squeezed him tight, not with as much force as Jay, but enough to communicate his intentions. Was this supposed to be a comforting embrace? If not, then why was Van stroking his hair with his left hand while Van's right hand patted his shoulder?

This was beyond weird and a little unsettling. No one had held him like this in more years than he cared to remember. Even stranger, why did he like it so much? "What are you doing?" he finally asked.

Van pulled out of the embrace. His big blue eyes didn't have that usual playful sparkle that had been the cornerstone of their friendship. They joked and poked fun. They didn't get all serious on each other. What new crazy shit had another day in P-town brought his way?

"I'm worried about you," Van said. His voice was soft, almost like a whisper. "And you looked like you could use a hug."

He gave Van his mischievous smile. The one that always started them down their usual path to banter. "I already got hugged real good last night," he admitted with a wink. "Damn, that guy's ass was fine. It probably could sharpen a pencil." The soothing calmness reflected in Van's eyes turned turbulent. He'd obviously pissed Van off with that comment. But why?

"Can you ever be serious?" Van asked as he dropped his hands from Nino's shoulders. He took two steps to the left and ran his hands through his hair.

"No," he admitted. "I can't."

"Why not? It's me, Nino. Not some random trick you picked up at tea. I'm your best friend, and I can tell that you're upset. But you won't let me in. You won't let me help you, and I really want to help you."

He waved off Van's concerns. "I'm good," he lied. Why had he just done that? Why couldn't he admit what was bothering him? Well, for one thing, he really had no clue *what* was wrong with him today. He'd been off lately because of the crap with Ford Michaels and his modeling career. But Teddy had helped him see what he should do about it. Once he finally got in touch with Ford, things would be better. *He* would be better. So if he had a plan, why wasn't he good right now?

"You're lying to me," Van said. "We both know it."

He appreciated Van's concern, but if he couldn't figure out what was wrong, then how could he possibly talk about it? He had to figure it out himself first, right?

"You've been weird since before Christmas," Van pointed out. "I chalked it up to the holiday blues, but it's only gotten worse. I rarely see you out and about, and when I do, you're moody and sulky. I thought that it would pass or that you'd approach me when you were ready. But you haven't, and you've only gotten worse. In fact, you've seemed to hit rock bottom ever since I saw that pocket bear leave your apartment the other morning. Does this have something to do with him?"

The pit in his stomach opened up once again. Like a black hole, it tugged on him and threatened to turn him inside out. "Why do you think Teddy has anything to do with my mood?"

Van studied him again. Perhaps he should just give Van a damn microscope. His best friend constantly scrutinized him like a scientist anyway. It would likely make his observations much easier. "So the pocket bear has a name now?"

"Of course he has a name. What the fuck's the big deal about that?"

Van sighed as if he had somehow become a frustrated parent trying to deal with a difficult child. Nino didn't appreciate being made to feel that way at all.

"Nino, when have you ever known the names of *any* of your tricks?"

Never. But Teddy wasn't a trick. They were friends. Wait a minute! When the fuck did that happen?

"You've always referred to your tricks by what they looked like or what they wore. Let's see," Van said as he gazed at the ceiling. "Most recently, there's been Bubble Butt, Backward Cap Boy, G-String, College Frat Boy and His Best Friend. What did you call the one with the cock piercing again?"

He sighed. "Princess Albert."

"That's right. Because he looked like a total top but wore lip gloss and painted his toenails red."

Nino chuckled. "Yup. That's him. The boy could power bottom, though, and he screamed like a real bitch."

Van smiled and closed the distance between them. "See, this is the Nino I know. The one who smirks like a bastard and treats everyone like shit. That hasn't been you these last few days. Something's happened to you. Something's changed. And I've got a feeling it has something to do with Teddy. The trick who somehow earned a name."

Was Van right? Was his current mood somehow connected to Teddy? He had been fine when they were at the breakwater and then later at Spiritus. After the churchyard incident, well, he'd thought Teddy's hard cock had been for him. So what if that hadn't been true? Had that really bothered him? And why the fuck would he care who Teddy sported wood for? He'd already been with Teddy, and rule number five expressly stated he was never to repeat a fuck.

"So tell me what's going on?"

The empty pit in his stomach unexpectedly filled with fire, fueled by Van's sudden interest in his life. Its snaking tendrils reached up through his throat until they could finally be set free. "What the hell do you care, Van?" he asked.

Van jumped back a little from the surprise force of his words.

"You've been off playing grab ass with Zach since the two of you decided to play house and fuck your days away. You've had no fucking time for me. You fell in love, moved out, and left me here all by myself. And now you come into *my* apartment and want to know what's wrong with me? Well, take a good hard look at yourself, buddy. You're part of my problem. You've just stood there berating me for not seeking you out, but in that same breath, you also told me how you've watched me change. Continue to get depressed. Did you ever seek me out? No. You went home to Zach instead. I thought you were supposed to be my friend. I was there for you. At the goddamn lowest points of your life. I expected you to at least check in with me every once in a while. Not just watch me fall apart from a distance. I was a better friend to you than that."

By the time he'd finished unloading a burden he'd carried for too long, his vision had turned blurry. What the hell was going on now?

First his heart and now his eyes. It was like looking through a windshield on a stormy day. And why the hell were his cheeks wet?

Holy fuck! Was he crying?

"Nino, I'm so sorry," Van said as he attempted to get closer. Nino wasn't ready for that, so he held out his hand for Van to stop.

If he was going to do this, he couldn't be stopped. He had to let it all out before it ripped him apart. Through tears that sometimes made it difficult to see or speak, Nino finally revealed how he'd felt abandoned by Van, about his modeling career, and about Teddy. When he finished, he was on the couch with his back against Van's chest and his best friend's arms wrapped securely around him.

Was this what happened when he let someone in? Would he turn into a blubbering mess and fall apart? He could handle the hug just fine. That part was pretty awesome, but he didn't care much for the crying.

"First of all, I'm sorry for being such an awful friend. I should've done something sooner. I can't deny that."

"You're in love," Nino said with a sniffle. A runny nose too? Yeah, he didn't like that part much either. "I'm happy for you. All I ever wanted was for you to be happy."

"That's what I've wanted for you too," Van said. "And I've let my happiness get in the way of being a good friend. That won't happen again. I promise."

That guarantee slowly filled up the hole that had been gaping inside him.

"As for the problems with Ford Michaels, that guy's a twat. Believe me, I know. I've seen him and his prissy little cunt boyfriend in action at the Nasty Boy Studio parties Tripp used to throw. They've got no fucking reason to blackball you, and they'll know it once you confront them. If they give you any trouble, I'm sure I can get Tripp to let me steal a couple of photos of them participating in an outdoor gangbang. I'm sure that wouldn't be good for business."

Nino laughed. No, that wouldn't be good for business at all. Especially since Ford marketed himself as a wholesome gay man. Pictures of him balls deep inside some random guy at a porn party would definitely shatter his public image.

"And now Teddy."

This was the part Nino dreaded the most. Did they really have to talk about him?

"You realize you like him, don't you?"

"He's a good guy," he admitted. "Not quite the furry little fucker I'd thought he was. He's proven to be a good friend."

Van repositioned himself on the couch so he and Nino could look each other in the eye. "No, you like him more than as just a friend."

He rolled his eyes. "You've got to be kidding me. Is that really what you think?"

Van nodded. "Think about it, Nino. You were down in the dumps yesterday, until you spent the evening with Teddy. You two had this amazing night on the breakwater. Which is a pretty romantic place. You go for pizza, which you actually ate, and then you get bummed out when you think he likes someone else."

"Loves someone else," he corrected. "He's still in love with his boyfriend from college."

It was Van's turn to roll his eyes. "It sounds to me like Teddy doesn't know up from down right now. He's even more clueless than you. If that's even possible. I think Teddy feels something right now, but it's not for his ex. I think it's for you."

Van had obviously lost his mind. "For me? Get real! We've hated each other for far longer than we've been nice to each other. That's a pretty quick turnaround."

"That's true, but it happened to me and Zach. I didn't want to fall in love with him, but I did. It just happened. It just sort of took over."

"I hope you're not saying that Teddy and I are in love with each other. Because that's not true."

"You're right," Van agreed. "Your situation is, well, hairier than mine was."

Nino groaned. "Really? You're gonna start with the bear jokes now?"

Van giggled. "Hey, you've gotta work with what you've got, and you, my friend, have the hots for a bear who thinks he's in love with someone else. That definitely makes your situation a tad hairier than me and Zach."

"I do not have the hots for a bear," he said. Good God, now he was pouting? Where was his pacifier and baby blanket?

"Look, I know beary boys aren't your usual thing. Lord knows you've complained enough about them over the years. But so what if you like this bear? Are you worried what people might think because his body isn't perfectly sculpted or his hair isn't waxed religiously? You don't like him because of the way he looks. You like him for the man he is. That's what makes him so different from all the other guys you screw. He's not a carbon copy. Teddy's been able to get this far because he's special. That has to count for something, right?"

He'd never thought of it that way. Maybe Teddy had become special to him. But how was that possible? Only a few days had passed since they woke up together. Could feelings like that develop that quickly? It had happened that way for Zach and Van.

Did it really matter, though? He didn't do feelings. They were much too dangerous. That was why, above all his other rules, he would never *ever* break rule number one, the most important rule of all.

He'd never allow himself to fall in love.

"What's the matter?" Van asked.

Worry had once again taken over Van's expression. He obviously sensed something within Nino had changed.

And it had. No matter what he might or might not feel for Teddy, he had no choice but to stop it.

"Thanks for the talk," he said as he stood up. He shook the unpleasantness from his body and then stretched. His muscles were no longer as tense. That was progress. "I think I'm good now."

"That's good, but what are you gonna do about Teddy?"

He shrugged. "Absolutely nothing."

"What? Why?"

Nino glanced down at Van. His standard casual approach to life had suddenly returned. He could sense it when his lips parted in his typical half grin. He was more himself now that he'd finally gotten all his problems off his chest. Thank God! That was obviously what he'd needed more than anything else. He didn't need Teddy. Or even want him in his life as anything more than a friend.

"Because there's nothing to do about Teddy. Whether you think he's in love with his ex or not, Teddy thinks he is. That's really all that matters, right? Besides, what's the number one rule I live by?"

Van frowned. "Don't fall in love."

Nino grinned and followed it with a wink. "Precisely. Love's not for me. Never has been. And I'm not about to start getting all mushy now." Van opened his mouth to speak, but Nino cut him off. "Now, enough of my shit. You're obviously going to the beach. You should probably get going."

Van sighed and stood up. "Fine. I'll let you off the hook for now." Was Van actually going to let a matter drop? Talk about a fucking miracle. "But if I do that, then you must do something for me."

"What is it?"

"Come to the beach with me."

"What? And watch you and Zach sneak off into the dunes all afternoon? No, thank you."

"That's not it at all. Gary and Quinn have the day off. They've invited us to the beach to hang out, drink, and have fun. I think it would be good for you to get out."

"The last time I went to a Gary and Quinn party, I woke up in bed with Teddy," he reminded Van.

"Well since rule number five in your insane guide to life says that you're never to repeat a fuck, I think you'll be safe."

He couldn't argue with that. He'd never dipped his wick twice before. He definitely wouldn't start today. "All right," he replied. "You've got it. Let me get my suit."

After a quick costume change and grabbing the essentials he'd need for an afternoon at Herring Cove, Nino followed Van out of his apartment and down to Commercial Street. The hole in his stomach had all but closed up. Sure, there was an empty spot here and there, but for the most part, he was back to being the Nino Santos he loved.

He wouldn't trade that for anything in the world.

Chapter Thirteen

WHEN NINO and Van arrived at the spot on the beach, the party was already in full swing. Gary was in total diva mode, walking around with a yellow parasol and carrying a green-tinted drink. He was gesticulating like crazy, something he typically did when he was trying to be the life of the party. The bears he was talking to, who just happened to be the ones from tea yesterday, seemed to enjoy it. Most of them sported smiles wider than their heads.

Poor Quinn just stood off to the side, shaking his head and talking to Zach. Quinn and Zach were definitely not as social as their boyfriends. They preferred to stand by and watch the show instead of take part.

"There's my fair-skinned man," Van said.

Did he have to sound like a fan girl spying her pop idol crush? When Zach saw Van, he about pissed his white swimsuit with excitement. The way they fawned over each other was sickening. They needed to bring it down by about a hundred notches. Not even Quinn could stand their squishiness. He walked away and stood over by Nino.

"He looks more red than fair to me right now," Nino replied.

Van nodded as he eyed Zach's sunburn. "I told you to put on sunscreen before we left," he chided Zach. "But do you listen to me? No!"

Zach pulled Van into his arms and squeezed his ass. "Maybe I was waiting for you to do it for me."

"Hmmm," Van said as he lingered on Zach's lips. "I like the way you think, Mr. Kelly."

"Why don't you two get a room?" Nino asked. "Or pull up a dune."

Zach peered over Van's shoulder at him and winked. "We just might."

"Might?" Quinn asked. "Who you kidding? You packed more lube in your backpack than sunscreen, and you know it."

"Well, if it isn't Humberto Santos," Gary said, speaking his name with almost perfect Portuguese intonation.

Why did Gary always have to use his first name? He hated Humberto. That was why people called him Nino. But that was just what Gary did, even though it irritated the crap out of Nino. Still, it meant that Gary liked him, so that made the annoyance somewhat bearable.

Gary then sauntered over to him and gave him a kiss. "Where have you been hiding yourself? You've been MIA for days, and I don't like it!"

"It's Bear Week," Quinn reminded Gary.

"Ah, yes," Gary nodded. "The week of your self-imposed exile."

The bears Gary had been chatting with inched over to where they stood. He eyed them suspiciously. If their judgmental glances from yesterday resurfaced, he'd put them in their place. He wasn't taking their crap today.

"Why do you hide from the bears?" the one he remembered being Rick asked. "We're not that bad, are we?"

"Or are you scared we might eat you?" his husband, Carl, asked.

"If you were hungry enough, you would," he bantered. The group chuckled at his comeback. He was pleased to see they were less hostile than they'd been yesterday. Maybe he'd read them wrong, or maybe they'd realized they'd been too hard on him too. If it happened to be the latter, he assumed Jay had a hand in that.

"No, really," Dave said—if Nino recalled his name right. "Why the exile?"

What was he supposed to say? That he didn't like bears? That he thought they were fat, smelly bastards he never wanted to have sex with? Although that was what he had once believed, his opinion had changed. Jay was a bear. A fucking big bear at that. And he'd come to really like that guy. Then there was Teddy. He'd had sex with him *and* become his friend.

He'd misjudged them mostly because they reminded him of the person he'd once been and no one had ever liked. How could he have been so blind as to have never noticed that before?

"Well?" Dave asked. "You gonna answer my question or are you just gonna stand there with your mouth open? What are you waiting for? A cock to magically appear before you to suck?"

As he was about to answer, Van's wide, panicked eyes practically begged him to be nice. Even Zach, Quinn, and Gary were obviously worried how he'd respond. They fidgeted and stared up and down the beach instead of watching what they apparently perceived as a disaster waiting to happen. "I don't hide from the bears," he finally said. "I just take the week off, usually. Twink week is right before Bear Week, and I'm usually too sore to walk."

The men laughed and nodded while his friends sighed in relief.

"Nino!" he heard someone scream from farther down the beach. When he turned, he spied Jay and Terry exiting the dunes to their left and walking over to greet him. He didn't need to ask what they'd been doing. From their messed-up hair and the semi-hard-on still visible in Jay's trunks, they'd just finished pumping out fresh loads on the beach.

Ah, the joys of Herring Cove!

"Hey, Jay," he said when Jay and Terry sidled up next to him. Naturally, Jay grabbed him for the usual bear hug, but this time Nino was ready. He quickly exhaled all the air from his lungs to make Jay's viselike grip hurt less.

After Jay put him back on the sand, Jay asked, "How are you? You were in quite a state after tea yesterday."

Everyone got quiet. They all evidently wanted to know the answer. "I'm fine. Nothing to worry about."

Jay looked him up and down, obviously trying to gauge for himself whether Nino was speaking the truth. Satisfied that Nino was,

Jay smiled and then patted him on the back twice, very hard. If he was this rough with a friendly pat on the back, how brutal was Jay when he was pounding ass? Poor Terry. Hopefully, the guy had good health insurance.

"I don't have to ask how you two are," he said with a nod to the dunes. "Looks like the two of you were having some fun in the sand."

"They've been there ever since we arrived," Gary said in pretend exasperation. "That was what? An hour ago?"

"At least," Quinn replied with a grin.

Jay turned four different shades of red while Terry beamed. How cute was that? Nino groaned to himself—if he could punch himself in the face without looking crazy, he would. He needed to stop thinking things were cute. When did he turn into Van?

"Can I talk to you for a minute?" Jay asked as he pulled Nino away from the others. The other men allowed them to walk off. Except for Terry, who followed Jay around like a puppy.

"What's up?" Nino asked.

"Listen, I want to prepare you for something. It may or may not be a big deal, but I want you to know."

"You're in love with me, aren't you?" he kidded. Terry obviously didn't think the joke funny, because he wrapped his arms around Jay's meaty midsection.

"Like you'd ever be that lucky," Jay remarked. He placed his arm around Terry's shoulders to reassure him that he and Nino were teasing. "Brody's going to be here."

Why the fuck would he care if Brody showed up or not? Although he typically didn't hang out with guys he'd already tricked with, he couldn't care less what Brody did. "Okay," he said in response to Jay's revelation. "I don't see why you'd have to prepare me for that."

Jay frowned. "Well, after yesterday, I figured he wouldn't exactly be your favorite person."

He laughed. This time he patted Jay on the back. He tried to put as much force behind it as Jay did, but he just didn't have the mass to carry it off. Jay barely flinched. "Don't worry about it. Brody and I worked through our issues last night."

Jay's frown widened into an impish grin. "You dog," he commented as he heartily punched Nino's shoulder. Nino stumbled twice before he caught himself. "Oops! Sorry. I don't know my own strength."

"Tell me about it," Terry commented as he rubbed his ass.

"Oh, shush," Jay told Terry. "You like it, and you know it!"

Terry's big-ass grin revealed that he did. That was just too much information for Nino.

On steady legs once again, Nino said, "Thanks for looking out for me, though. I appreciate it."

"What are friends for?" Jay asked as he placed his free arm around Nino's shoulders. They then walked back to the group of guys, who all had an alcoholic beverage in their hands.

"Is your tête-à-tête over?" Gary asked. He handed Jay and Nino a beer each. "You know how much I hate private conversations when they don't include me."

Jay took a long swig before answering. "Sure do."

"When is Tara getting here?" he asked. It was always a good idea to divert Gary's attention when he was fishing for information. "I thought she was coming."

"She'll be here in an hour or so," Gary replied.

"Will that be everybody?" Zach asked.

Gary answered with an exaggerated headshake. "We've got two more joining us. They are renting the condo you stayed in last summer."

Zach grinned ear to ear and then gazed at Van. "That place has great memories."

"Yes, well, that magic won't repeat with these two. It's an old friend of Bobby Quinn's and mine from our Boston days. And his horrendous fag hag."

The bears groaned in unison.

"Is she that bad?" Nino asked.

"You have no idea," Quinn commented. "But you should know, since you've already met them."

"I have?" He didn't recall ever meeting friends of Gary and Quinn.

Quinn nodded. "At the beach party a few days ago. You don't remember?"

Nino exhaled. "I don't remember a lot from that night."

"Well the two of you hit it off. The last time I saw you boys that night, I left you behind in the dunes."

Fuck! Quinn was talking about Teddy. Why should that surprise him? Everywhere he went, Teddy seemed to be there. How was he going to handle that today? He'd started to feel more like himself after his talk with Van this morning, but would that last with Teddy around?

Maybe what he needed was to find out how all this had started at that beach party he couldn't remember. Perhaps if he understood how it began, it would help him deal with the damn pit that had once again opened in his gut.

For that, though, he needed to get Quinn alone.

"WHAT'S UP?" Quinn asked after Nino had safely led him away from the group.

"This guy who's renting your condo. What's his name?"

"You really don't remember his name?" Quinn asked. A mocking grin clung to his lips before a sip from his beer washed it away. "I shouldn't be surprised, though. You were pretty wasted."

"Well, I had a lot going on. You know that."

Quinn nodded. "How are things going? I've been worried about you." He motioned toward Gary, who was currently singing a show tune to his captive audience. "We both have been."

"I'm better," he admitted. "I've talked things out. Gained some perspective on what I've got to do."

"Good. I'm glad. And just so you know, I threw out all our Ford Michaels shirts. Fucking bastard!"

He really had some good friends. He'd never realized that before. He'd only ever taken notice of Van's friendship, but he apparently had more than he'd realized. He wasn't that poor, fat, unloved kid anymore, was he?

"You really remember nothing from that night?" Quinn asked.

"Not a thing. I'm hoping you can fill in the gaps. Starting with the guy's name."

"His name's Teddy," Quinn replied after he downed the rest of his beer. "I think he's a pretty great guy. You seemed to think so too. Which surprised the fuck out of me."

"What do you mean?"

"You've had a serious hate on for bears all these years. Naturally, I was sorta thrown when the two of you seemed to hit it off."

"How so?"

"Damn, Nino," Quinn said with a shake of his head. "How drunk were you?"

"Can you just tell me what happened, please?"

When Quinn next spoke, his words parted the fog of inebriation.

"THIS IS a great party!" he told Quinn as he stood next to him to take a piss. They had left the others and walked around the nearest dune to relieve their alcohol-heavy bladders.

"Great?" Quinn asked as his urine stream struck the sand. "It's awesome! There's more hot bear flesh than I can shake my stick at." He punctuated the statement by waving his cock around.

"Watch it!" Nino warned. "If you piss on me, I'll make you lick it up."

"Promises, promises," Quinn replied.

For some reason, Nino found that comment hilarious. He couldn't stop laughing, which made it difficult to pee. Every time another round of laughter hit him, his flow stopped. God, how drunk was he? He'd lost count after the sixth tequila shooter. There'd been at least four more drinks of that awful trash-can punch Gary made. He hadn't drunk this much since his early twenties.

All this alcohol wasn't exactly great for his figure, but who the fuck cared? It wasn't like he was working right now or anything. Fucking Ford Michaels!

"Stop thinking about your problems," Quinn ordered. "Enjoy yourself. Let your hair down. That's why I made you come in the first place." Quinn was obviously pretty drunk too. His slurred speech told him that much, but what made it more obvious was that Quinn couldn't even stand still while taking a piss. He swayed back and forth as if the ocean breeze was knocking him around.

"What's this?" a voice behind them asked. "A piss party?"

He peered over his shoulder at the furry little bear who'd spent most of the evening dry humping his much larger counterparts. He couldn't have been taller than five six, which basically made him a pocket bear. There was nothing small about his cock, though. Damn! When he stood next to Nino to take a piss, he'd expected a small cock to flop out of the guy's suit. The little bear surprised him. His dick had to be at least six inches soft, which would make it quite the party favor when it got hard.

He was also sort of cute. For a bear.

He had a furry chest and belly— the latter wasn't as bloated as most of the other bears on the beach. It certainly wasn't flat and chiseled like Nino's, but the little guy carried off the look. He probably wouldn't even look as cute without the belly. How fucking weird was that?

Christ, he was even drunker than he'd thought!

"Take a picture," the little guy said to his right. "It'll last longer."

"What?" Nino asked. He hadn't realized he'd been watching the guy pee this whole time. "Oh, shit! Sorry."

The guy shrugged. "No worries. You've got a nice cock too."

When he gazed downward, he realized he'd stopped peeing and had been standing there holding his semihard dick in his hand. What was up with that?

Suddenly Quinn stood between them. He wrapped his arms around both of their shoulders as they put their dicks back in their

Speedos. *"Well, since you've seen each other's cocks, I guess I should introduce you. Teddy, this is Nino. Nino, this is Teddy."*

"Hey," he said. *Why did this guy look so familiar? The haze of alcohol made him unable to make any connections. It was someone from back home, though. Someone who once meant the world to him. Who the hell could that be? He didn't exactly have childhood memories he treasured.*

"Hi," Teddy replied. *"You having a good time?"*

"Not really," he replied. *"But I think I'm about to."*

"On that note," Quinn interrupted. *"I'll leave you both to get better acquainted."* He patted Teddy on the back and then winked at Nino before stumbling back over the dune to rejoin the party.

Why couldn't he stop staring at Teddy? Was it the bearded face that he found absolutely adorable? If that was what drew him, it would be a first. He'd always enjoyed clean-shaven men, who wouldn't leave razor burn after a long night of kissing and fucking.

No, it wasn't Teddy's face. As fucking cute as it was. Maybe it was his eyes. They were a warm and inviting brown, like the sand on a hot, sunny day. He loved lounging on the beach more than he did fucking. On the beach and under the sun, he was alone, where he could just be the man he truly was. Not the Nino he often pretended to be.

Was that what he saw? Someone similar to him? They might look like two very different people on the outside, but inside they were the same. But how did he know this? Was he just able to spot another person who'd lived through hell too, or was it something else?

"You're kinda freaking me out."

Teddy's voice dragged him out of his thoughts. *"I'm sorry. What?"*

"You're just staring at me. Not saying a word. It's a little weird."

He shook the thoughts from his head. *"My bad. You just remind me of someone."*

"Who?" Teddy asked.

"That's what I was trying to figure out."

"Well, if you tell me it's your favorite aunt, I'll deck you."

He laughed. "No. It's definitely not anyone in my family. I hate most of them."

A wistful look flashed in Teddy's eyes before he blinked it away. "Yeah, me too. Except my family is my mom and me. And we don't exactly like each other much."

"Yeah, well, my family's much bigger. Five sisters and two parents. Who all hate me for liking cock. So I guess I win."

"Oh, so it's a contest, is it?" Teddy asked.

He nodded. "Maybe it is. Let's see whose life actually sucks the most."

"Fine," Teddy said as he sat down. He patted the sand next to him. "But I play to win."

Nino plopped down on the sand beside Teddy and grinned. "You may play to win, but I always win."

"Get ready to lose for the first time, then," Teddy announced as he discussed his stripper mom who had verbally and emotionally abused him his whole life.

"That all you got?" Nino asked. After he shared the awful way his sisters treated him and the parents who turned a blind eye to the bullying, he allowed a smug grin to hook his lips to the left. "There's no way you can beat that!"

Teddy snorted. "I'm just getting started. I'm still in love with my ex, and we broke up over ten years ago."

"Yeah, well, I've never been in love. So there!"

Why was he telling Teddy all this? There was no way he could blame it all on the alcohol. He'd been shitfaced before. He hadn't turned into a chatterbox any of those other times. In fact, he'd never talked about his past with anyone. Well, except Van, who knew all the gory details.

What was it about Teddy that broke through all his barriers and made him open up like this?

"Now, that is sad," Teddy offered as he playfully shoved Nino. Under normal circumstances, he would have been fine. But his equilibrium was already off because of the excessive drinking. That was why he sprawled backward into the sand.

Why was he laughing like an idiot, though? It hadn't been that funny. Teddy apparently found it humorous as well. He'd fallen back in the sand next to Nino, clutching his stomach and lost to the laughter that shook his body.

What a strange moment this was in his life. He'd always been guarded with people. He didn't cut loose and laugh like some silly boy. That kid had been beaten out of him in his youth. Yet here he was, giggling on the sand with Teddy like they'd been best friends forever. Instead of strangers who'd just met during a potty break.

After his giggles subsided, he turned on his right side. Teddy's warm, extremely handsome face gazed back at him.

"You've been hurt as much as I have," he stated. It wasn't a question. It was a fact.

"Yeah," Teddy admitted. "It sucks, but what can you do? Bitch about it until the end of time? Nope. I had to move on or I'd always be stuck in the past. I'm sure that's what you've done too."

Maybe. But he wasn't so sure he had. His past had such a bearing on his present that he found it hard to differentiate them. The pain of yesterday still stung just as harshly today. "I think you've done a better job of it than I have. At least from what you've said."

Teddy shrugged. "Doesn't matter, really. All that really counts is what we do from today forward."

That made sense. But what could he do? He couldn't just change years of repressed anger and hurt and suddenly be someone else. Could he? No. That was only done in the movies. Real life was more complicated.

"It's easier than you think," Teddy commented. How the hell did Teddy know what he was thinking? That was just bizarre. It reminded him of those crazy silent conversations couples like Zach and Van or Gary and Quinn had. "I don't usually get this philosophical, so let's chalk it up to the alcohol. Okay?"

He smiled and nodded. He somehow didn't buy that it was the liquor talking, but he wasn't going to burst Teddy's bubble. If it was easier for him to open up and blame it on being inebriated, who was he to tell Teddy differently?

"I've lived my life in the past," Teddy admitted, "for far too long. I realized that tonight on the beach. I'm here with all these fine guys, but I can't stop thinking about my ex. That's not healthy. I can't put my life on hold and revisit the past whenever something reminds me of him."

"What reminded you of him tonight?" he asked.

"Truthfully?"

"Sure, let's give honesty a try. I don't go that route too often."

Teddy stared at him, no doubt wondering what that comment meant. "Well, to be honest, it was you."

What the hell? He wasn't expecting that one. "How do you mean?"

"The two of you are similar in body type. I mean, look at you," Teddy said as he waved at Nino's body. "You're perfect. I hate you for that, by the way."

Nino smiled. "Lots of people hate me because I'm beautiful."

Teddy groaned. "And modest too."

"Naturally," Nino added with a nod.

"Anyway, back to me," Teddy said, trying to sound annoyed. The chuckle in his throat gave him away, though. He was enjoying himself. Surprisingly, so was Nino. "When I first saw you on the beach, I thought 'Damn, he's fine!' With your hot, trim, perfect body, that got me thinking about my ex. And how happy I'd been when we were together. I didn't feel like a complete loser when I was with him. When we broke up, well, all my insecurities came tumbling back on my head. I haven't been in love since."

"Okay, so where does the 'it's easier to change than you think part' come in?"

"Well, I've decided to move on. After tonight, I'm not letting my past hold me back anymore. I'm forging ahead. Seeing what else is out there. I refuse to believe that I already missed my chance at happiness, and it's time to go wherever I'm supposed to be."

That was ballsy. Nino doubted he could ever just let go of his crap. He lived pretty routinely. Who would he be if he suddenly changed everything up? He wasn't sure he wanted to find out. He might not be happy right now, but he wasn't miserable. That had to mean something was working out.

"I just hope I remember this epiphany tomorrow morning," Teddy joked. "I anticipate a major hangover tomorrow."

"You and me both," he agreed.

"Can I tell you something, Nino?"

"Why the hell not," he said.

"When I look into your eyes, I see such sadness. And it looks like it's been there for a long time. But I also see something else. I see a little boy just waiting for someone to pick him up and give him a hug. And I just want to tell you, it's going to be okay. I promise."

Why did he suddenly want to hold Teddy close, to feel his little furry body against him? And why the hell did he think it would chase all the demons from his past and present away?

Teo had been the only one who'd ever done that for him in his life.

That was it! He sat bolt upright and stared down at Teddy. Teddy reminded Nino of his childhood teddy bear. The best friend who'd always been there for him. The one he told all his troubles to and the only one who'd ever loved him no matter what.

It was as if Teo had somehow come to life as Teddy. Was that why he opened up to Teddy so easily?

"What's wrong?" Teddy asked as he sat up. He moved closer to Nino so their knees just barely touched. The warmth of Teddy's skin filled the tiny gap that separated them, then rode up Nino's body in never-ending waves. His cock sprang to life, and he almost crossed the distance between them to bring Teddy into his embrace.

"Are you okay?"

The tenderness of Teddy's question fanned the flames of his desire. Perspiration dripped down his face and his back. He was also trembling—not in fear, but in an indescribable need to pluck this man from the sand and never let him go.

Could he really do that, though? No one had ever stirred such emotions within him before. Sure, he'd found lots of guys hot. He had bedded all that he could. This was different.

Teddy didn't just make his cock hard. That was easy enough to do. Talking with Teddy, hell, just being there with Teddy, filled the emptiness he'd carried around with him from Sao Paulo. How the hell was that possible? Not even Van had accomplished that. And he'd known Van for years. He and Teddy had just met!

"Nino?" Teddy repeated. He brushed his hand across Nino's cheek. His fingernails scratched a slow path along his jawline. A low moan escaped his throat before Nino could stop it. He didn't just want Teddy. Now he needed him.

"I just realized who you remind me of," he admitted. His voice was low and throaty.

Teddy unfolded his legs and scooted closer. He now sat before Nino with his legs parted on either side of Nino in the sand. The hair from Teddy's calves tickled his skin like dozens of soft feathers. "Who's that?"

"My teddy bear," he answered. "He was my best friend."

"Aw, that's so cute," Teddy said as he leaned closer. His voice had also softened and grown deep. "I like teddy bears. What was his name?"

"Teo."

"Do you still have him?"

He shook his head. "He was donated to the church a long time ago. But he was always waiting for me when I got home. With his arms wide open. Even to this day, I sometimes check my bed to see if he's returned."

"Well, I might not be Teo," Teddy said. He decreased the distance between them until Teddy's hot breath rushed against Nino's lips. "But I'd like to be your Teddy bear right now."

In reply, Nino bridged the gap remaining between them. When their lips touched, it was like the waves finally crashing upon the sand. One kiss quickly followed another as their bodies, which had been silently pulling upon each other, finally surrendered to nature's will.

Nino freely gave up the reins, which he'd so strictly held onto. They weren't needed right now. He had to trust, and he had to let go. If Teddy could do it, then so could he. Who else would be better to help start him down this path than his Teddy bear brought to life?

But for now, he drew Teddy's tongue into his mouth. Underneath the bitter alcohol, he tasted the sweet promise their lips somehow exchanged. What that meant, he had no clue. Right now, he didn't care. He enjoyed how his body came to life, responding like a seed to water. So much that had been dormant inside him had awoken, and he had Teddy's lips and arms, holding him close, to thank for such a gift.

"Should we go back to my place?" he asked once their lips hesitantly parted. They were both out of breath and very hard. Teddy's cock snaked across his hip. The fabric was losing the battle of containing the bulge.

Teddy grinned. "Whatever for?"

"I think it's time to see how this Teddy bear looks on my bed."

Teddy accepted the offer by once again brushing his lips against Nino's. While Teddy's tongue lolled inside his mouth, he gingerly trailed his fingertips down Nino's chest. He traced slow, lazy circles around his nipples before descending down his stomach to where his cock peeked out over the fabric of his swimsuit. He squeezed Nino's hard dick and pushed him down onto the sand.

Apparently, Teddy wasn't willing to wait. That was fine by him.

They were obviously both in for a night they'd never forget.

"NINO, YOU okay?" Quinn asked.

Okay? No, he was far from okay. He'd just remembered everything about that night. He and Teddy hadn't accidentally stumbled into bed in a drunken stupor. They had both wanted each other.

On that beach, while everyone else was partying, they'd shared a special moment. Something within him had instantly responded to something in Teddy. Were they kindred spirits? Did such things really exist? Van believed in that. He never had.

Had he been wrong all this time?

If what they shared was so special, then why hadn't they remembered any of it? Being drunk didn't explain all that away.

Had it been because they'd both let down their defenses? Had the alcohol allowed them to momentarily be true to who they were? But when they woke up the next morning, their self-defense systems had rebooted. They then suppressed the memory of how vulnerable they'd been to each other.

What else could explain the memory gap?

"Nino," Quinn repeated. This time Quinn grabbed him by the shoulders and shook him. "What's the matter, man? You look like you're ready to pass out."

"I remember," he admitted to Quinn, but mostly to himself. Right now, his head spun and the ache in his stomach had returned. It wasn't just loneliness that had caused the emptiness within to come back. It was his desire to be with Teddy. It was the same hollow feeling he'd suffered through once he realized his Teo was gone and would never come back.

"That's good, right?"

Nino shook his head. "I don't know." That was an honest reply. What was he supposed to do with these feelings? Teddy was in love with his ex-boyfriend. Could he pursue someone who didn't want him in return?

But Teddy had wanted him that night on the beach. Maybe he wanted him still and didn't realize it. Just like Nino.

There was only one thing for Nino to do. He had to talk to Teddy.

Chapter Fourteen

EVEN THOUGH they were an hour late, thanks to Irene's search for the perfect swimsuit, Teddy, Irene, and Louie—who'd fallen asleep in his arms—had finally made it to the beach. Now, where the hell was Brody? Gary and Quinn were there, laughing it up with Jay, Terry, and the bears. Next to Jay stood a couple he'd never seen before. One of the guys had bright-red hair and extremely fair skin, while the man he had his arms around had a perfectly tanned body and light-brown hair. What a contrast in color palettes. They had to be Zach and Van, the ones Jay had told him were invited to this get-together.

Off to the group's right, Tara chatted with Nino, who was clad only in a very tight red Speedo. Seeing Nino both surprised him and made him smile, although he didn't see why he should be so shocked. Nino somehow managed to show up wherever he was. It was like the universe was trying to tell him something about the man who'd become his friend.

But why was Nino staring at him that way? He'd been talking with Tara just fine, but as soon as he glanced up and saw Teddy, he became nervous. As if he couldn't decide whether to run or come say hi. What was that all about? Hadn't they worked through their issues last night?

"Theodore Miller!" Gary shouted. He waved his arms wildly in the air. He obviously wanted Teddy to head over to him first. If homage wasn't paid to Gary before all others, there would be hell to pay. No one wanted that. No matter how much he wanted to learn why Nino was acting weird, it would have to wait.

He strolled over to where Gary stood, but he kept a watchful eye on Nino, who seemed to be watching him too.

"It's about time you showed up," Gary said once he and Irene made it to his side. His wide, friendly smile faltered a bit when he gazed upon Irene.

"Tell me about it," Teddy grumbled. "Someone just had to play supermodel and try on all the swimsuits she brought with her from Boston. Naturally, she ended up choosing the first one she had tried on."

"What can I say?" Irene asked. "I dress to impress."

Gary eyed her attire up and down. She had on a bright neon-yellow one-piece, pink sunglasses, and hair teased tall enough to touch the sun. She reminded Teddy of a blonde Kelly LeBrock from the eighties classic *Weird Science*.

"Well, you certainly are impressive," Gary told Irene.

Irene smiled at Teddy as if Gary's comment vindicated her for taking her sweet time getting ready. She apparently failed to hear the mockingly critical nip in Gary's tone.

A muffled snuff from his arms told him Louie had awakened. His pooch opened one eye to peer at Gary, yawned, and then promptly fell back to sleep.

"Nice to see you too," Gary said to Louie.

"He's tired," Teddy told him. "And hot."

"He isn't the only one," Irene pointed out as she wiped the sweat from her brow. Not even the humidity, perspiration, or sea breeze could unmake Irene's do. Did she use hair spray or super glue? "It's like a hundred degrees in the sun. Isn't there any shade around here?"

"There is," Gary pointed out. "Back at the condo."

Irene caught the sarcasm in that comment. Before she could respond, Teddy asked, "Where's Brody?"

"Who?" Gary asked. His question created an abrupt cease-fire, even though he could tell Irene was still ready to launch a salvo of bitchiness.

"Brody O'Shea," he said. "Jay told me he'd been invited."

Gary shrugged. "Never met him."

"Jay said he was coming. Brody's his roommate."

"And your ex," Irene added.

Gary's eyebrows arched higher than a McDonald's sign. This turn of events evidently met with his favor. "Your ex-boyfriend?" he asked. "You haven't had a man ever since I met you in Boston. This sounds like a fantastic story. Naturally, I must hear it at once."

"Only if you like tragedies," Irene commented with an eye roll.

Gary switched his gaze from Teddy to Irene. "I *love* them," he practically tittered.

"Please don't," he begged Irene.

"Why not?" she asked. "Maybe if you hear what I've been telling you all afternoon from Gary, you'd actually listen."

"Irene Frost, your words are not only wise, but you have piqued my interest. Theodore is sometimes far too bullheaded for his own good."

"Tell me about it," she said.

Irene Frost? Gary was using her full name now? When the hell did he start liking her? It couldn't just be the fact that she had gossip she was evidently willing to share, could it? But as he observed Gary and Irene huddling together to talk about him as if he wasn't there, he realized that was exactly why.

The fastest way to Gary's heart, after all, was through talking about others.

He was just about to interrupt them when Louie sat bolt upright in his arms. He sniffed the air intently, and his bat ears perked up. They twitched to the left and then the right, searching for something familiar.

When Louie finally spotted Nino, he wiggled about. He obviously wanted to be set free so he could be reunited with his new friend. Teddy set Louie down and watched his handsome boy bound through the sand toward Nino. When he reached his destination, he hopped into Nino's waiting arms and delivered several kisses before finally snuggling in Nino's lap and arfing at Teddy.

That was Louie's way of commanding *him* to come.

Teddy sighed. "I'll be back," he told Gary and Irene. "Louie beckons."

They both waved him off as if he didn't exist. Teddy shook his head at them. He'd never understand either Gary or Irene. Somehow his problems brought the two of them together. If he didn't suspect they would be ganging up on him later, he might be thankful of their newfound appreciation for each other.

"I see your daddy hasn't learned his lesson yet," he overheard Nino say to Louie as he drew closer.

"And what lesson would that be?" he asked. Instead of staring at *him* with loving eyes, Louie gazed up at Nino as if he hung the stars and the moon. The little traitor! Louie was supposed to only look at him that way.

Nino glanced up at him with the devilish grin that had once pissed him off. Now it made him smile. But Nino's smile caused another surprising reaction. A storm of butterflies fluttered in his stomach. It made him anxious, like last night at the church when he realized he had to see Brody. Why was he having that reaction again? With Nino?

Maybe it was because there was something underneath Nino's typically puckish demeanor. Something that seemed both familiar and foreign at the same time.

"What lesson?" Nino asked as he stood. His question pulled Teddy away from identifying the strange emotion he'd been experiencing. "You mean besides the fact that you don't have Louie on a leash? Again!"

"It's not like he's going to get away from me," he pointed out. "There's nowhere for him to go."

"Except into the ocean," Nino said in mock horror. "It's okay, little guy. You stay here with me, and I'll keep an eye on you."

Louie arfed in thanks to Nino and then turned to stare at Teddy. His puppy expression seemed to communicate complete disappointment in Teddy. When they got back to the condo, someone wasn't getting his favorite treat, that was for sure.

"He's such a cutie," Tara said. She knelt down next to Louie. He studied her out of the corner of his eye before moving to the other side of Nino. "He doesn't like me," she said with a pout as she stood up.

"He doesn't like anyone," Teddy clarified.

Tara pointed to the look of absolute adoration on Louie's face. "Tell that to him. He apparently loves Nino."

Yeah, Teddy didn't understand that either. Not that he hated Nino anymore. But how could his dog, who'd never liked another soul before, be drawn to Nino? "Maybe he's just slumming it."

"You mean like you did the other night," Nino replied with a playful wink.

Whoa! Since when were they going public about their one-night stand?

Tara grinned as she looked from Nino to Teddy. "I can see it," she said with a nod. "Very nice."

What the hell did that mean? See what? And just what was nice?

"Well, I'm gonna go see what Gary and Irene are whispering so intently about," she told them as she walked away. "You boys have fun," she added with a wink before turning around and leaving them alone.

After Tara left, they stood in silence. Louie gazed up at the two of them, glancing back and forth as if expecting them to do something. What did Louie want them to do? Whatever it was, he was getting impatient. He chuffed at them and then yawned. He then jumped up on Nino's legs and then on Teddy's, as if that would somehow jump-start some grand event.

"How are you?" Nino asked.

Why did Nino look so miserable and nervous? He darted his eyes from Teddy to Louie and then gazed down the beach. He refused to look Teddy square in the eyes. Nino reminded him of some poor soul who anticipated disaster. What could that possibly be?

"I'm good," he finally replied. "I've never been better, in fact."

"Oh," Nino replied. His one-word response was barely a whisper. "You must've found your ex, then. How'd it go?"

"I actually didn't," he answered. Why did Nino look relieved to hear that? What was going on here? "I went home to think about everything we talked about. To make sure I was making the right decision."

That apparently got Nino's attention. His eyes suddenly locked on Teddy's. "And?" he asked in a tone far more positive than before. Why did Teddy hear hope in that question?

"And even though Irene doesn't think it's a good idea," he admitted, "I'm going to talk to him later today. See where he stands with everything."

Nino nodded. "So there's time, then."

Time for what? And why did Nino seem to be saying that to himself? "I don't understand."

Nino opened his mouth to respond, but no words formed on his lips. Only a soft sigh escaped his throat. Although he hadn't known Nino for long, he recognized this was abnormal behavior. He'd always come across as cocky and confident. As if the world lay at his feet and all he had to do was choose which direction to go. Now Nino reminded him of someone walking down an unfamiliar path and trying to find his footing. When did that happen? Did it have something to do with Ford Michaels? Oh, God! Had his advice further damaged Nino's career?

"Is everything okay?" he asked. "You're acting a bit weird. Even for you."

The uncertainty from before vanished. The corner of his lips hooked up to the left in Nino's typical smug expression. It was like one switch had been turned off and another flicked on. What decision had Nino just made? And why had the butterflies that had settled in Teddy's stomach suddenly flittered back to life? "Okay, now you're scaring me," he admitted as he stepped back. "Why are you staring at me that way?"

"Because it's time for Nino and Teddy's day of fun."

What the hell did that mean?

Before he had a chance to reply, though, Nino suddenly swept him off his feet and cradled him in his arms. "What are you doing?" he asked as Nino held him close. He wrapped his arms around Nino's neck to steady himself. The move closed the distance between his and Nino's lips to mere inches, and the butterflies in his stomach swirled around so quickly that he became light-headed. He also noticed a change in Nino. His heart thundered so forcefully that its reverberations pulsed through Teddy's body.

"You didn't hear me the first time?" Nino asked. His voice was low and tender. Teddy almost didn't hear him this time either. He was too busy studying the gentle movements of Nino's succulent lips as he spoke.

Instead of replying, Teddy shook his head. The butterflies in his stomach had somehow stolen his words. Nino didn't respond either.

His smug grin exploded into a haughty smile as he took off running down the beach and toward the water with Teddy still in his arms.

"DON'T YOU dare!" he screamed as Nino waded into the water. The cold Atlantic splashed up from Nino's legs onto Teddy's back. The chill made him clutch Nino harder and try to squirm his way higher up Nino's body. "That water's fucking cold!"

Nino only laughed in reply. Louie's arf drifted from the shore to where they stood. One peek over Nino's shoulder revealed that Louie had followed them to the shoreline. He entered the ocean only briefly before darting back from the cold water and arfing at them some more from the beach. He obviously wanted them to get the hell out of the water. Teddy couldn't have agreed more.

Not heeding Louie's arfs or Teddy's pleas to turn back, Nino continued forward into the cold water, which had risen all the way to Nino's midthighs. How could Nino stand it? He had absolutely zero body hair or fat to keep him warm. Teddy had an excess of both, and he could never stand more than a few seconds of the ocean before he had to head back to the beach.

"Why are you doing this to me?" he asked. He'd planned on coming off irate. Instead, he laughed and held tightly onto Nino, fearing the inevitable plunge they would take under the water.

"It's Nino and Teddy's day of fun," Nino replied, as if that somehow explained why he'd suddenly held Teddy hostage in the middle of the ocean.

"Does that translate into torturing me?"

Nino peered down at Teddy, his damn grin still lingering on his face. Why did he find that smug look so charming now?

"Maybe," Nino replied. "If you're lucky."

He could be wrong, but was Nino flirting with him? No, that couldn't be what was going on. He'd obviously imagined that. Right?

"The water's getting higher," Nino reported as he continued his progress into the water. He tensed and let out a hiss. "It's up to my junk now."

"Is this really worth shrinkage?" Teddy asked.

Nino scoffed. "Shrinkage isn't a problem for me. It just brings me down to average." He wiggled his eyebrows at Teddy.

Damn! Why had he gotten so fucking drunk that first night? If he hadn't, he'd actually remember how impressive Nino's dick really was. Of course, Nino could be boasting, but he didn't believe so. Nino already had a perfect body, flawless skin, and a gorgeous full head of curly hair. Why wouldn't God have also blessed him with an amazing cock? The lucky fucker!

He even briefly entertained the idea of reaching between their bodies and copping a feel for himself. It wasn't like he hadn't already touched it. He just didn't remember doing so. Stupid alcohol!

But grabbing a handful of Nino's package might upset his stranglehold around Nino's neck. He didn't want to unbalance them and end up in the ocean. After all, he still held out hope that he could convince Nino *not* to dunk him under the chilly water.

"Uh-oh!" Nino exclaimed.

"What?" he asked as he followed Nino's eyes to a passing ferry. Its passage had started a series of waves that, at this moment, rolled toward where they were. "Nino!" he shouted as he pointed to the approaching waves that would surely drench them.

"I see them," Nino replied. "This is going to be fun!"

"I hate you right now," he told Nino as he observed the advancing waves.

"No, you don't," Nino said. "Maybe you'll even figure that out too."

What the hell did that mean? He'd thought they'd become friends. Wasn't that why Nino was tormenting him right now? Was something else going on? When he looked up at Nino to see if he could discern what was happening, he became even more confused. There was more than just Nino's standard cocky expression sparkling in his eyes. Something new had taken residence inside Nino. He was still the same smug bastard Teddy had come to actually like, but the biting sting had been removed. A new radiance shone from within. He looked somehow lighter, as if he would suddenly sprout wings and fly.

What had caused that?

"Get ready," Nino advised as his attention returned to the ocean.

As the waves drew closer to the beach, they had increased in size. The swell must have been at least as tall as Nino now. This was not going to be good.

"You'll pay for this," he whispered in Nino's ear.

Nino turned to him and rested his forehead against Teddy's cheek. Their lips were a few breaths away from touching. "That's the plan," Nino said before the wave struck.

WHEN TEDDY broke through the surface, he was greeted with Nino's laughter. He'd obviously gone under as well. Nino's curls were gone, replaced by straight, wet strands that he pushed back over his head in one swipe. Water trailed down his face in steady rivulets. The slow, snaking trails poured down his cheeks and across his jawline before once again rejoining the ocean that still swelled around them.

How did Nino manage to emerge from almost being drowned by a ginormous wave and come out ready for a photo shoot? If he still hated Nino, this would have made him dislike him much more.

Despite this most recent event, though, he really did like the perfect bastard. Even more so today. Yesterday, he'd seen the vulnerable side of Nino, a side he guessed not many people saw. He'd been lost and unsure where to go. Two very uncharacteristically Nino qualities. Today, though, the insecurities had vanished, but they weren't replaced by cold distance, which was what Teddy had originally feared when Nino had been acting weird on the beach.

Whenever people like Nino let their guard down, their walls immediately sprang up around them. They isolated themselves from those they'd made themselves vulnerable to as a self-defense mechanism.

Teddy understood that because he did that too. The only person he'd ever let in since Brody was Irene. No one else had made it past the first barrier. But Nino had. He'd allowed himself to be just as vulnerable as Nino had been. What did that mean?

"Are you treading water?" Nino asked. He waded over to Teddy, his body glistening from the chilly water, which also made his nipples hard and perky.

"You have a problem with that?" he asked in reply. He needed to stop staring at Nino's hot, wet body. It was making him hard, and he'd die of embarrassment if his cock burst free of his blue swimsuit and bobbed up to the surface to say hello. He had to focus on something else. Like Brody. Brody was the man he loved. B-R-O-D-Y. Brody. "Some of us aren't giants."

Nino chuckled. "Nope. Some of us are munchkins."

"Fuckwad," he teased as he splashed water in Nino's face.

Nino accepted the challenge by floating on his back and kicking at the ocean's surface. The resultant spray created yet another icy deluge that washed over Teddy.

"Okay, fine," he muttered after spitting out half the ocean. "I give."

"Round one goes to me!" Nino cried out as he breached the water like a whale. Naturally, Teddy was soaked again.

"You did that on purpose," he complained.

"Who? Me?" Nino asked as he swam closer.

"Yes, you." He paddled backward to put some distance between his persistent boner and Nino. If the two met, well… it was probably just better if they didn't. "Now, stay back. I no longer trust you."

Nino pretended to be hurt, but his Cheshire grin gave him away. He absolutely loved this. When had their relationship become this playful? Not that Teddy was complaining. It was certainly better than bitching at each other.

"Shall we swim back to shore?"

Teddy eyed Nino suspiciously. Why did he suspect Nino wasn't quite done plaguing him? "That depends," he said. "Are you going to behave yourself now?"

Nino stared at him as if he were stupid. "When do I ever behave myself?"

He had a point. "Okay. That was a dumb question." Nino nodded in agreement. "How about this? Are you done tossing me in the ocean?"

"I'm done tossing you in the ocean," Nino said. He even crossed his heart and hoped to die. Why didn't that make Teddy feel any better?

"Then let's head back to shore."

Nino gave him a thumbs-up. He then dove under the water and swam for shore. The bastard even swam like a superstar. Teddy, who'd never been a huge fan of the water, began his standard dog paddle.

Louie still arfed at him from the beach. He was evidently telling Teddy to hurry the hell up. If he could, he would. He wasn't exactly built for speed, though. He'd get there when he got there. Louie apparently realized this and sat on his haunches to wait for his slow master to once again set foot on dry land.

His friends, if he could still call them that, were on the beach drinking and having a grand old time. Not a single one of them came to his rescue when Nino spirited him into the ocean. It wasn't like they hadn't noticed. He'd observed their open-jaw amazement when Nino had first scooped him up. Those nosy bitches watched the whole thing unravel, and they just stood there. When he made it back, he planned on giving them an earful. Especially Irene. She knew he didn't swim very well, but had she come to his defense? No.

He might just toss her in the ocean for that. With his luck, all the hair spray she had applied before they left might weigh her down. She'd probably sink like a rock.

Suddenly his toes met sand, and Teddy was able to once again stand instead of paddle like a puppy. Thank God. When he looked around to celebrate his victory, he couldn't find Nino. Nino had been beside him for part of the way, but he'd become so focused on reaching shore that he stopped taking notice of where Nino was as he swam.

"Nino!" he called out into the ocean. He surveyed his right and his left, hoping to discover that Nino was playing some trick and had swum farther out to scare him. But he couldn't find him anywhere. "Nino!" he yelled. This time his voice had more urgency. Panic also seized control of his muscles. What he should be doing right now was getting help, alerting people to help him find Nino.

He couldn't move. His stomach, which had once been a flurry of butterfly activity, turned hollow and empty.

Where was Nino? He couldn't be...? No. He couldn't allow himself to think that way. "Nino!" he shouted at the top of his lungs. This time his hysteria was even more apparent, and it also crossed the beach to where his friends had been partying.

Some called out to him, but others, like Gary, Quinn, Zach, and Van, sprinted through the sand toward where he had been paralyzed by fear.

"Nino!" he screamed again.

Then something brushed between his legs. Before he registered what was happening, he was being lifted out of the water on Nino's shoulders while also screaming like a little bitch.

"I'm right here," Nino snickered while he blew the seawater out of his face. His hands wrapped around Teddy's thighs and held him secure.

"You bastard!" he cussed as he swatted the top of Nino's head three times. Very hard.

"Ouch!" Nino complained. "Do that again and back in the water you go."

He had no choice but to comply, even though he really wanted to chance it and smack Nino again. But when Nino gazed up into his eyes, his previous panic and anger drifted away. How could he be so pissed off when Nino smiled at him that way? Only Louie had ever looked at him like that.

"You scared me," he finally said.

"I'm sorry," Nino replied. He squeezed Teddy's thighs and then gently rubbed them as he carried Teddy aloft and out of the water. "I didn't mean to. I promise."

Had Nino ever been this conciliatory this fast in his life? He seriously doubted that. What happened to the sharp tongue and quick comebacks? Evidently, they'd been traded in for sincerity and reassurance. Nino was even rubbing his hands up and down Teddy's thighs to communicate his apology. Instead, Nino ended up causing Teddy's flesh to break out in goose pimples as Nino's surprisingly warm hands stroked his chilled skin. The combination of his touch and his body heat turned Teddy's cock rock hard.

Could this be any more horrifying? Not only did Teddy have a boner, but his erection was practically poking into the back of Nino's head. He expected Nino to toss a wisecrack any moment now.

What he didn't expect was for Nino to smile up at him and then push his head back against Teddy's straining erection.

Chapter Fifteen

AFTER EVERYONE gave Nino a hard time for scaring the shit out of them with his little stunt, they finally calmed down and sat around the small fire Quinn had built on the beach. The dipping sun turned the air cold, and Teddy couldn't stop shivering. He hadn't planned on being out here this long. He originally intended to find Brody, admit his feelings for him, and then head back to his condo for a marathon round of fucking.

Brody had never shown up.

Surprisingly enough, he hadn't been as upset or disappointed as he expected. Instead, he had been having a good time. He hadn't spent much time with anyone except Irene and Nino over the past few days, and it had been good to reconnect. He even liked Nino's best friend, Van, and his hottie boyfriend, Zach. They were nice guys. Although he didn't understand why Van kept stealing glances at him and Nino for most of the evening. What was that about?

"You cold?"

"What gave me away?" he asked in reply to Nino's question. "My chattering teeth or the fact that I can't stop shivering?"

"Neither," Nino replied as he reached into his backpack. He pulled out a Provincetown hoodie and handed it to him. "It was the blue tinge to your lips that clued me in."

He stuck out his tongue in reply but still snatched the sweater from Nino's outstretched arm. "Well, if someone hadn't thrown me in the ocean, I wouldn't be about to catch frostbite." He then quickly put his arms into the sleeves. Once he zipped up, his chest and arms weren't as numb. Too bad he didn't have anything for his ice-cold legs and feet.

"I told you to bring a sweater," Irene scolded from within the confines of the sweater she'd brought with her. It had so many bright colors it looked like she might have stolen it from Bill Cosby's closet.

"Yeah, well, I didn't think I'd be here this long," he reminded her. She replied with an exaggerated eye roll.

"What?" Jay asked. "Don't tell me you were planning on bailing on us?"

How was he supposed to respond? Should he admit he'd come looking for Brody? No. He didn't need to add any more wood to the Gary-and-Irene pyre that already blazed. They had bonded over his plans, and Gary's frown communicated how displeased he was to hear what Teddy had wanted to do.

He'd more than likely get an earful later. He couldn't be less excited about that if he tried.

"Well, I think it worked out for the best," Gary commented. He glanced from Teddy to Nino and smiled. "Sometimes what we want isn't what's best for us."

What the hell did that mean?

"I agree," Van added. He sat between Zach's legs, and Zach practically draped himself over his man. They couldn't look cozier or happier. He envied their happiness. Especially now that he wanted that for himself again. "If I would have had my way, I wouldn't be here now with this gorgeous man."

"Who's that?" Zach asked, surveying the group. "I'll kill him!"

Van snickered as he lifted himself off the sand to kiss Zach. "It's you, you silly man."

Zach beamed. "I'm glad to hear that."

"Could the two of you be any sappier?" Nino asked. He sat to Teddy's immediate left, with Louie sound asleep in his lap. They hadn't been alone since they emerged from the water, and he was thankful for that. That whole scene still confused him. Then, when he recalled how Nino seemed to enjoy his hard cock pressed against him, well, it made his head spin.

Just what the hell was going on with Nino?

"We actually could get sappier," Zach responded. "We're toning it down just for you."

Nino groaned.

"What do you have against love?" Jay asked as he drew Terry into his arms. "It's a wonderful feeling."

Everyone, including Teddy, stared at Nino. He looked like a rabbit who'd been cornered by a pack of hunting dogs. His wide eyes were clearly requesting Teddy's assistance. Since when had he been able to read Nino so well?

"Yeah, tell us," Quinn prodded. He placed his arm around Gary. In fact, all the other couples, including the bear trio, scooted closer together, waiting for Nino to reply. Tara and Irene, the only other people on the beach who weren't a couple, also leaned forward in interest. When did those two become chummy?

That didn't matter right now. There was no way he could let Nino face this horde alone.

"Well, speaking as a single gay man myself," Teddy said. "I think that seeing couples so much in love only reminds us what we don't have."

"That's part of it, I guess," Nino admitted. "But it also makes me feel excluded. Like I'm a part of the group but not really a part of it. I mean, you all have each other. You even talk to each other with only your eyes." The couples around them had to nod in agreement at that one. "You start a sentence...."

"And then the other finishes it," Teddy continued. "You have your own private jokes and stories. You can be chatting with us about some dinner you had, and then one of you says something like—I don't know—cabbage, and then the other one starts laughing...."

Nino nodded. "And then you start talking to each other and leaving the other person out. Saying stuff like 'Oh my God, that was so funny. Right, honey?' And the person you've been talking to has no fucking...."

"Clue what you're talking about," Teddy finished up. "It can be very...." He couldn't find the right word. Frustrating wasn't it. Neither was infuriating. He turned to Nino, who also looked at him. He was obviously searching for the word as well.

Then it came to him. "Aggravating," he said at the exact same time that Nino uttered the same word. He glanced over at Nino and nodded. But when he turned back to the group, they all stared at him and Nino in amazement.

What the hell was going on now?

"What?" he and Nino asked in unison.

Everyone immediately broke out into laughter. He glanced back at Nino, who shrugged.

"You're right," Gary chuckled. "It is pretty annoying. I've never noticed it before."

"I actually have," Zach admitted. "It used to drive me crazy too. I just didn't realize Van and I did that."

"Well, you do," Nino said.

They all stared back at him and Nino and burst out laughing again.

"Would you mind filling us in?" Teddy asked.

Tara shook her finger. "I think we should leave that for you two to discover."

Everyone agreed with a synchronized head nod and then burst into laughter once again. The only one who didn't seem as amused was Jay. Instead of laughing like everyone else, he shifted his focus between Teddy and Nino, and a worried expression twisted his face.

What did Jay know that the others didn't? Whatever it was, from the tortured look on Jay's face, it promised to be disastrous. Why did that suddenly make him feel very nervous and extremely vulnerable?

"AW, COME on," Nino insisted. "It's part of Nino and Teddy's day of fun."

"No," Teddy replied. "I don't want to go to the Vault at Large." Apparently everyone, with the exception of Tara and Irene, was going to the bear-themed leather party at the Crown & Anchor tonight. It wasn't that he didn't enjoy a room filled with hot men or the intoxicating odor of leather and musk. Also, the idea of Nino in leather was actually quite tempting. It would be interesting to see how naughty an all-American boy looked all geared up.

But he still had to find Brody.

"Why not?" Van asked.

How was he supposed to answer that? The truth would only elicit scowls of disapproval from Irene and Gary, but they didn't pay his bills. He was going to do it whether they thought it was a good idea or not. Plus, he didn't want to hurt Nino's feelings. He obviously still wanted to hang out. What a difference time made. Just a few days ago they couldn't escape each other's company fast enough. Now Nino actually wanted to spend time with him, and truth be told, he would like to do just that.

But he couldn't. Brody was out there somewhere, and he had to find him.

"I've just got plans," he finally said. Why did everyone react like he'd just shot someone? Gary and Irene's eye rolls were obvious enough; they needed no further explanation. But the bears? Why were they so shocked and why was Nino so obviously disappointed? Sure, he and Nino had had a good time. There was no denying that. He'd love to continue their day of fun, but he had to finish what he'd already set his mind to do. He'd make it up to Nino later. After he found Brody.

As for Jay, well, just what was his problem? He'd had a pained expression on his face for quite some time now, but it had worsened. If he didn't know any better, he'd say the big guy was getting ready to hurl.

"Well, I'll be there," Nino said. He zipped up his backpack. "In case you change your mind."

"Don't forget your sweater," Teddy said as he took one arm out of the hoodie Nino had loaned him.

Nino shook his head. "Keep it," he told Teddy. "You've still got a long walk back. You can return it later."

"You sure?" he asked. "Aren't you cold?"

"Nah," Nino replied. "You know me. I don't feel much." He offered Teddy a smile, but it failed to reflect any joy at all. The high spirits Nino had been in while they were in the ocean or sitting around the fire had vanished entirely. Nino couldn't be that upset that he wasn't going clubbing with them. Could he?

"Well, thanks," he replied. He flashed Nino a super-big grin. So big that it hurt his face. He'd hoped it would bring that delightful spark from earlier back, but it only seemed to darken Nino's mood further.

"You have fun," Nino said as he pulled the backpack over his shoulders. "And good luck with, well, you know." Nino then walked over to Van and Zach, and the three of them headed down the beach.

Louie snorted in disapproval of Nino's departure. He even trotted over to Teddy and arfed at him. He then stared back in the direction Nino had left. What did Louie expect? For him to run after Nino?

No, it was time to go.

Evidently, everyone else agreed. They, too, had started to pack up, and Gary and Quinn finished putting out the fire. He needed to grab his belongings as well, but he couldn't move. He just stood there staring after the shadowy outline of Nino as he strolled away with Van and Zach.

Before leaving, Nino had wished him good luck, and he had obviously meant it. He sensed that much. But there was something else lurking beneath the well-wishes. A deep sadness that threatened to swallow him whole. As if saying those words had been like pulling teeth out with pliers and no Novocain. That was weird. Even stranger, though, was that he had to stop himself from chasing Nino down the beach and making sure he was okay.

Since when did he long to be a source of comfort for Nino? And what was with that empty feeling in his gut? Earlier, he'd been full of butterflies. It seemed they had all abandoned him now.

"We need to talk," Jay said. His sudden appearance at Teddy's side caused him to jump.

"I can't right now," he replied. He shook the unpleasant feelings from him as if they were pieces of Louie's shedding coat. "I have to find Brody. He was supposed to be here. Remember?"

"All too well," Jay answered. His face contorted in absolute misery. Was Jay sick to his stomach or something? "But we still need to talk."

"It's gonna have to wait, Jay," he said. "I need to snag Irene and get going."

"She's already gone," Jay revealed. "She took Louie with her."

"She what?" he asked as he surveyed the beach. Irene and Louie were both gone. In fact, the only people left were Gary and Quinn. Even Terry had apparently left. When the hell did that happen? Had he been so wrapped up in watching Nino head off into the darkness that he hadn't even noticed she had slipped out with his handsome boy? Also, it wasn't like Louie to be so easily taken from him. "When did they leave?"

"When I asked her to give me some time alone with you," Jay said. "And while you were staring after Nino."

None of that made a bit of sense. If Irene came with him, she left with him. That had been their routine. Why had she changed the rules on him now? "That's not like Reenie at all," he commented. He then continued packing up his stuff. "I'll get to the bottom of that later. After I see Brody."

"We need to talk first," Jay said. His stern expression communicated that this conversation would not be put off.

Teddy exhaled and set his backpack on the sand next to him. "What's got your panties in such a bunch? You're obviously upset. Upset enough that Terry's not here with you. Have the two of you even been apart since you met?"

"No," Jay replied. "But this isn't about me. It's about you."

"Me?" he asked. "I don't understand."

"I had no idea about you and Nino," Jay admitted. "If I had, I would have said something sooner. I just want you to know that."

How did Jay find out about his and Nino's one-night stand? Had Nino suddenly decided to tell the world? "Don't worry about it." He shrugged. "How many times have you woken up drunk next to someone you didn't remember from the night before?"

Jay's big face scrunched up. Was everyone doing Louie impersonations these days? "What are you talking about?"

"What do you mean, what am I talking about?" he asked. "You just told me that you knew Nino and I had hooked up."

"You did? When?"

"Okay, now I'm confused." That was the God's honest truth. It was like he and Jay were having two different conversations. "Nino and I hooked up the night of the bonfire. Remember, when I was supposed to meet you for lunch the next day?"

"That was who you'd hooked up with?" Jay asked. "I had no idea. I didn't even see the two of you together at the party."

If Jay had no idea, then what the hell had he been talking about earlier? This conversation needed a map, so they could both get from point A to point B together. "I'm really lost now," he admitted.

"So it's been going on that long, then?" Jay asked, more to himself than to Teddy.

Jay wasn't being much help in fixing their communication troubles. "What are you talking about now?"

"You and Nino," Jay said.

"What about me and Nino?"

Jay put both hands on his hips. If he weren't such a big guy, it would make him appear quite girly. "You really don't know, do you?"

How many times did he have to tell Jay he had no clue what he was talking about? "I think I've made that pretty obvious," he finally said. "I'm completely clueless here."

"No truer words have been spoken," Jay said with a nod.

"Will you just cut the crap and tell me whatever it is you have to say?"

"You like Nino," Jay said.

Was that all? Good Lord. The way Jay had been going on he would have thought some grand deception had been taking place. "I didn't at first," he admitted. "But he's not the complete ass I'd thought he was. He's a good guy. He even helped me see that I want to work things out with Brody."

"You what?" Jay asked. Why did Jay look like he wanted to pass out? "Are you fucking serious?"

"What's wrong now?" he asked. He'd thought they'd begun to move forward. Evidently, they had just stalled.

"You're not into Brody," Jay announced. "You're interested in Nino."

"I'm what?" he asked. Their stalled conversation just hit reverse.

"I've been sitting here watching you and Nino this afternoon. The two of you are obviously into each other. How else do you explain away his taking you in his arms and playing with you in the ocean? That was some pretty romantic shit."

Romantic? It had just been two friends goofing around. Hadn't it?

"We were all talking about it while you guys were out there," Jay continued. "Believe me, we were all as surprised as hell. Then when you're back on the beach, the two of you were finishing each other's sentences and talking to each other with your eyes. The same thing you both accused the rest of us of doing. It was so damn cute, and pretty fucking funny when you didn't even realize what you were doing."

Was that true? Had they been doing that?

"And he was so damn disappointed when you turned him down. You do realize he had just asked you out on a date, right?"

Really? Was that what that had been? That would certainly explain why Nino had looked so disappointed. Fuck! He needed to sit down before he fell over. He plopped down onto the sand in front of Jay and stared up at him.

"You see why I don't buy that you're into Brody? I think you're just one extremely confused motherfucker right now."

"But I've always been in love with Brody," he admitted. "You've been asking me since we met why I didn't have a boyfriend. Well, that's why. I'd been in love with Brody since the day I met him. I didn't realize that until recently."

"That's bullshit!" Jay said. "Brody's just an excuse. You've told me before that you'd been hurt by some guy you couldn't even talk about. At first I felt sorry for you, but after I witnessed you in action at the clubs and here in P-town, I realized that it wasn't pain that was keeping you from moving on. It was you."

"What the hell does that mean?"

"You conveniently place all the blame for your past on Brody. When you'd meet guys, you were all about the fun and the sex, but when it got too real, you bailed. That wasn't the pain of your past. It was your fear of being hurt again."

"So what?" he asked. "What's wrong with not wanting to go through that again?"

"Nothing at all," Jay admitted. "But don't be a pussy and blame Brody for your shit. Yeah, it hurts to get dumped. We've all been there, but it happens. You've been using that pain as an excuse to not get serious, and now, when you're feeling something for someone, you do it again. Except this time, you're claiming to be in love with Brody so you don't have to deal with what you're really feeling. For Nino."

This was getting out of hand. He loved Jay, but he didn't appreciate anyone telling *him* how *he* felt. Besides, when had Jay suddenly become the relationship guru? "Look, I know you mean well. I really do," he said as he stood back up. His knees were no longer wobbly, and his world had stopped spinning. "But I don't feel anything for Nino. Except friendship."

"Oh, really?"

"Really," he said with a firm nod.

"Let's put that to a test, then. What do you say?"

"What are you going on about now?" he asked. "I'm not in the mood for games, and I see no need to prove anything."

"That sounds like someone who's afraid he'll be proven wrong."

He wasn't afraid of a goddamn thing. "Go for it," he finally said. "Hit me with your best shot."

"This was what I was actually going to tell you earlier," Jay began. "Before we got sidetracked. Like I said, I didn't know about you and Nino before, or I would have said something."

"Yeah, yeah," he said, waving Jay along. "We don't need to rehash the prologue. Just tell me."

Jay sighed. His face twisted in pain again. For someone who'd been so eager to spill his guts, he sure didn't look that way anymore. "It's about Brody and Nino."

"What about them?"

"They hooked up last night," Jay revealed.

"They what?" he asked. The sand beneath him somehow turned to quicksand. It dragged him downward until he was kneeling before Jay again. "I don't understand."

Although it took some effort, Jay knelt down with him. "I don't know the details," he admitted. "And they're really not important. Are they?"

No. They weren't. But why did he really want to throw up right now? Those butterflies in his stomach had returned. With a vengeance. And they were pissed off.

"I just learned about it this afternoon. When I saw how you and Nino were acting together, well, I figured you needed to know. Especially considering your past with Brody."

"Don't you mean my *love* for Brody?"

"Search your heart, Teddy," Jay said. His kind eyes practically begged Teddy to do as he suggested. "Look inside yourself. What's really gotten you upset? I mean, look at yourself. You're on your knees, trembling. What's done this to you? Is it that Brody slept with Nino or is it that *Nino* slept with Brody?"

Teddy didn't have an answer. Not right now. He just had to get the fuck out of there.

So he jumped up and sprinted down the beach and away from Jay, who yelled for him to come back. But he couldn't. He had to run until his legs gave out.

Maybe when he stopped, he'd have the answers he needed.

Chapter Sixteen

WHEN TEDDY finally stopped running, he stood before the breakwater. The long, rocky wall reached through the ocean to the curl of land on the other side. Not more than a few dozen feet of the breakwater was visible this late at night. Occasionally, the moon broke through the clouds, spotlighting small patches of the structure. They appeared to be isolated islands cast adrift from the Cape, an oasis from the troubles that waited on the land.

He'd been there not too long ago, and he'd even made a friend out there in the middle of the ocean.

Fuck! This was the last place he needed to be right now. He'd sprinted from the beach to forget about Nino fucking the man he loved. The last place he wanted to be was where he and Nino first started liking each other.

Out there, they had opened up their hearts and their souls and had allowed the other to see the scared, insecure freaks they really were. He'd never had that with a relative stranger before. It had been a special moment.

Or so he'd believed.

It turned out to not be so extraordinary after all.

What had Nino and Brody shared with each other before getting naked? He remembered how Brody used to enjoy pillow talk before and after sex. He'd claimed it made him feel closer to Teddy. Did Brody do that with other men too?

No. He couldn't go there. If he did, he'd sprint across the breakwater like Nino had done to escape the demons that had been chasing him that night. It was pretty ironic, though. That Teddy would be here now, after running until his legs gave out. Nino had told him that was what he'd used to do as a child. To escape the awful way other children and his family had treated him.

Is that why he'd hauled ass after Jay dropped his little bomb? Because he'd subconsciously remembered what Nino had told him?

Those answers didn't really matter right now. He had to figure out why he was so upset. Whether he wanted to admit it or not, Jay had been right. He needed to figure out what the fuck had made his chest feel like it was caving inward when he learned about Nino and Brody.

It wasn't like he and Brody were together anymore. They hadn't been for quite some time. Brody no doubt had bedded scores of men since then. So had Teddy. And Nino? Well, Nino got more ass than just about anyone he knew. At least that was what Nino claimed. Besides Nino's one-night stand with Teddy and then with Brody, he hadn't observed Nino getting lucky with anyone else.

What was that dry spell about? Had the lack of tricking really been a result of Nino's problems with bears or his career? Or had it been something else?

If Jay were here, he'd be saying it was because Nino liked him. That was why Nino hadn't been hooking up. But could that even be true?

He doubted it. If it had been, Nino wouldn't have happened to fall into bed with the only man Teddy had ever loved.

Damn! How did his life get this screwed up?

He took a deep breath, trying to center himself. If he couldn't focus, he'd never find his answers. Once he managed to get the roiling emotions within under control, he once again stared at the breakwater. Perhaps the tranquility of the ocean would help him, if he surrendered his thoughts to the lapping waves and the cool ocean breeze.

But as he gazed out into the bay, a lone figure emerged out of the darkness. He strolled across the breakwater, making his way back toward land. Was that Nino? He appeared to be the right height. Plus, the guy didn't have a bearish figure. He could discern that even from this distance. It had to be him, since there weren't many other guys in P-town this week with Nino's build.

But what was Nino doing here? He was supposed to be going to the Vault at Large with everyone else. Had he changed his mind once Teddy turned down his invitation?

He still couldn't even be sure it was Nino at all. The night's shadows made it impossible to be certain.

If it was Nino, what should he do? Should he confront him with what he'd learned? No. Confront was too strong a word. No one had cheated on anyone here. The three of them were single men in P-town, and random tricks seemed a part of the vacation package.

He couldn't hold what had happened against Nino or Brody. He sure as fuck didn't have to like it, but there was no villain here. Besides fate. She apparently was a big bitch. If he could, he'd push her into the ocean and hold her head under water.

Now, *that* might improve his mood.

What he needed to do was talk to Nino. To tell him he was upset about what he'd learned. That was something he could do, and being upset was human. Why he was so upset would be harder to explain right now. Maybe once Teddy started down that path, he'd find the answers he needed.

After all, Nino had been there for him before. Why not now?

Teddy rounded the small fence that separated Commercial Street from the breakwater and headed down the path. The man, who he was pretty sure was Nino, had just hopped off the rocks and back onto land.

When the man stepped into the cone of light cast from the parking lot of the Provincetown Inn a few feet away, he gasped.

It wasn't Nino after all. It was Brody.

"WHAT ARE you doing here?" Brody asked.

He had walked over to where Teddy still stood, too paralyzed to move once he realized it wasn't Nino. Why was he also more than just a little disappointed? He'd been chomping at the bit to find Brody all day long, and here he was.

"Just out for a jog," he finally replied. He patted his belly. "Trying to get my fat ass in shape."

Brody shook his head. "You're not fat," he said. "I've always thought you were perfect just the way you were."

Really? He could've said that more when they were dating. It certainly would have made him a little less self-conscious about dating the perfect Brody O'Shea. "Yeah, well, don't worry. I'm not getting rid of the belly. Too many bears like to rub it for luck." He followed his comment with a wink. He hoped he came across far more casual than he actually felt. He couldn't lose it in front of Brody like he'd done at tea. He had to be stronger. To show he had changed from the insecure wreck Brody had dumped in college.

"I've no doubt about that," Brody replied. He then placed his hand at the small of Teddy's back as they walked down the sidewalk. The comfortable weight of Brody's touch made him shiver. He'd always enjoyed it whenever Brody touched him like that when they used to stroll across campus or do laps in a bar.

It made him feel special.

Right now, though, the contact made him tremble for a different reason. No matter how much he enjoyed the touch of this hot man, his body wasn't surrendering to the sensation like it once had. It seemed to be trying to shake it off. Like Louie often did when he got wet.

"I've been meaning to talk to you," Brody said as he led Teddy to a small bench. They now sat across from the breakwater in a small, tree-lined area known as the Pilgrim Park.

"About what?" he asked. Brody scooted closer to him on the bench until the side of Brody's left knee rested against his right. The last time he'd touched knees with someone it had been Nino. That had been an electrifying moment. Their essences had bridged the gap between them until it seemed that they were touching even though they hadn't been.

That wasn't happening right now. Brody's typically warm skin had turned strangely cold.

"About a lot, actually," Brody said after a moment's thought. "I need to apologize to you first, though."

"Apologize? For what?" He couldn't look Brody in the eyes. He was too focused on their knees and the strange absence of emotion that had overcome him. Those butterflies from earlier on the beach were long gone.

"Well, for a lot of stuff. I'm sorry for just leaving you like that in college. Like I said, I'd thought it would be easier that way. But I couldn't have been more wrong. Especially since you made it very clear at tea the other day how devastated you'd been. I guess the road to hell is paved with good intentions, huh?"

"You're not going to hell for dumping me," he admitted. He was finally able to force his attention from their knees to the conversation. When he gazed into Brody's gorgeous green eyes, true repentance for what Brody had done reflected back at him. He appreciated that after all these years. But was it even necessary?

Maybe Jay had been right. Had he been using Brody as an excuse to not get involved with other people?

"Thanks for saying that," Brody admitted. He closed the gap between them further. He leaned across the bench and wrapped his arm around Teddy's shoulder. "I've been feeling awful about what happened at tea."

Yeah, so awful he slept with Nino. How horrible that must have been!

"It's one of the reasons I didn't go to this beach party," Brody continued. "I needed to think. To understand what I'd been feeling since I saw that hurt look in your eyes."

"I know the party," he said. "I was there."

"You were?"

Teddy nodded. "Yes, it was lots of fun." He left out the part about going there specifically to find Brody. That information was no longer as important as it had once been. Why exactly was that?

"I wish I would've gone now," Brody added. "I haven't seen you in a swimsuit in a long time."

Instead of sitting face to face with Brody, he repositioned himself so that he looked forward. He then stared at Brody out of the corner of his eye. Brody was coming on to him again. Just like he'd started to do at tea, before Irene stopped him. All day long, this was what he'd been hoping would happen. Hell, he even had condoms and lube waiting for them on the nightstand in his condo. Now that it looked like he and Brody might just hop back in the saddle, why was he pulling back on the reins?

"Yes, well," he said after a long, awkward pause. "Not much has changed since then. I'm still fat and hairy."

"Will you stop that?" Brody asked. His face widened into the smile Teddy would once have done anything to see. It was still perfect and gorgeous, but his cock didn't seem to think so anymore. Instead of standing at attention as it typically did, it remained asleep and unimpressed. "Do you not remember how much I loved your body?"

Oh, he remembered. In fact, those memories used to be standard jerking-off fodder. He and Brody shared some great times together. More than a few of them were also pretty fucking hot. But they had happened over ten years ago. He wasn't the same Teddy Miller who'd been in love with Brody O'Shea.

In fact, he remembered saying to someone quite recently that he'd been pining over Brody for too long. But who was that? Had it been Irene? Whoever it was, he had told them his past couldn't hold him back anymore. That he had to move on. No, that wasn't quite right. He had to forge ahead. Yes, those were the words he'd used.

When had he said these things? He couldn't recall, but he did recollect that he had wanted to see what else was out there. To find his happiness and go wherever that took him.

He tried to force the memory of this event from his mind, but it wouldn't budge. His head, however, did start itching really badly. No matter how vigorously he scratched, it wouldn't go away. It was like the damn irritation somehow originated *in* his head instead of *on* it. What the fuck was that about? Was he getting ready to have a seizure?

Wouldn't that just be the best way to end today?

"Did you hear me?" Brody asked.

He'd almost forgotten Brody was there. "Sorry," he said. "I was just lost in memory."

"Me too," Brody acknowledged. Brody repositioned the arm he had rested around Teddy so Brody's hand gently rubbed his shoulder. With his free hand, Brody stroked the length of his exposed thigh. He traveled all the way from Teddy's knee to his groin, where he gingerly brushed against Teddy's balls before once again sliding back to his knee. "We were good together. Weren't we?"

He nodded in reply. He couldn't speak. Not with Brody intermittently fondling his ball sac. This had been what he wanted. All he needed to do was reach out and grab Brody the way Brody was grabbing him.

"I realized something tonight," Brody said. The hand on Teddy's shoulder moved to his chin. Brody hooked it and brought Teddy's gaze to meet his. "I've missed you. I didn't realize how much until I saw you at tea. When you left, I was worried I'd never see you again. And I've been going crazy trying to figure out what it all meant. It was like a whole new world opened up in front of me, and I realized that I wanted back what I once had."

Was he hearing this right? "You mean me?" he asked.

Brody nodded. His lips drew closer to Teddy's. "Yes, you. Before today, I hadn't realized that you were the last person I'd ever truly loved. I've had boyfriends, but I've never felt for any of them what I feel for you. You've always been my very special—"

"Teddy bear?" he asked. Why did that answer seem both right and wrong at the same time?

Brody chuckled. "Well, I was actually going to say sexy little man."

That was right. Sexy little man had been Brody's term of endearment for him. Teddy bear had been what Nino had called him that night on the beach.

And just like that, the forgotten events of the beach party broke through the drunken haze that had once suppressed them. He recalled everything about his first night with Nino. How he had walked up to Nino and Quinn. How they had talked and gotten to know each other. And how he wanted to be Nino's teddy bear to replace Teo, his childhood best friend.

"But if you want," Brody whispered, "you can be my teddy bear."

Chapter Seventeen

JUST WHY had Nino allowed Van to dress him up in this outfit? Just because he'd finally agreed to attend a leather event didn't mean he had to arrive all geared up. He was perfectly comfortable in his standard, and far more fashionable, jeans and skintight shirt.

This leather bulldog harness that stretched tightly across his chest wouldn't exactly have been the hit of any runways he'd strutted down. He must look ridiculous. As if he were trying to be someone he wasn't. The same couldn't be said for all the other guys crammed into the outdoor patio of the Paramount, one of the three clubs at the Crown & Anchor, where the Vault at Large took place. They looked quite at home strolling about in their second shiny skins and dancing to the thumping house music from the dance floor inside.

Just why the hell was he here again?

How could he have forgotten that answer? He'd been stupid enough to hope that Teddy might change his mind and show up. He even purposely didn't wax his chest today. When he ran his hands across his skin, his typically smooth flesh had turned prickly. He'd been ready to hate the sensation, but it really wasn't that bad.

And he'd done that for Teddy. To show Teddy that he'd changed. And maybe the gesture might actually mean something to him.

But as the night wore on, he doubted Teddy would show up.

If Teddy wasn't coming, why the fuck was he still making a complete ass of himself?

"Oh, loosen up," Van teased from his left. Unlike Nino, Van looked quite at home in his holster harness, with his leather collar around his neck. Attached to the collar was a leash that extended to Zach's hand. He quite proudly led Van through the crowd, displaying to everyone who saw them that Van was his property, and that by holding the leash, his heart belonged only to Van.

How did Van and Zach manage to turn gear into sappy, sentimental crap?

"I'll loosen up when I'm drunk and fucking some tight bottom," he said. He didn't really believe that. Since Teddy rejected him, he had spiraled downward quickly. Thankfully, Van and even Zach had been there for him. They refused to leave him alone and made him gear up for this featured event for Bear Week.

"You're not fooling anyone," Zach told him. His harness was identical to Van's, and they even wore the same tight black denim. Were they wearing matching cock rings too? Knowing them, they probably were. "So you can stop acting like you're not in pain."

"I'm a heartless fucker," he reminded Zach. He then took a swig of his beer. "Have you forgotten?"

"You've never been one," Van said. "I know that better than anyone. You're good at faking it, but I've always seen right through that charade."

"Not a charade," he said with a shake of his head. "It's the truth."

"No, Nino. It's not," Van replied. "You actually let your guard down for someone. You let Teddy in. You like him so much that his not being here is killing you, and you know it."

Van was right. It hurt. Bad. But what could he do about it? He had hoped maybe he and Teddy had something. Especially after he remembered their night on the beach. But that wasn't the way Teddy felt. He wasn't going to mope about it. That didn't accomplish shit. He needed to pull up his big-boy undies and deal.

That was the Nino Santos way.

Teddy had made his choice, and it wasn't him. He'd tried to respark their initial encounter on the beach—the night Quinn had thankfully made him remember. He'd hoped that by being flirty this afternoon and getting him alone it might have worked. That he'd forget all about the ex-boyfriend. It seemed to have been working for a while there. Teddy even got a boner when Nino carried him out of the ocean. That had been damn promising. Then Teddy's interest stopped. Pretty abruptly.

Maybe he had made Teddy uncomfortable. Teddy probably only saw him as a friend. When he had started blurring the lines, Teddy possibly didn't know how to respond. That seemed logical enough.

It also made him one of the biggest losers in the world. The one time he actually developed real feelings for another man, it happened to be the one guy who seemed virtually unresponsive to his charms. Over the years, his looks and his flirtations had gotten him tons of hot men.

When it mattered the most, though, he couldn't seal the deal.

"Do something about it," Zach said. "Don't just stand there moping."

He snapped his attention to Zach. If looks could kill, Zach would be a bloody mess right now. "I *don't* mope."

"Well, you're doing one hell of an impersonation, then," Zach said.

Nope. Not a bloody mess. They wouldn't even be able to find his pasty-ass corpse. "Fuck you, carrottop."

"You can cuss me out all you want," Zach replied. "That's fine. I can take it. But that's not going to help. The only thing that will is if you make some move that lets Teddy know you want him."

"What the fuck do you think I was doing on the beach?" he asked. Did he have to sound like a whiny child? He needed to get a serious grip, starting right now.

Zach nodded. "That was a good start, but far too subtle."

"I'd have to agree with that," a voice said behind him. It was Gary and Quinn. Dressed in tight leather pants and a rubber polo-style button-down shirt, Gary resembled a preppy butcher. Quinn was attired in his standard leather vest and tight jeans.

"I don't remember asking," he replied. He hated to come off as such a bitch, but he didn't want to talk about this anymore. It was done.

"Oh, Humberto, since when do I need to be asked?" Gary inquired. "We all saw how you were acting with Theodore on the beach. I'd never seen that from you before. Ever. Sure, I've seen the horndog who went sniffing after tail all over town. But that's not what today was about. I was so happy that you'd finally met someone special enough to affect you that way."

"Look, can we drop this, please?" he asked. "Teddy doesn't want me. I think he made that perfectly clear."

"That's not what I saw," Quinn offered. "I think he wants you more than even *he* realizes."

"I agree," Zach said. "That's why you need to stop being subtle. If you want him, go get him. That's what I did last summer. Remember? I had to get over my fears and just accept the fact that I had fallen in love with Van."

"I'm not in love with Teddy," Nino pointed out.

They all glared at him. They obviously didn't believe a word he said. Well, he didn't need to convince them how he was feeling. He was the expert on Nino. Not them.

"Then what do you feel?" Van asked.

That was a good question. One he didn't really have the answer to. He gave a fuck about Teddy. That much was obvious and pretty damn irritating since he'd spent all his life doing his best not to care about anyone else. Teddy had not only helped break that rule, he had practically obliterated it.

Damn him!

"Well?" Van asked. His left eyebrow arched upward. He obviously wouldn't stop until he got an answer.

"All I can say is that I do give a fuck about him. How's that?"

"So, you've broken your own sixth rule, then?" Van asked.

"So what?"

"Are you serious?" Zach asked. "Van told me about these lame-ass rules of yours that you've lived by for most of your adult life. You've practically dedicated yourself to never breaking them, but you have. For Teddy. You don't think that means something?"

"Because I broke one rule?" he asked. "Not at all."

"You've broken more than one," Van told him. "You let him spend the night."

Yes, he'd broken that rule too. But he'd been drunk, so that didn't really count, right? It's not like he'd broken any of the other rules for Teddy. Well, that wasn't entirely true, was it? They had sex that night on the beach and then again back in his apartment. Which meant he'd also broken rule number five.

He'd repeated a fuck. With Teddy.

Did that mean his friends were right? Was he in love with Teddy? He'd never been in love before, so he had no clue what that even felt like.

When he held Teddy in his arms in the ocean, it had been one of the most intimate events of his life. He'd never been that close with anyone before. At least not when his cock hadn't been buried up inside them. If he wasn't naked with another guy, he saw no reason to hold them. That was just silly. And then there was the breakwater and Spiritus. They hadn't really been touching there, but that same closeness he'd experienced in the ocean had been there too.

It had been nice. It made him feel special. Did love have anything to do with that?

And what about when he had left Teddy on the beach? His chest had hurt. He had chalked it up to being rejected. But was it more than that? Was that why a chasm had suddenly opened in his gut?

"I need to talk to him," Nino said before his defenses refortified. "Does anyone have his phone number?"

"I do," Gary said. With a satisfied grin, Gary took his cell out of his pocket. "Here you go," he said after dialing Teddy's phone.

Teddy's line immediately went to voice mail. That meant he was most likely with his ex-boyfriend right now. Probably on his back with his knees behind his ears. That seriously pissed the shit out of him. He couldn't have Teddy fucking someone else. Teddy should be in his arms. His cock should be lodged in Teddy's butt, not some random fuckhead's who dumped Teddy more than ten years ago.

Why did he suddenly want to kill someone?

"Don't worry," Quinn said. "You'll get in touch with him."

"You could always go looking for him," Zach said with a wink. "That's what I would do."

"What do you want me to do, Zach?" Nino asked. "Go shouting up and down Commercial Street for him?"

"Of course not," Gary said. "That would just be stupid. Especially since you already know that he's staying at Zach's old condo."

That was right. He'd totally forgotten about that. "Okay," he said. "I will."

All his friends cheered.

"About damn time," Van said.

"Nino, there you are!"

He turned to see Jay, sporting probably the biggest harness he'd ever seen in his life, and Terry, who was wearing a blue rubber wrestling singlet.

"I've been calling you for the last hour or so," Jay said. He was out of breath and sweating profusely.

He didn't have time for this. "Sorry, big guy. But I've got to get to Teddy's."

"That's why I've been looking for you. It's about Teddy and Brody."

Teddy and Brody? What the hell?

When Jay finished talking, Nino bolted through the crowd and out of the club.

How the fuck could Brody be Teddy's ex? But more importantly, had his cock ended his chances with Teddy even before they had started?

NINO HAD been to Gary and Quinn's place many times, but none more important than this. He had to get to Teddy, to explain about him and Brody. He only hoped his explanations made a difference.

What was he going to say, though? An apology for tricking with the only man Teddy had ever loved just didn't seem to cut it. There weren't words big enough to express that regret. It didn't matter that he had no fucking clue. He'd done it, and he had to pay the price. Whatever that happened to be.

But maybe, just maybe, Teddy could forgive him.

Was that even possible? Was his one mistake going to be the final nail in the coffin? Hell, would they even be friends after tonight?

For the first time in his life, he wished he could go back in time and undo what he'd done. Along with his feelings for Teddy, that was also something new to him. He'd always been fine with his choices. He had never given one fuck how what he did affected anyone else. After all, it was his life. Wasn't it?

But what he did mattered. Especially if it hurt the people he loved.

He stopped in his tracks. The gravel drive that led to Gary and Quinn's complex lay only a few feet away, but his feet refused to budge.

Holy Fuck! He *did* love Teddy. Everyone else had been right. He must be the biggest idiot to have ever lived. But how could he have seen that one coming? From the day they woke up together, they hated each other. They quarreled pretty much every time they saw each other.

Except on the breakwater. After that, something had changed between them. He hadn't been able to identify it because he was clueless about how to handle real emotion. He had spent most of his life making sure he kept everyone at arm's length. To protect himself. But Teddy had just slid right under the barricades without effort and without Nino even realizing it had happened.

If he truly loved Teddy, how was he going to handle it if Teddy couldn't forgive him? Or worse—if he chose Brody instead.

No, he wouldn't let that happen. It wasn't an option. And he'd do everything in his power to remind Teddy of their first night on the beach. Because what happened to him that night had happened to Teddy as well.

Teddy just couldn't remember it. By the time Nino was done, he'd make sure neither he nor Teddy ever forgot that night again.

Appropriately motivated, he sprinted down the driveway and up the small deck to Teddy's condo. Just as he was about to knock on the glass patio door, Teddy exited the stairwell just opposite the front door. He couldn't see Nino. The porch light was out, which hid Nino in the darkness outside, but more than just the bad lighting kept him from

Teddy's sight. Teddy was distracted. He was still chatting with whoever was descending the steps after him. That would most likely be Irene.

As he stood in the darkness, he couldn't help but notice the big grin Teddy wore. He obviously wasn't as distressed as Jay had led him to believe. Jay claimed Teddy had been so upset Nino had hooked up with Brody that he took off running down the beach.

Maybe Jay had exaggerated the story for effect. What else could it be?

"Get your ass down here already," Teddy said into the stairwell.

When Brody turned the corner, Nino's stomach sunk to his feet. The grin made perfect sense now. Teddy had obviously reunited with Brody despite learning about the two of them.

Apparently, Brody was all Teddy wanted.

If that was the case, then what the fuck was he still doing standing there like an idiot? He sure as hell didn't need to watch Teddy grinning at Brody or whatever else they might do right there in front of the stairs. His feet, however, wouldn't obey. They rebelled, forcing him to witness Teddy hugging Brody. It was his body's way of repaying him for breaking his number one rule.

He had fallen in love, and it had bitten him in the ass.

No. He wasn't giving up. Not after coming all this way. Zach had told him he needed to do something. To make a move and let Teddy know exactly what he felt. Maybe he was about to make the biggest mistake of his life, but he was going to do it anyway.

He shoved the patio door open and stepped inside.

Teddy and Brody jumped in surprise when the patio door slammed shut. They were still in each other's arms. If he had a crowbar, he'd pry them apart and then smash in Brody's perfect white teeth.

"Nino?" Teddy asked. "What's going on?"

"I know I have no right to be here," he said. "But I'm not leaving until I've spoken my piece."

Teddy stepped out of Brody's arms. "Nino, there's no need for this."

"Yes, there is," he stated. "I'm sorry that I slept with Brody, but it's not him you should be with. It's me."

Teddy's wide eyes clearly revealed his shock. Even Brody couldn't hide his amazement. His lips had drawn themselves into a perfect "O."

"I know you think you're in love with Brody. The two of you have a history together. I realize that. But that's all it is. History. If you two were meant to be, then you would never have broken up. Brody would've accepted your marriage proposal, and the two of you would be one of those couples so in love with each other that it makes everyone around you sick. But that's not what happened."

He crossed the room and stood before Teddy. Teddy's brown eyes gazed up at him, and the smile that had once rested on his lips now reflected in Teddy's gaze. Was he somehow getting through? If so, he couldn't stop now. "I get it, Teddy. I really do. You've been afraid to open yourself up to someone since Brody. It hurt you so badly when he left. I understand because I've lived pretty much the same way my whole fucking life. How could I trust anyone to not hurt me when my entire family spent so many years making my life miserable? If you can't trust your family, you can't trust another damn soul in this world. And that's what I believed. Until I met you."

He reached out and placed his hands on either side of Teddy's stubbly face. More than anything, he wanted to taste Teddy's lips, to draw his tongue into his mouth and live solely on the breath that escaped Teddy's body. But he wasn't finished. Yet.

"I know you think we've hated each other since that first morning. But that's just not true. I remember that night on the beach now. It was such a special evening, Teddy. Even better than the breakwater. Because we fell in love that night. Well, at least I did. Maybe it was the alcohol or what I instinctively sensed in you, but I knew that I'd met a man who'd never hurt me. And who I'd never hurt."

"But—" Teddy began. Instead of letting him finish, Nino pressed his thumb and forefinger against Teddy's lips. If he was interrupted now, he might not ever get out his true feelings. And they needed to be said. More importantly, Teddy needed to hear them.

"There are no buts," he continued. "I think we were just scared the next morning. That's why we reacted to each other the way we did. We'd let our defenses down. By the time we woke up, they were back up. We've been fighting our feelings for each other since then because we've been too stupid to see how great we are together. Everyone else can see it. They've told me that. But you know what? I can see it. Now I need you to see it too. I need you to look past the mistake I made with Brody. Because that's all it was. A mistake. It meant nothing. I need you to look past the fear, and I need you to see past whatever you think you might feel for Brody." He pressed his forehead against Teddy's. "See us, Teddy. See what we can be."

Teddy's hands came up and rested against Nino's cheeks. He stroked them before his hands traveled through Nino's curly locks and then descended to his neck. There, he wrapped his arms around Nino's neck and pressed his body against Nino. With a smile, he said, "I see it, Curly. And I've never seen anything more beautiful in my life."

The few inches that separated them seemed more like miles, and Nino wanted no more of it. He wrapped his arms around Teddy's waist and leaned down. When their lips brushed together, the emptiness that had opened up within him on the beach and threatened to swallow him when he saw Brody here in the condo immediately filled back up.

Teddy's hot breath occupied all available space within his body, and he wanted more. Of everything. But they couldn't have that with Brody still standing there playing peeping Tom. He hesitantly pulled away from Teddy's kisses and peered over at Brody. "I'm in. You're out. So get out."

"Nino!" Teddy exclaimed. "That's not very nice."

"Nice or not, you're mine. He had his chance, and he blew it."

"I did," Brody said. He then crossed over to where Nino and Teddy still held each other and patted them on the back. "I never had a shot," he told Nino. "Teddy made that very clear to me tonight."

Nino looked down at Teddy. "You mean you two didn't—?" He couldn't even think about it, much less say it.

Teddy shook his head. "Nope. We came back here to talk."

"To let me down easy," Brody clarified. "After he did, I needed to use the restroom. That's the only reason I was upstairs."

Nino couldn't help the smile that broke across his face. "Thank God!" he said. He then lifted Teddy into his arms and nodded to Brody, who got the hint. He crossed through the living room and left the condo.

"Are you ready?" he asked Teddy.

"For what?" Teddy wiggled his eyebrows provocatively.

"For Nino and Teddy's *night* of fun."

Teddy grinned, and it was one of the most beautiful sights Nino had seen in his life. It took his breath away at the same time as it breathed new life into his body. "Sounds like a wild ride," Teddy replied.

"Only the best for my Teddy bear," he said. Nino then climbed the stairs with Teddy still in his arms.

Chapter Eighteen

NINO KICKED the door to Teddy's room closed and then crossed over to Teddy's bed. If he wanted to do all the naughty things to Teddy that currently played through his mind, he would have to set him down. He just couldn't bring himself to do it. It had taken them so long to finally get to this moment. The thought of not holding him was more than Nino's body could bear.

So, instead, he pulled Teddy closer to him until their lips brushed together again. Their kiss was soft and gentle, nothing like he had ever experienced before. Whenever he'd kissed another man, it had been fueled only by the desire of getting off. Nothing more. There had never been a connection. His lips had merely been a vessel of selfish pleasure.

That was no longer the case. Whenever Teddy's lips met his, pure lust raged throughout his body as before, but it was a fire far richer and deeper than any he'd previously experienced. This flame consumed his soul and his heart as much as it burned across his flesh. It promised not just the release of sexual energy but the liberation of his spirit.

He sought not only to receive pleasure as he'd done it the past. He now longed to give it in return.

"Aren't I getting heavy?" Teddy asked. He gnawed on Nino's bottom lip, and the scruff on his chin scraped against Nino's flesh. Each scratch acted like a flint and sparked his desire even further. His body smoldered. He longed to experience Teddy's beard searing across his chest, his cock, and his ass. He wanted Teddy's face to consume his body at once like a wildfire.

It was a completely new desire, and one Nino suddenly couldn't live without.

"I could hold you like this forever," he panted. He darted his tongue inside Teddy's mouth, where Teddy's tongue wrapped around his. They coiled and pulled, their tongues jostling like competing flames between their open mouths, which could not contain the passion they had created together.

Teddy trailed the fingers of his left hand up and down the curves of Nino's back. Paths of fire triggered by Teddy's touch spread further across his body, snaking across his skin until he seemed made more of flame than of flesh. Teddy's right hand clawed at his cheeks and his chin, and his eyes glowed like a bonfire. The passion that raged across Nino obviously blazed inside Teddy as well. His body radiated heat in pulsing waves that reached across the distance that still separated them and threatened to consume them whole if their desires weren't immediately sated.

"Put me down," Teddy begged between ragged breaths. Beads of perspiration broke forth from his forehead and snaked lazy paths down his cheeks. Although he had asked to be released, Teddy wrapped his arms around Nino's neck, forcing their lips even harder together.

"I can't," Nino replied. "You feel too good. You taste too good." He then lapped up the sweat from Teddy's chin, which was like adding gasoline to the fire of Nino's passion. Consuming such a small part of Teddy drove him crazy. The taste hadn't been enough. He needed more.

"Please," Teddy whined. "I need to feel you against me," he said in between the hot, breathy kisses he delivered to Nino's lips and throat. "Everywhere."

Nino nodded and reluctantly released Teddy's legs. As he set him delicately on the floor, he drew Teddy's body against him. While he might not be cradling Teddy in his arms anymore, that didn't mean he'd sacrifice the comforting warmth of his body against his skin. "You have on too many clothes," he complained as his mouth once again enveloped Teddy's.

"I know," Teddy mumbled around Nino's lips. He kicked his tennis shoes from his feet without breaking the seal of their kiss. "Why do you think I wanted you to put me down?"

"So I could do this," he announced as he tugged Teddy's shirt from his body. Teddy's fur-covered chest was now in plain sight. Before, the idea of body hair had made Nino wince, but now he couldn't imagine Teddy without the dark coat of hair that spread across his chest and around his pink, perfect nipples. From there, the pelt descended down to his adorable belly, where it looped around his belly button. It then disappeared beneath the waistband of Teddy's shorts, which tented outward from the hard cock that obviously wanted to be released. "You look beautiful," he said.

"Really?" Teddy asked. The confusion in his voice was apparent. "I thought you didn't like—"

But he didn't allow Teddy to finish. "Not on other men," he admitted. He then ran his fingers through the dark forest. It was soft yet rough at the same time, an intoxicating mixture of the smooth flesh he desired and the manly essence Nino craved. "But I love it on you. I can't imagine you without it."

"Are you sure?" Teddy asked. He ran his fingers up and down Nino's sides. The feathery touches made him shiver in want. "I can always trim or wax it."

"Don't you dare," Nino replied. He had followed the trail down to the boundary where flesh dipped beneath fabric. He curled his fingers around the waistband and pulled Teddy against him. Teddy's bare chest now rested against his midtorso. "This is how my Teddy bear is supposed to feel against me. All warm and hairy. Please don't change that."

"I won't," Teddy agreed with a kiss that fanned the flames of their passion once again.

Nino unfastened the button of the pesky shorts that kept Teddy's hard cock from him. He then undid the zipper. Teddy slid his hands underneath Nino's, and, together, they dropped the remaining clothes from Teddy's body.

With the material removed, Teddy's hard cock bobbed between them. It protruded about eight inches out from a dark thatch of pubic hair, and the shaft appeared at least two inches thicker in the middle than at the head or its base. Gazing at it made Nino immediately hungry. While he had seen numerous men over the years naked and ready to go, none of them were as beautiful as Teddy was now. And none of them had ever filled him with such longing.

In fact, he couldn't even recall what any of them looked like.

"You're so fucking hot," he muttered. He then descended once again upon Teddy's deliciously sweet lips. He lapped at them, licking a scorching trail across the top, down the bottom, and then back up the other side. With his free hand, he gripped Teddy's shaft. He stroked its thickness, working it until Teddy's cock throbbed in want. When a small pool of clear liquid had formed at the tip, Nino sank to his knees.

He fluttered his tongue along the swollen head, tasting the precious pearl that had formed. It tasted sweet, like apple, and he craved even more. With the base of Teddy's dick in his hand, he wrapped his lips around the head and sucked, hard.

"Oh, God!" Teddy moaned. He laced his fingers within Nino's curls. "Your mouth feels so good on my cock." He then started to pump himself in and out of Nino's throat until his nostrils nestled within the musky patch of Teddy's dark hair. The heady aroma fanned the raging flames higher, so he forced even more of Teddy inside his mouth. The thick middle made it difficult for Nino to swallow, but he was determined to make Teddy feel good. Nothing else mattered to him. Not his own cock, which still strained against the denim, or his aching, cum-filled balls.

Right now, this was about Teddy, and he wouldn't have it any other way.

With Teddy's cock lodged in his throat, he swirled his tongue along the engorged shaft and constricted his throat muscles. Teddy grunted in appreciation. Was this what it felt like to give pleasure to someone else? His cock had never been this hard, and he feared if he touched himself he would splooge his underwear. That had never happened to him before. He'd given blowjobs in the past, but none of them had ever made him as sexually crazed as he was right now with Teddy fucking his face.

"You've gotta stop," Teddy pleaded. "I don't want to come yet." Teddy's fingers pulled desperately at his hair as he obviously tried to force the rising cum back into his balls.

With one final slurp, Nino allowed Teddy's rigid dick to slip free of his throat. "Fine," he said. "But I'm not done playing yet." He then sucked one of Teddy's balls into his mouth. He rolled it around, using his tongue to tease the sensitive flesh.

"Fuck!" Teddy called out. He then reached down, grabbed Nino by his underarms, and lifted him upward. "You've seriously got to stop that."

"What?" he asked. He'd only been working Teddy's balls for a few seconds. He intended on getting right back to where he was. But Teddy grabbed him by the harness and yanked him back up.

"It's my turn," Teddy said. He shoved Nino backward onto the bed. "I'm thinking that harness is going to come in handy," he said before falling on top of Nino.

"You like it?" he asked. "I thought I looked silly."

"Are you fucking serious?" Teddy asked as he peered down Nino's body. "You make everything look good. Guess that's why you're a model."

"The only thing I want to look good on me is you," he said.

"That's both the worst and the best line I've ever heard," Teddy replied with a grin.

As he gazed up into Teddy's smiling, warm brown eyes, he wrapped one arm around Teddy's neck. The other caressed his cheek before traveling through the short-cropped hair on the top of his head. "No line," he clarified. "Just truth."

"Well, then," Teddy uttered. "For that, I'm going to drive you as crazy as you've driven me."

"Too late for that," he sighed. "I'm already stark raving mad." He then turned onto his side, Teddy fell into the space on his left, and their tongues once again came to life inside the other's open mouth. With every kiss, he inhaled a part of Teddy, and the hole that had existed since his childhood filled with Teddy's presence. He was now completely the man he was always meant to be. He had to share the gift, so when Teddy filled his lungs to capacity once again, he forced the air back out and into Teddy. He wanted to be as much a part of Teddy as Teddy had become a part of him.

Teddy's eyes closed as Nino's breath filled him. When Teddy exhaled, he opened his mouth and said, "That was hot." He then shoved Nino onto his back and straddled his legs. "But I need something else inside my mouth right now." He then leaned down to deliver dozens of light kisses across Nino's face as he fumbled Nino's jeans open. Once they'd been unzipped, Teddy plunged his hand inside and took ahold of Nino's rock-hard cock. He jacked it with his left hand while his right squeezed Nino's balls through the jeans.

"Shit!" he moaned. He'd never almost come just by someone touching his cock, but that was what almost happened. Nino had to bite his lip to keep himself under control. "I need to calm down before you do that again."

"Too bad that's not gonna happen," Teddy said. The devilish glint in Teddy's eyes told him he was in trouble. Before Nino could respond, Teddy had yanked his jeans down to his ankles. He then scooted downward and started to lick the length of Nino's shaft.

Nino gasped and clawed at the bed as he kicked his jeans free. Teddy continued to slide his tongue up and down, teasing the sensitive skin at the junction of the shaft's base. He then followed the same tortuous path back up, where he swirled lazy circles around the head before sucking the entire length into his mouth.

As Teddy bobbed up and down on his hard cock, he fondled Nino's balls. With each downward motion, he'd tickle the gathered flesh, and when he slid back up, he'd lightly tug on the entire sac. The combined motion, along with Teddy's wet, wicked tongue, brought him quickly to the edge of no return. "You're gonna make me come," he warned.

Teddy pulled off his cock and grinned up at him. "I like making you moan like a bitch."

"How about we make each other moan at the same time?" he asked.

Teddy sat on his haunches and winked. "I like the way you think, Curly." He then repositioned himself so his rigid cock dangled in front of Nino's face. "You ready?"

Instead of answering, he swallowed Teddy's cock whole. Teddy inhaled sharply as Nino began working Teddy's throbbing dick.

"Cheater!" Teddy replied before he fell back upon Nino's cock.

While Teddy fervently feasted upon him, Nino gobbled up Teddy as if he were his last meal. He wrapped his arms around Teddy's waist, trying to drive Teddy farther and deeper down his throat. The faster and harder he slammed Teddy into him, the more precum coated his mouth. He swirled his tongue along the head, savoring the musky, sweet flavor as he thrust his own cock up and into Teddy's hot, willing mouth.

He was getting close. His balls were churning. But he couldn't get there. Not without Teddy. So he grasped Teddy's ass, which was covered by a thin sheen of sweat. He used the handhold to slide Teddy faster and faster into his slick mouth. Yes, he wanted to come, but he wanted Teddy to explode at the same time.

Teddy responded with a grunt. His hard cock grew even stiffer, and his body tensed—the universal sign of a cock about to shoot.

"Oh, God," Teddy moaned as his cock spewed forth seed into Nino's mouth. He swallowed Teddy to the base and wrapped his lips around the girth. Thick, creamy spurts of cum filled his mouth, and he worked to swallow every single drop. As soon as the first barrage of spunk hit his tongue, Nino also erupted inside Teddy. His body fired five heavy volleys down Teddy's gullet until, spent and out of breath, he had no more to offer.

"Damn!" Teddy exclaimed, then rolled onto his side. "That was awesome."

"Awesome?" Nino asked. He moved so that he rested his head on Teddy's legs. "I came so hard I almost blacked out."

Teddy chuckled. He then mimicked Nino's posture and rested his head on Nino's legs. "I guess that means Nino and Teddy's night of fun was a success?"

"It's not over yet," he said with a wink. "Give me about fifteen minutes, and we'll kick it into high gear."

TEDDY HAD to give Nino his due. It was only ten minutes before Nino was once again at full mast. His gorgeous nine-inch cock lay rigid across his flat, toned stomach, and it throbbed in time to the heart that beat within Nino's chest.

He gazed up into Nino's eyes from where his head rested on Nino's once-smooth chest. The telltale prickles of chest hair tickled his face. Apparently Nino hadn't waxed today, just for him. It was sweet but unnecessary. Nino was perfect just the way he was. "Looks like someone's ready for round two," he replied with a smile. "And it hasn't even been fifteen minutes."

Nino nodded. "I've been staring at your cute ass," he said with a grin. "I already know how hot your mouth feels. I'm thinking I need to visit your backyard now."

"I don't know if you can handle it," he commented with a smug jut to his chin.

Nino rolled on top of him, parting his legs with his hands and resting his hard cock against Teddy's lengthening shaft. "You doubt my skills?"

Teddy looked off into the distance, pretending to be in deep thought. "Well, I haven't actually experienced them firsthand. At least not when I wasn't drunk. So until I do, I remain a skeptic."

Nino sneered down at him playfully and then brushed his lips across Teddy's. As before, a flash fire raged across his skin whenever Nino's lips pressed against his. He opened his mouth and drew Nino inside. As Nino invaded him, he reached around and grabbed Nino's steel-hard ass.

Fuck! Was there any part of Nino that wasn't perfect? Not that it bothered him anymore. Since Nino had declared his intentions and practically shoved Brody out of the condo, his fears and insecurities had vanished. Their body types were different, but Nino obviously didn't care. If he did, he wouldn't have come looking for Teddy. Much less fallen for him.

And he had fallen for Nino too. On that very first night on the beach. It had hit him so hard that he'd suppressed the memory. Like he'd been doing for most of his life, he ran away from real emotions. It was how he'd kept himself safe since Brody.

He wasn't going to do that anymore. Not with Nino in his life and in his bed.

No, it was time for Teddy Miller to give up the fight and rejoin the world.

And there was no better way to do that than by letting Nino into his heart and into his body. He increased his grip on Nino's hot, tight ass and forced Nino's hard cock against his own. The sweat from their previous encounter still covered them, and their cocks slid over their slick skin. "I need you inside me," he told Nino. "So bad."

"I want that too," Nino replied as he kissed his way down Teddy's cheeks to his neck.

There he nibbled like a hungry man, and Teddy cried out in pleasure. Nino's persistent lips slid like butter across his coarse, hot flesh, and it made Teddy's toes curls. When Nino started to lightly bite his way from Teddy's neck to his chest, he had a hard time catching his breath.

"Oh, Nino," he moaned. He rubbed his hands up Nino's back, following the dip and curve of each muscle. He charted a path across his broad shoulders and back down his deltoids before returning to his firm ass. Once again he grabbed a handful and resumed grinding their bodies together. "I can't wait anymore," he whispered. His voice was low and urgent. "I've waited long enough."

"We both have," Nino murmured in his ear. He then nibbled his way from Teddy's neck down to his chest. Nino's tongue fluttered across his nipple, causing him to gasp. The warm, wet flutters were almost too much for him to bear. When Nino gently bit down on the sensitive skin, rolling the nipple slowly between his teeth, Teddy arched his back off the bed and howled. Never had anyone been able to bring him this much pleasure by playing with his nipples. He grabbed Nino's head and forced him harder against his chest.

"That feels great," he purred.

Nino released the nipple from between his teeth and looked up at him. "Just wait," he grinned. He then proceeded to chew his way from Teddy's nipple down to his belly button. His tongue flicked inside, causing Teddy's cock to jump. "Somebody liked that," Nino said as he took Teddy's cock in his hand.

When Nino's hand enclosed his dick, he whimpered and instinctively thrust his hips up into Nino's grasp. "I like everything you do," he moaned. "I love the way your body feels against mine. But what I really need is for you to fuck me. Right. Now."

Nino wiggled his eyebrows as he licked circles around the head of Teddy's hard cock. While his tongue drove Teddy crazy with want, Nino squeezed the base of his cock before working his fist up in one tight motion.

"Fuck!" Teddy groaned. The pressure against his dick was intense. It was like being milked. "What are you doing?"

Nino didn't answer until his fist reached the head and a milky drop emerged from Teddy's slit. "Getting a snack," he replied. He then swabbed his tongue over the head, rolled the precum onto his tongue, and swallowed. "Yummy," he said after smacking his lips. He then swallowed Teddy's cock to its base, and Teddy almost lost his mind.

His hips arched up to meet Nino's greedy throat. He dug his fingers into Nino's hair and shoved him farther down on his cock. "Damn!" he yelled. "You feel so good."

"You taste good," Nino told him after swirling his tongue around the weeping slit once more. "I couldn't help myself."

"Well, if you do that again, you're gonna make me come," he panted. "And I want to come with your cock up my ass."

"I don't know," Nino teased before he increased the suction. "I may need some refreshment first." He swallowed Teddy down his throat again as he furiously pumped his cock. His eyes burned with an apparent need for more of Teddy's juice as he resumed his milking process. Teddy cursed and groaned as he fought against the blinding pleasure that spread throughout his body. He wanted to give Nino what he wanted. He longed for it. Few things would be better than to explode for the second time today and have Nino drink him down. But he fought his body tooth and nail. He willed the rising flood of semen back into his balls.

"Spoilsport," Nino playfully chided. "I almost had you that time."

Teddy nodded. His body was now drenched in sweat, and his chest hair had matted to his flesh. "I know," he panted. "I almost lost it too."

Nino gripped Teddy's cock again tightly and aimed it for his mouth. "Maybe this time, I'll get what I want."

"Please, Nino," Teddy begged. He stroked Nino's face as he struggled to breathe. Nino closed his eyes and leaned into his palm. "I need you. Now."

"Okay," Nino said in tentative surrender. "But I'm coming back for more later."

"It's yours," Teddy replied. "I promise."

Nino smiled and then scooted himself between Teddy's open legs. He grabbed Teddy underneath his knees and pulled them up and forward. "Is this what you want?" he asked as he nudged his cock in the crevice of Teddy's ass. "For me to plunge deep inside you?"

"Oh God, yes," he pleaded. Teddy pushed back against Nino's hard cock, nudging the full head of his dick closer to his puckering center. "That's what I need."

"Then hold your legs," Nino commanded.

Teddy immediately obeyed. There was no way he was going to do anything less. He grabbed his knees where Nino had previously held him and pulled them back to rest against his chest. Staring down his body at Nino kneeling just at his back door made his cock turn harder than it had ever been in his life. It also leaked a fair amount of precum onto his furry belly. Nino noticed the glistening pool and immediately craned his neck down to greet it. As he slurped up the juice, the wet, sucking sound caused Teddy to groan in anticipation. His breathing turned even more rapid.

If Nino didn't fuck him now, he would likely pass out.

"Please, Nino. Do it. Now."

The sly half grin that he loved so much once again made its appearance on Nino's lips. "Almost," he replied.

"Almost?" Teddy asked. His skin burned, and he was about ready to leap out of it. "What does that mean?"

Instead of replying, Nino dove in between Teddy's cheeks. His tongue swirled around Teddy's opening, slobbering gobs of spit all over his butt. Teddy moaned and writhed under Nino's expert tongue. It pierced his flesh, twirling around inside him. Nino flicked it to the left and right, creating circles inside him with only his tongue. The motions drove Teddy to the brink of insanity. He grunted and clawed at the covers, ripping the fitted sheet free from the right corner. He balled it in his hand and shoved it into his mouth to keep from screaming at the top of his lungs.

"That good?" Nino asked from between his ass cheeks.

Words wouldn't form on his lips because he was so out of breath. All Teddy could do was nod.

"Let's try this, then," Nino teased as he slid his index finger inside Teddy's spit-slick ass.

"Oh, fuck!" Teddy cried out. Nino worked his finger quickly in and out of him. He repeated the circular motions he'd previously done, except this time with his wiggling digit. After a few blissful moments, Nino plunged even farther inside. Teddy responded by grinding his ass against the insistent finger, working it farther and farther up inside him. When Nino found the bundle of nerves that was his prostate, Teddy yelped. Nino massaged the button with the finger, rubbing tiny circles around the pleasure center inside his body. Sparks of light flashed in front of Teddy's eyes.

"How's that?" Nino asked as he prodded further, increasing the pressure he applied to Teddy's prostate.

"It's fucking great," Teddy whimpered. His body twisted on top of the sheets as Nino's finger took complete control. What would it be like once Nino's cock entered him?

When Nino pulled out his finger, an emptiness immediately opened inside Teddy. Before, he had been filled with more than just Nino's tongue or finger. He'd been filled by the promise of what they had. With Nino no longer inside him, his body cried out in loneliness. He couldn't stand it. He longed to have Nino inside him again, so he sat up and scooted his way closer, trying to impale himself on Nino's hard, jutting cock. "I need you," he demanded. "Now."

Nino took Teddy's face in his hands, running his fingers lightly down his cheeks and along his bearded jawline. His lips then lighted on Teddy's for a few seconds before his tongue once again danced in Teddy's mouth.

Teddy wrapped his arms around Nino's neck, moving himself ever closer to the cock he so desperately needed buried inside him. He clawed at Nino's back as he devoured Nino with his kisses. He then arched his hips, sliding Nino's shaft along his crevice. When Nino's cock head nudged against his opening, he gasped. He ground against it harder and faster, trying to force it past the ring that would allow Nino to finally enter his body.

Nino then shifted his weight so that they slowly fell back onto the mattress. Teddy wrapped his legs around Nino's waist, bearing down against the hard dick that teased his center. With Nino's full weight now upon him, Teddy panted and shuddered as Nino's warm, wet body slid on top of him. He kissed his way from Nino's lips to his neck, drawing in the heady scent of sex and sweat that emanated from Nino's skin. The aroma almost tipped him over the edge. "Please, Nino," he urged.

Nino snatched a condom and the lube from the nightstand. He tore open the condom and handed the lube to Teddy. He immediately squirted a generous helping into his hand and applied it to his ass while Nino rolled the rubber onto the dick Teddy needed inside him.

"You ready?" Nino asked. His lips hitched up to the right.

Damn, he loved that smile. "Are you fucking serious?" Teddy replied. "I've been ready for like an hour."

Without another word, Nino held his cock at the base, aiming it to where it belonged. Teddy reached down and spread his ass. He wanted no resistance. Just Nino sliding inside him and replacing the emptiness with the one thing that would keep him full forever.

As Nino slipped in, Teddy held his breath. His body opened up, pulling Nino farther and farther inside until Nino's balls rested against his ass. Nino's dreamy eyes and slack mouth told Teddy he enjoyed the sensation of Teddy's body closing around him.

"You feel so wonderful," Nino whispered. "I've never felt this close to anyone before."

"Me either," Teddy replied as he wrapped his arms around Nino's neck. "Now kiss me."

Nino lowered himself completely onto him, and their lips once again found their home. As they drank in each other's sweetness, Nino rocked inside him. With tongues jostling, Teddy slid his hands down Nino's straining, wet back. He surfed the sweat until he arrived at Nino's ass. There, he held on and used the leverage to move up against Nino's rhythmic thrusts.

With each moist slap of their bodies, he groaned while Nino panted into his mouth. Nino's hands clutched at his sides before he slid them down to cup Teddy's ass. He squeezed as he continued to pummel his way farther inside Teddy.

Their grunts and moans filled the tiny bedroom, reverberating off the walls and resonating within Teddy's chest. The pulsations drove him even crazier than he already was. He bore down on Nino's cock, using his ass muscles to clench the invading dick so tightly that the move made Nino shudder.

"Fuck!" Nino panted. "Keep doing that."

Teddy responded by increasing the pressure. He skimmed his hands from Nino's ass to his shoulders, gaining the leverage he needed to squeeze his ass muscles and move himself up even harder into Nino's frantic hip thrusts.

Sweat poured down Nino's face, drenching his curls until it looked as if he'd just exited a swimming pool. Then Nino's jaw went slack, and his eyes almost rolled upward. Teddy understood what this meant.

His lover was ready to come.

Nino then moved his hands from Teddy's ass to the headboard, which he gripped with white-knuckle intensity. He used the headboard to pull himself harder and faster into Teddy. The increased power rattled Teddy's teeth and also further stimulated the button within his body. Electrical currents jolted through him, sending waves of pleasure that brought Teddy ever closer to the shore of release.

He palmed his cock, furiously jacking it with the same voracity with which Nino drove into him. "I'm so close," he told Nino.

"Me too," Nino huffed. "Come with me."

Nino then howled as his body stiffened. His cock pulsated to life inside Teddy, filling the condom with the result of their frenzy. As Nino spasmed inside him, Teddy jerked himself to a creamy finish. Jets of spunk flew from his cock, landing on his furry belly and chest.

When their orgasms subsided, Nino let go of the headboard and collapsed on top of him. The come coating Teddy glued their bodies together, making them one even as Nino's cock slowly withdrew from his body.

"Oh. My. God," Nino forced out in ragged breaths. "That was amazing."

"Yes, it was," Teddy nodded as he reached up to kiss Nino's cheek and then his lips. "You were amazing."

Nino shook his head. "It wasn't me. It's what you do to me."

Teddy grinned. "It's what we do to each other."

"I like that," Nino replied. "A lot."

"Me too, Curly. Me too."

Nino frowned. "I'm stuck with that name now, aren't I?"

"I'm afraid so," he replied. "You better get used to it."

"I suppose I could do that," Nino said as he snuggled into the crook of Teddy's neck.

As he lay there with Nino in his arms and on top of him, Teddy finally understood what finding a home felt like. He'd just never imagined it would be with the man he woke up next to after a drunken night of partying.

That was part of the beauty of Provincetown.

Chapter Nineteen

"IT'S BEEN two days. I think it might be time for us to actually leave the condo," Teddy announced. He then extended into a big stretch that allowed the covers to dip past his waist and reveal the cock Nino had come to thirst for.

"No," Nino complained. He drew Teddy's naked body to him. He loved the way Teddy fit so perfectly in his arms. Whenever Nino held him close, Teddy made sure to nuzzle Nino's cock between his butt cheeks. Naturally, that got him hard, and then they'd end up having sex again. Not that he was complaining. He could have sex with Teddy every day and that would be just fine with him. Damn, what a difference a few days made! "If we leave, we can't be naked. So no."

"But I think our friends are missing us," Teddy replied. He scooped his phone from the bed stand and turned it on. The move revealed Teddy's cute furry butt. Fuck! He wanted to eat Teddy alive right now. "I have ten texts from Irene. Her last one says we're going to die from dehydration."

"No, we won't," Nino replied as he kissed Teddy's neck and ran his fingers along Teddy's crack. Perhaps if he touched him just right, Teddy would stop worrying about their friends and let him back into his cave. "We produce all the milk growing boys need."

Teddy nodded in agreement. He obviously couldn't argue with that. Things were definitely headed in the right direction. "Okay. What about all these missed calls from Jay? Or the voice mails from Gary?"

"They're in love too. They'll understand."

Teddy turned around in his arms. He rested his forehead against Nino's as a big grin spread across his face. "You have an answer for everything."

"That's me. Mr. Know-It-All."

Teddy kissed the tip of his nose before pressing his lips against Nino's. The slow, leisurely kiss quickly turned into one of their openmouthed tongue-dueling sessions. Nino had never kissed a man who'd made him want to devour him whole. But that was just what Teddy did to him. He couldn't get enough of Teddy's spit on his lips or Teddy's tongue on his. When Teddy was sucking him off or bucking back against his cock, he wanted the moment to last forever. Fucking had always been about the eventual cum shot. With Teddy, release was just the literal icing on the cake.

They didn't have sex. They made love. He'd never done that in his life, and he wanted it again. If he could get Teddy to stop talking.

"What about Van?" Teddy asked as their kisses slowly subsided. "He's called you at least a gazillion times."

"A gazillion and one," he corrected. Getting Teddy back into a naughty frame of mind was proving difficult. Maybe he just needed to shove Teddy's face in the pillow and start eating his ass. That would get Teddy going. "But I can see Van any old time. Besides, you head back to Boston tomorrow, and I want to spend this time with you."

Crap. What had he just done? He'd been avoiding this subject for the last twelve hours, and now there he was bringing it up. From Teddy's knitted eyebrows, Nino could tell he wasn't going to let the matter drop so easily this time. Nino tried to pull him back into a kiss, but instead of relenting, Teddy raised his head from the pillow and rested it on the palm of his hand. His plans for more Teddy loving were falling apart.

"I think we need to talk about that," Teddy finally said.

Nino exhaled. This was precisely why he hadn't wanted to leave the condo. Out there, the real world waited. With adult responsibilities and the reality that they didn't live in the same town. Sure, Boston was only a two-hour ferry ride away, but it wouldn't be the same. He'd just found Teddy. The idea of not seeing him, or feeling him, or tasting him every day turned the pit that once existed in his gut into a bottomless cavern.

After tomorrow, a whole bay would separate them, and he didn't want to think about it.

"I don't wanna." He pouted. He then pulled the sheets over his head and burrowed away. If he couldn't have sex to take his mind off things, then hiding was the best alternative.

"Oh, stop it, you big baby," Teddy chided.

Now why did Teddy have to yank the sheets off the bed? He couldn't hide without his covers. When Teddy climbed on top, he grinned. *That* was a step in the right direction.

"Now you can't run or hide."

"I don't want to hide from you," he said as he craned upward to steal a kiss. "I'm hiding from reality."

"Well, we can't hide from that either," Teddy commented. Even when he was trying to be serious, he was so damn cute. His wide eyes and stern expression made Nino want him more. What spell had Teddy cast on him? Whatever it was, he wanted Teddy to do it again. "Don't you think we've done that enough in our lives? That's what almost kept us apart."

He didn't want to discuss life outside these walls. What he wanted to do was slip back inside Teddy's warm ass. With Teddy straddling him, his tight butt rested right on top of his cock, which was getting harder by the second. The fact that Teddy was restraining him made this position even hotter. "Let's fuck instead," he said with the grin that typically made Teddy lose his resolve.

Teddy's frown made it apparent that his usual ploy wouldn't work today. Why did he have to fall in love with someone who wouldn't always give in to his charms?

"Aw, come on," he complained. He thrust his hard cock up against Teddy. "I want you real bad right now. And it's your fault for being so damn sexy."

"Are you going to make me put on clothes?" Teddy asked.

Nino and his cock grew alarmed. "What? No! Are you out of your mind?"

"Then let's talk."

"Fine," he replied. His erection deflated when it realized it wasn't going to get what it wanted after all. "But you're ruining Nino and Teddy's day of fun!"

"It's been two days!" Teddy exclaimed.

"So you've been counting?" he asked. "You bored with me already?"

Teddy rolled his eyes. "Bored? No. Sore? Yes."

"I've got some cream for that."

"I'm serious, Curly. I will put clothes on." Over the last two days, Teddy had only called him Curly when Nino was exasperating him. If he didn't start talking, Teddy would get dressed. He'd rather have this talk and keep Teddy naked than have him upset and fully clothed.

"Okay, fine," he huffed. "You win."

"Thank you," Teddy said as he released his grip around Nino's wrists. "Because I really think this is important."

"What? Talking about you going home?" The idea filled him with dread. What if the distance became too much? What if absence didn't make the heart grow fonder? Or even worse, what if some other fucker made Teddy fall in love with him while they were apart? What would he do then?

"Yes," Teddy replied.

He sat up, and his naked body loomed over Nino. It made him instantly hard again. Damn! He just couldn't get enough of Teddy. He'd become an addict.

"Pay attention," Teddy scolded before he reached under to squeeze Nino's hard cock. "I can't have all the blood leaving your brain right now. I want us to be on the same page, and in order for that to happen, your brain must be properly oxygenated."

He preferred being hard to talking. Expressing how he was feeling left him defenseless. What if Teddy didn't feel the same way? He'd never been in love before. How was he supposed to handle such a foreign emotion?

"Okay," he conceded. It was obvious Teddy wasn't going to give up. If they were going to talk, he was going to have to be bold, like he'd been two nights ago. It had worked then. Maybe it would work now too. "But I want you to know something first."

"What is it?" Teddy asked. He absently rubbed his hands over Nino's chest. It was something Teddy had done whenever they had talked. Like touching him was some kind of security blanket for Teddy. It made Nino feel good, but it also revved him up. If Teddy didn't stop touching him like that, they wouldn't be talking for much longer. He'd flip Teddy over and head back inside his happy place. Teddy evidently realized that and crossed his arms over his chest. "Sorry," he said. "Now, you were saying?"

"I'm new to all this and not really good at saying what I'm feeling," Nino admitted with a sigh.

Teddy nodded. "I know you are. Just speak from the heart. Like we did on the beach. Like you did the other night."

Nino grinned. Teddy could read him like an open book. He rather enjoyed that. He at last understood why Zach and Van, and Gary and Quinn, relished their intimate connection. "I can do that." For a few moments, he actually listened to his heart. It anxiously thudded in a mixture of fear and anticipation. What were those feelings about?

He'd changed so much over the past few days that he barely recognized himself. The heartless prick he'd always pretended to be had been discarded for the new Nino, the guy who actually took the time to get to know people. To see them for who they were instead of what they looked like. He'd even made new friends and had fallen in love. These were the things he'd wanted but had always been afraid to allow himself to have.

But he had them now. Partially because of Teddy.

The promise of what they could be filled him with hope and anticipation. His future was no longer one endless trick. It had direction, but that was where his fear resided. His destination wasn't one he could, or even wanted, to reach alone. He not only wanted Teddy. He needed him.

That was why he was so afraid. Loving Teddy made him a new and better man, but it also made him far more vulnerable than he'd ever been in his life. Being rejected by his family had devastated him. Losing Teddy might completely destroy him.

"Are you okay?" Teddy asked.

He nodded. It was now or never. "I've broken pretty much every rule I've lived my life by for you. I never cared about the guys I slept with. They were just there to get me off. That's all. But with you, I care so much. And I have since we met. Which is pretty damn crazy. So for me, this isn't some relationship that'll last only as long as you're in P-town. I want it to be so much more than that. I've never felt this way before. About anyone. And it scares the shit out of me." Teddy opened his mouth to speak, but Nino pressed his fingers against Teddy's lips. He wasn't quite done yet. If he didn't say it all now, he might lose his nerve. "I know we've just met, and this may sound like an odd request, but I don't want you to date other guys in Boston. The thought of someone else touching you quite frankly might turn me homicidal. I just want it to be you and me. No one else."

When he finally stopped talking, Teddy stared down at him. Teddy's smile radiated on his scrumptious lips and in his beautiful eyes. "You know, for someone who claims not to be good at expressing his feelings, you're actually quite a natural."

"What do you mean?"

Teddy leaned over him, bringing the face Nino wanted to cover with kisses only a few inches from his lips. "What you said was perfect. I'd been wondering the same thing. Where would we go from here? What would we do once I went home to Boston? I know how these things usually go in P-town. You make a connection, but once the week's up, the connection always seems to be lost when the bags are packed for home. But I didn't want that for us. I've lived without love for so long. Like you, I thrived on the thrill of sex. And while it was hot, being with you has been the hottest experience of my life. It's not one I want to end. I want it to grow. I want us to grow. I just wanted to know if you felt the same way."

"Really?" Nino asked. If he were any happier, he'd be a character in a Disney cartoon.

Teddy nodded. "So we agree. You and me, despite the distance?"

"You and me," Nino repeated. "And to hell with the distance."

Teddy closed the space separating them. When their lips touched, Nino's body came to life once again. The response was more than just a physical reaction to Teddy's tongue on his lips or his hands traveling up and down Nino's body.

He released the fear he'd held onto for so many years. Only hope and love remained. And the man in his arms that made it all possible.

WHEN THEY finally descended the stairs after another round of hot loving, Teddy was surprised to find Tara and Irene in the kitchen, making breakfast. They hadn't been in the condo since Nino and Teddy had holed up in the bedroom a couple of days ago. But here they were, dressed only in long T-shirts that barely covered their behinds. Tara's curls were even wilder than usual, and Irene's hair was straight and not teased. What had happened to her typical '80s do? He'd also never seen either of them look more radiant. What the hell had been going on in the world since he and Nino had been screwing the last two days away?

He looked over his shoulder at Nino, who shrugged. His lips hitched up to the left in that damned smile that almost made Teddy surrender to him right there in the stairwell. How could anyone look that sexy just by standing still? But he couldn't think about Nino's stiff cock inside his ass or the smooth stomach he longed to kiss. He'd finally managed to convince Nino to get dressed and come downstairs. Teddy couldn't very well be the one who escorted him back to bed. They'd never leave if he did that.

No, he had to focus on getting an answer to his question. What was going on with Irene and Tara?

"Well, well, look who's up," Irene commented from the kitchen. She'd just finished putting cream cheese on the bagels while Tara portioned out the eggs onto four plates.

"We thought you boys might actually rejoin the world today," Tara said with a grin. "So we made enough for an army."

"With the way they've been going at it, they might eat enough for two armies," Irene said with a wink. "Then again, so might we."

Did he hear that right? Had Irene and Tara hooked up?

The two women giggled at his obvious confusion. When Irene reached out to brush away the hair that had fallen in front of Tara's eyes, Teddy had his answer. They'd definitely been naked together.

"Okay, spill," Teddy said. "Just what have you girls been up to?"

Nino groaned. "Do you really need them to spell it out? I mean, just look at them!"

Tara wrapped her arms around Irene's waist and peered at them from over her shoulder. "Let's just say that we've gotten to know each other better."

"A lot better," Teddy pointed out. "I'm going to need the details."

"Not me," Nino announced before he crossed to the kitchen to help Tara with the plates.

"Not those details," Teddy clarified. "I want to know when this happened."

"While the two of you were fucking," Irene admitted. She picked up two of the juice glasses and stuck her tongue out at him. She was being difficult, and she was enjoying it. She then motioned for Teddy to bring the remaining two glasses and follow her and the others outside.

"No shit," he commented once the drinks were in his hands. When he walked onto the patio, he placed the glasses in front of his and Nino's chairs and then sat down. "But how?"

"We hung out together after the beach party," Irene revealed.

Tara nodded. "She was bummed that you were so obviously into Nino. She didn't know what she was going to do with herself if you left her for another man."

Left her? They were best friends. Not a couple. "What does that mean?"

"It's been the two of us for so long, Teddy. I didn't know what I would do if you suddenly had someone else in your life. And I could tell on the beach that Nino was exactly what you wanted. It was all over your faces. It got me thinking. We've hung out together for years. It had been you and me against the world, and I guess I suddenly realized that I hadn't been living my life because I've been so wrapped up in helping you live yours. That was no one's fault but my own. I mean, I'd spent so much time with gay men that I actually started to think I was one. How many damn gay guys have I hit on all these years?"

"All of them," he replied before placing a forkful of eggs in his mouth. It was now his turn to be difficult. She flicked a piece of egg at him in reply. Luckily, it landed on his plate, so Teddy picked it up and plopped it into his mouth. "I just figured you were attracted to gay men. That's what you'd always told me. Although there were times when it seemed like an act or something. Was that what you were doing? Pretending?"

"Pretending isn't the right word. I think I've been hiding from everyone. Including myself." Irene then reached over and grabbed Tara's outstretched hand. "I don't know why, but it was okay for other people to be attracted to someone of the same sex. I never gave myself the same permission. So I chased after gay boys knowing I'd never land one. Kinda like how you chased after bears but didn't really want one. But when Tara and I were alone, and we got to know each other, well, something just came over me. I just had to have her."

"I know how you feel," Nino replied. He scooted his chair closer to Teddy and grabbed his hand. "I never wanted anyone before like I want this man. It's taking all my willpower not to strip him naked right here. Right now."

Irene grimaced. "Please don't." She pointed her fork at them. "Keep that between the two of you."

"I'm planning on it," Nino added with a wink.

"Can we please get back to the identity crisis at hand?" Teddy asked. "Are you telling me you're a lesbian now?"

Irene shook her head. "Tara and I have talked about that. I think I'm more bisexual than anything else. I still find men attractive, just not as attractive as Tara."

Tara beamed. She evidently liked Irene just as much as Irene liked her. He'd always sensed something weird between them. He always assumed it was a general sense of loathing. But there was a fine line between hate and love. He and Nino knew that better than anyone.

"It's been the same way for me," Tara finally said once she was done mooning at Irene. "I think men are hot, and with the exception of the man who fathered my daughter, I've only ever fallen in love with women."

Teddy was speechless. Irene's constant grin told him she was deliriously happy. Still, had he been the world's worst friend? If Irene had been this unhappy with her life and in herself all these years, shouldn't he have noticed? The fact that he hadn't told him he'd only ever been concerned about his feelings. "I'm sorry for being so selfish," he finally told Irene. "I should have been a better friend to you."

"What are you talking about?" she asked. She appeared genuinely shocked. "You've been the best friend in the world to me."

"I don't see how that's possible. A true best friend would have seen this coming or noticed how unhappy you'd been. I've been too wrapped up in my own shit to notice."

Irene rose from the chair and crossed over to Teddy. She held his head to her stomach. "Oh, Teddy. You couldn't have seen it because I hadn't seen it yet. Plus, you're a man, and men aren't exactly the most observant of creatures."

"Amen," Tara added.

"I even have to agree with that one," Nino said with a nod.

"But you and I are in a much better place now. You're finally happy with your life and the direction it's going." She looked to Nino when she said that. Nino smugly grinned back at her in reply. She rolled her eyes at Nino and returned to staring at Teddy. "And I'm excited about what my future holds too. For the first time in years. We'll still be there for each other, I know that now. Except maybe now we'll be happy."

Teddy stood up and squeezed Irene tight. "We deserve it."

She nodded. "Yes. We do."

"I just have one question left for you."

"What is it?"

"Where's Louie?"

She swatted him on the shoulder. "I don't know why I've been fretting, telling you all this. It always boils down to that damn dog, doesn't it?"

"Hey now," Nino admonished. "He's not a damn dog. He's adorable."

That comment made Teddy want Nino more.

Irene rolled her eyes and glanced to Tara for support. "Do you see what I have to put up with?"

"You know boys," Tara said with a smirk. "They just love their dogs."

Nino woofed in reply, and they burst into laughter.

AFTER BREAKFAST, Nino and Teddy headed down the walkway to Gary and Quinn's. Apparently, while he and Nino and Tara and Irene had been getting their respective freaks on, Gary had been babysitting his handsome boy.

They'd never been apart for two days before. Would Louie forgive him or stare at him in disdain for abandoning him?

"It's going to be fine," Nino told him as they walked up the three steps to Gary and Quinn's condo.

Teddy liked that they could read each other so well so quickly. It boded well for the future. But could Nino sense what he was thinking right now?

"Now let's get Louie and get back to naked time," Nino said while Teddy knocked on the patio door. Evidently, Nino and he were in complete synch. Well, at least they'd managed to stay dressed for about an hour. That was a new record.

"How'd you know what I was thinking?" he asked.

"Because we're perfect for each other," Nino answered with a smile.

Damn, Nino knew just how to melt his butter. "Good answer."

"Good answer? That was a *great* answer." Nino then flashed his full set of teeth at him. If Nino weren't so damn cute right now, he'd smack him upside his head for being so cheeky. But instead, he rose up on his tiptoes to plant a long, leisurely kiss on Nino's lips.

Suddenly, a loud bang shook the patio door in front of them. What the fuck was that? When he gazed down, his answer came in the form of a smooshed-up face and a set of paws pressed against the inside glass. Louie's ears were peeled back in absolute joy, and he arfed at the two of them.

"I'm coming," Gary said as he exited the stairwell. By the time Gary opened the door, Louie had about wagged his cute little butt off his body.

"There's my boy," Teddy called out as Louie hopped over to him. He knelt down to Louie's level and basked in the sweet doggie kisses generously delivered. When he'd been appropriately greeted, Louie then turned to Nino and leaped up at him.

He sniffed around Nino's legs intently before hopping back down and snorting around Teddy's legs. He'd apparently caught a scent he liked, that he and Nino had been together the past few days. The subsequent arf told Teddy Louie was pleased, but when he snorted twice after that, he also obviously wanted to know what took them so fucking long.

He just loved that crazy dog.

"It takes us longer to figure things out sometimes," he said to Louie.

In reply, Louie yawned and then snorted. That was his way of saying "No shit!"

"We can't all be perfect like you, Louie," Nino added.

Louie gazed up at Nino and wagged his butt in agreement.

"Are the three of you done with this private conversation?" Gary asked. "And weren't you two the ones complaining about couples excluding others when they talked?"

"Yes, well, I think we've joined your ranks," Teddy replied.

"About damn time," Gary said with a smile. Louie yawned and snorted again.

"All right, that's enough out of you," Teddy told Louie, who immediately sat down and pretended to be a good boy instead of a troublemaker.

"So what are your plans for your last day in P-town?" Gary asked.

"I know what I want to do," Nino said as he wrapped his arms around Teddy's waist.

"Well, we better see you bitches at tea," Gary announced. "More than just Tara and Irene becoming sisters of Sappho has occurred in your absence."

Oh Lord. What now? "Tell us," he said.

Gary grinned at them. "You'll find out at tea," he said before waving good-bye and closing the door.

That wasn't like Gary at all. Whenever he possessed information, he couldn't wait to share it. If he was keeping mum, that meant whatever he knew was pretty damn good.

"I guess we're going to tea now. Aren't we?" he asked Nino.

Nino nodded as he bent down to pick up Louie, who snuggled into the crook of his arm and proceeded to fall asleep. "But first, it's back to Nino and Teddy's day of fun."

"But we'll wake the baby," Teddy whispered.

"Yeah, well, he better get used to it," Nino said with a grin. "There's gonna be many more sleepless nights in all of our futures."

Those words were music to his ears. "Then let's go," he said as he led Nino back down the walkway. "We only have four hours before tea, and I plan on using every minute."

They then hurried down the walk and back to their condo. Four hours just wasn't enough.

Chapter Twenty

NINO HATED that he was at tea by himself. Teddy apparently had some secret errand to run. When he complained and pressed Teddy for details, Teddy had told him it was a surprise. He didn't need that. He needed Teddy. And that was just what he had said.

His words had fallen on deaf ears.

Teddy sent Nino down Commercial Street by himself while he went off in the other direction. Just where was Teddy going?

Maybe Teddy was buying a new jockstrap. He just loved the way the fabric framed Teddy's ass while they had sex. He loved it so much that he'd accidentally ripped one during their last romp. That had been fucking hot. Or maybe Teddy was picking up some whipped cream and chocolate syrup. Teddy had mentioned he liked it when food and sex was combined. He could go for some chocolate-covered Teddy right about now. Talk about yum.

Whatever the surprise was, he suspected it had something to do with the fact that he'd finally called Ford Michaels and got him to stop blackballing him from modeling assignments. The dumbass quickly backpedaled when he threatened to go public with the fuck parties Van had told him about. The ones Ford and his boyfriend often frequented. Once he dropped that little nugget, Ford practically pissed all over himself to hire Nino for an upcoming shoot in Milan.

With his career back on track and with Teddy in his life, everything was good. While he had no doubt the gift would be sweet, all he really craved was Teddy standing next to him.

God, he'd become just as sappy as Van. What surprised Nino even more was it didn't make him grimace. It actually made him smile. He had great friends, and his Teddy bear was on his bed again.

What more could he possibly need?

"There he is," a voice called out. There was no mistaking Jay's booming voice. It clearly cut through the thumping music blaring from the speakers. Now he just had to find him in the middle of all the bears that swirled about the deck of the Boatslip. It was the last tea of Bear Week, and they were out in full force. "Over here," the voice cried out again.

A hand waved above the crowd about fifteen feet to his left. Using it as his beacon, he cut through the hairy men until he was standing next to his friends. They had all assembled next to the deck railing overlooking the bay.

"Nino!" Jay shouted. He then practically squashed the life out of Nino with his standard bear hug. His ribs were definitely going to be sore in the morning. "I've missed you so much!"

"I've missed you too, big guy." He then patted Jay's back and returned the squeeze. "How have you been?"

"I've been great," Jay replied as he returned to holding Terry's hand. "It's been a wonderful week."

"Yes, it has," he agreed.

"It's good to see you smile," Van told him. He left Zach's side to give Nino a hug. "I'm glad you got your man."

"I'm glad to see Teddy didn't eat you alive," Zach told him as he slapped his hand against Nino's shoulder. Zach's friendliness had always irked him. He'd always thought that the only reason Zach was nice to him was because of Van. Zach, however, had been the one to urge him to make his move on Teddy and to stake his claim. He'd be forever grateful to Zach for the advice. Not that he'd actually tell him that. He hadn't changed that much.

"Oh, he's eaten me all right," he replied with a wink.

"Such vulgarity!" Gary exclaimed. He was dressed as his drag queen alter ego Penny Poison. He flipped the green locks of his wig out of his face in pretend horror. "I love it!"

"Yes, honey, we know," Quinn responded with a frown. Nino was actually surprised to find Quinn there, with Penny's arm draped around his shoulder. Whenever Gary donned the black leather bustier and miniskirt that was Penny's trademark, Quinn typically hightailed it in the other direction. What had brought that change about?

"I don't think I've ever seen you and Penny together," he told Quinn. "This must be a special occasion."

"It is," Gary said. "One I'm thrilled to be a part of."

"What is it?" he asked.

"You'll just have to wait," Tara said at his side. She and Irene had brought over a waiter, who carried a tray full of Planter's Punches. "That's the price you must pay for not answering any of our calls or texts these last two days."

As Irene and Tara helped distribute the drinks, Nino studied the knowing faces of his friends. "Am I the only one who doesn't know what's going on here?"

"Well, you and Teddy," Irene announced. "He's being punished too."

"You know?" he asked. He couldn't cover the astonished tone of his voice. Irene hadn't exactly been a favorite among the group. Evidently that had changed too.

"Why wouldn't I?" she asked. "I've been hanging out with these guys for the last two days. I was even there when it happened."

"When what happened?" He surveyed his friends, who all appeared quite pleased with themselves. He didn't like these people anymore, and he told them so by flipping them off.

"Don't fret," Jay said with a pat to his back. "We're just waiting for Teddy before we fill you in."

"You're waiting for me for what, now?" Teddy asked as he suddenly appeared at Nino's side. Having Teddy next to him again made him happy. So happy that, if he were the old Nino, he'd be annoying himself right now. Now that Teddy was here, maybe his friends would stop torturing him with whatever they knew.

"Apparently something big went down while we were otherwise occupied," he revealed. Nino then stepped behind him and wrapped his arms around Teddy. He wanted the whole world to know Teddy was his. When Teddy snuggled back into the embrace, he couldn't stop from sighing in happiness.

"Now who's being sappy?" Zach snickered.

"Stuff it, carrottop," he said with a grin. Was he ever going to stop smiling? As he gazed down into Teddy's brown eyes, he accepted the answer would now always be no. That made him smile so big his face hurt. "So tell us," he said as he stared back at his friends. "What's going on?"

Everyone in the group switched their gazes to Zach and Van. Fear slowly crept its way back into Nino's heart. Were Zach and Van moving? Zach used to live in Texas, and they'd been spending a lot of time in the Lone Star State these days. Especially now that Zach had patched up his relationship with his family. Were things going so well that they were leaving P-town to be closer to family?

While Nino and Van hadn't spent much time together recently, Van was practically his brother. What would he do if he had to live in P-town without Van *and* Teddy?

"I wanted you to be the first to know," Van told Nino. "Seeing as how you're my best friend and all, but Zach here just couldn't wait for the two of you to come up for air."

"Just tell me," he said. Teddy must have sensed his apprehension because he began stroking Nino's arms in comfort. Nino gave himself over to the sweet gesture, and his muscles slowly relaxed. Whatever the news was, Teddy would be there for him. That gave him the strength to not only handle his best friend's departure but to also be happy for him.

Van held up his hand. A silver band now resided on his right ring finger. "Zach and I are engaged."

Everyone around them cheered. Even Teddy joined in with the congratulations. Nino, however, remained speechless. He'd never been a proponent of gay marriage. Why did homosexuals want to mimic an institution that had proven to be a complete failure? Just because marriage was legal in Massachusetts didn't mean a same-sex couple was obliged to walk down the aisle together.

But when he gazed down at Teddy, who jumped for joy for his best friend, he understood for the first time in his life why anyone would want to commit their lives to someone else.

"Congratulations!" he finally said. He then crossed over to Van and Zach and gave them both hugs. "I'm so happy for the both of you."

"Really?" Van asked. "I know how you feel about marriage."

Nino looked over his shoulder at Teddy. "I've changed my mind about a lot of things these days."

"Glad to hear it," Van said with his usual wide-mouthed, cheesy grin. "Because I need a best man, and you're it."

"I'd be honored," he replied with a hug. "When's the wedding?"

"Next summer," Zach answered with a sigh. "I wanted to do it sooner, but Van wants to plan a big wedding."

"Of course I do. I'm only getting married once," Van pointed out. "And even though it's not till next year, we have a lot of planning to do."

As Van droned on about the wedding, Nino glanced over at Teddy, who stood there smiling at him. Nino didn't see him in the shorts or T-shirt he now wore. He was suddenly imagining what he'd look like in a tuxedo.

"ALONE AT last," Teddy sighed. He then collapsed onto the bed that Louie had already been asleep on. Louie opened one eye, peered at them, and then snuffed before falling back to sleep.

The sight of the two of them on the bed filled Nino's heart. They had become his family. In a few days, they had come to mean more to him than even Van. If someone had told him that last week, he would have told them to get the fuck out of his face. He'd never imagined this would be possible.

But it was. As much as he loved Van, Teddy and Louie occupied a special place in his heart that was only for the two of them.

"What's wrong?" Teddy asked.

In reply, he fell back onto the bed next to Teddy and the already-snoring Louie. How had his mood changed so quickly? He'd had a blast celebrating Zach and Van's engagement. They drank far too much at tea and then drank even more at after-tea. Now that they were alone, *blam!* Instant dread!

The specter of Teddy's impending departure was obviously to blame.

How was he going to handle saying good-bye to Teddy when he drove away tomorrow? He'd see him again. They had talked about visiting each other every weekend, but that left five days without each other. Could he really handle that separation?

Right now, he seriously doubted it.

Why did he have to fall in love with someone who didn't live in the same town? He'd never been in love before, and he deserved to be able to experience it every day. Not just a couple of days a week. That was why Townies and tourists shied away from each other for more than just hookups. The pain distance caused ate away at long-distance relationships. He'd seen it happen to other guys before. He didn't want that to happen to the two of them. But what could he do?

"Stop it," Teddy said. He turned on his side and faced Nino. "We're going to be fine. You're going to come up to Boston next weekend. The weekend after that I'll come back to P-town. Now that I have a place to stay rent free, it will make coming back much cheaper."

Teddy's lips broadened into a Cheshire grin. He obviously meant for his comment and his smile to lighten the moment, but for Nino, it only made him sadder. Tomorrow night, he'd go to bed without his Teddy bear, and he didn't like that one bit. "I'm going to miss you," he said. He scooted over until his head rested on Teddy's pillow. With Louie still between them, he draped his left arm around Teddy's shoulder and nuzzled his leg across Louie. Nino needed to be as close to them as possible right now.

"I know," Teddy sighed. "I'm going to miss you too. I know it's only been a few days, but I can't imagine not waking up next to you next week. It's been nice. I've become used to your presence. And even your nightly gas bombs."

Nino grinned. "I have no idea what you're talking about."

"Please," Teddy laughed. "Your farts are even worse than Louie's. It's lucky for you that I've lived with him all these years. He sorta prepared me for you on that front."

Nino reached down and patted Louie's head. "Thanks, boy."

Louie replied with a snort.

"Now, I know tomorrow is going to be hard. For both of us. But I got you something that might make the time apart a little less difficult."

He'd forgotten all about his present. He sat up on the bed and started bouncing up and down like a little boy on his birthday. Louie didn't appreciate the disturbance. He clearly communicated that by chuffing three times in rapid succession. "Oh, hush," he told Louie.

Teddy reached under the bed and pulled out a red box wrapped with a golden bow.

"Give it to me," Nino said as he reached for the gift. "It's mine, mine, mine."

Teddy held the box out of reach. "It's just a little something to remind you of me while I'm gone."

"Gimme," he insisted. He reached across the bed and snatched the box from Teddy's hands.

"Good Lord," Teddy said in obvious exasperation. "You're worse than Louie before I give him his treat."

Louie snorted twice. He evidently found that funny.

In no time at all, Nino undid the bow. When he opened the box, he stopped breathing.

Inside rested a teddy bear. It was extra fuzzy. Just like his Teo. "How?" he asked, unable to form any more words than his one-syllable question.

"Don't you remember describing him to me that night on the beach?"

Nino nodded. He did recall that. He just didn't think Teddy would remember what Teo looked like with such detail. "But it looks almost exactly like him."

"I should hope so," Teddy replied. "I scoured through the stuffed animal section at Puzzle Me This. When I found this guy, I couldn't believe my luck. I know he's not identical to Teo, but he's close."

"Pretty damn close," Nino said as he hugged the teddy bear to his chest. "Thank you. I love it."

"Good," Teddy said. "Now, when I'm not here, you'll have this teddy bear to keep you company. At least till we're together again."

The fear that had previously descended upon him drifted away. He would never be alone again. That was what this gesture told him, and that was the gift that meant more to him than anything else.

He placed the new teddy bear beside him and took his real life Teddy bear in his arms, the one that would forever be at his side. "I love you," he said as he drew closer to Teddy's lips.

Teddy smiled up at him. "I love you too, Curly."

With a huff and a snort, Louie got up and leaped off the bed. He then trotted down the stairs and out of sight.

"What's up with him?" Teddy asked.

"He just knows where things are going, so he decided to give us some privacy."

Teddy's lips parted in the grin Nino hoped to see for the rest of his life. "And just where are things going?"

"Well," he replied as he gently nudged Teddy back on the bed. "It's time for Nino and Teddy's day of fun."

"Just a day?" Teddy pouted.

"How about *every* day?" Nino asked as he lowered his body on top of Teddy's.

"Now *that* sounds like my idea of fun."

JACOB Z. FLORES lives a double life. During the day, he is a respected college English professor and mid-level administrator. At night and during his summer vacation, he loosens the tie and tosses aside the trendy sports coat to write man-on-man fiction, where the hardass assessor of freshmen level composition turns his attention to the firm posteriors and other rigid appendages of the characters in his fictional world.

Summers in Provincetown, Massachusetts, provide Jacob with inspiration for his fiction. The abundance of barely clothed man flesh and daily debauchery stimulates his personal muse. When he isn't stroking the keyboard, Jacob spends time with his husband, Bruce, their three children, and two dogs, who represent a bright blue blip in an otherwise predominantly red swath in south Texas.

You can follow Jacob's musings on his blog at http://jacobzflores.com or become a part of his social media network by visiting http://www.facebook.com/jacob.flores2
or http://twitter.com/#!/JacobZFlores.

Provincetown Stories from JACOB Z. FLORES

http://www.dreamspinnerpress.com

Also from JACOB Z. FLORES

http://www.dreamspinnerpress.com

For more of the
best M/M romance,
visit

Dreamspinner Press

www.dreamspinnerpress.com

CPSIA information can be obtained at www.ICGtesting.com
Printed in the USA
LVOW01s0812231213

366531LV00001B/4/P